LONG DAY FOR RAY

BONNER LITCHFIELD

BOOK DAWG PUBLISHING

PART ONE
MEAT PACKING

CHAPTER 1

RAY CALDWELL'S skull was too small. There wasn't any give at all. So the pain was a single never-ending throb of agony. He'd been prepared for that. Nothing to do but sit still and ride it out. Do nothing. So simple. Except that the pain level made him scared to open his eyes for fear they'd pop out of his head.

He sat and waited without allowing any thoughts to emerge. The slightest brain activity—even a single, fleeting thought— would crank up the pain volume. Even reminding himself that an end was near, that what seemed an eternity was really only two minutes and seventeen-point-six seconds, reflecting even on that would only make things worse. He might have wished for death, if wishing hadn't been a thought, and thereby off limits.

He sat and waited and endured till he blacked out.

———

The room swam into focus. A ratty couch solidified under him. An old TV occupied most of the space on a pressboard table. He was in a trailer with a den and kitchen combined into a one-room box.

Ray Caldwell's home.

The nauseating aftertaste of stale beer had as much to do with getting him to his feet as his mission. The carpet crunched under his feet as he made his way to the kitchen in search of water. There was a sink overflowing with dishes, but nothing fit to drink from. And he knew better than to even look for bottled water. Not here. Not in most places in the 1980s.

Putting his head under the faucet, he let the water run into his open mouth. Bitter and warm. But wet. It blunted out the nasty staleness in his mouth to some extent.

Something else: the smell of cheap perfume made his nostrils burn. That was notable. A thing out of place. Because Ray Caldwell couldn't get laid in a morgue. He filed that away in the back of his mind for future reference.

Grateful that his head was only throbbing like a sledgehammer hitting him between the eyes, he went down a hallway with the cheap paneling that would shatter if you breathed on it and found the bathroom.

It was as disgusting as everything else in this pit. The toilet was clogged with stagnant water right up to the rim. And a rotted floorboard almost gave way underneath him. Step hard enough and you'd wind up breaking a leg.

But that's how Ray Caldwell lived. That was the best he could do.

Then he looked in the mirror. Seeing Ray Caldwell staring back at him sucked worse than he'd thought it would.

Disappointment gnawed at him. Yeah. He was Ray Caldwell, alright. Granted—becoming Ray Caldwell had been the goal all along. But there was still no way to totally prepare for the letdown of actually *being* Ray Caldwell. A thin human wannabe who looked more like a praying mantis. Several inches shy of six feet tall. Gray skin with a lantern jaw and mouse-colored mullet. It wasn't the face of a genius or a scholar.

His muscles felt somewhat wiry, though. Not completely

useless. And, thankfully, the grayish eyes were at least proportional, not so wide or tiny as to signal birth defects. A somewhat normal brain with a low IQ ... that was the ideal.

All by design.

The dullness in his eyes was evaporating; a sharp vitality was beginning to emerge. He'd have to tamp that down. Ray Caldwell didn't have any sharp features. Nope. Nothing sharp about Ray at all.

CHAPTER 2

AT FIRST, he thought something had gone wrong with his vision, even knowing that Ray Caldwell had superb eyesight. Another reason Ray Caldwell had been selected. Funny, that a guy who could read fine print from across a room could barely comprehend the funny papers. Nature was like that sometimes.

There was a wallet in his back pocket. He opened it up and found nine dollars, an expired driver's license, and a battered matchbook. The matchbook was black with "Shelly's Gentlemen's Club" emblazoned on the cover in gold lettering that looked hot to the touch.

He pocketed the cash along with the matchbook and discarded the wallet. Then he quickly tossed the place with machinelike efficiency. Every drawer emptied onto the floor. Closets ripped apart. Mattress and cushions flipped. Couch capsized. All done in a matter of minutes.

Aside from old luncheon meat and spoiled milk in the refrigerator, all he found was some pills that could have been anything. Wasn't touching them. And a sharp hunting knife with a sturdy six-inch blade in a leather belt sheath. What the hell Ray Caldwell ever thought he was going to do with that was anybody's guess. But it would work. He grabbed a belt out of the closet and looped it through the sheath. Then he found a flannel shirt on the floor. It was hot for long sleeves during September in Raleigh, North Carolina, but the shirt would hang down past the waistline, hiding the blade he was carrying.

Finally, he rifled through magazines and old papers, but he couldn't find anybody's number written down anywhere. Just as well, because the phone was dead.

That was the bitch about transfers. Being in Ray Caldwell's body and taking over his mind ought to mean access to everything Ray knew, which would eliminate having to root around this rathole for information. But transfers didn't work that way.

One good thing: he'd been thinking with Ray Caldwell's brain for almost ten minutes, and it didn't hurt. Well, not much anyhow. A very good thing, because this was what he had to work with—at least till the transfer ended. Regardless of how long your mission lasted—days, weeks, even months—you always returned to your real self a split second before midnight on the same day you left.

It could be a long day sometimes.

CHAPTER 3

So NOTHING TO eat or drink. And he'd found everything in the trailer that was of any use. He might as well get out of here. There was a set of keys on the kitchen counter. That might mean a vehicle parked outside.

He could hope.

He stepped outside onto a rickety deck and immediately spotted a dirt road that curved out of sight about thirty yards away. The road came to an end between his and two other rusty trailers in the vicinity. There were no vehicles parked at either of his neighbor's abodes, which probably meant nobody home.

Ray Caldwell, however, had a '74 Chevy Impala parked at his trailer. The car's interior was every bit as disgusting as his living quarters. It stunk of stale smoke and vomit, was littered with empty glasses and bottles, and its ashtray overflowed with cigarette butts. Gas needle just a smidge above empty.

Again, disappointment hit him hard. Ray Caldwell was nobody you'd ever want to become. But most somebodies you'd want to become were unsuitable candidates; the strong-minded could sometimes fight off yielding control of their very being to a total stranger. It had happened before.

Searching the car took half a minute. Expired registration. No maps. Nor spare change. Absolutely nothing to find. Driving this trash-barrel-on-wheels around would be an unpleasant experience, assuming it even ran.

The engine started, but the red temperature light stayed on. Killing the engine, he checked underneath the car and found the dirt saturated with a mix of oil and engine coolant. That meant multiple leaks, or that Ray Caldwell hadn't been paying attention. Or both.

He saw the cloud of dust before a huge truck, a black Dodge Ramcharger jacked up tall on oversized wheels, barreled around the bend. Definitely headed his way. Ray Caldwell stayed where he was. Hidden underneath his car was as good a place as any for now.

The truck skidded to a halt at his trailer. Two people got out. He could see their feet from his prone position under the car. A male and female, judging from their shoe sizes. What people would have dealings with Ray Caldwell?

A big man's voice said: "You wait in the truck."

The woman didn't answer, but her sneakers disappeared from sight and a truck door slammed shut. The man's boots thudded across the deck. He pounded on the door a couple of times, then went inside.

Under the car, Ray Caldwell began to focus on his mission; he cleared his mind and then concentrated on one thing for a couple of seconds. And again. Rinse and repeat. The thing he focused on was irrelevant. In this case, the object of his focus was a two-foot patch of weeds about eight inches tall with no other vegetation surrounding it. Didn't matter. It was all about fitting into his new being, a lot like breaking in a new pair of shoes.

The man from the truck stormed out of the trailer. Down the steps over to Ray's car. He opened the driver-side door and rooted around inside. Then he slammed the door and kicked it.

A solid thump with the heel of his boot. One of the side windows was next.

Under the car, Ray Caldwell focused on the weeds, studying the ragged growth of each greenish stalk, and weighed his options. Like as not, he could remain under the car and not be found. His visitors would drive off. And he'd be left with no map, very little money, and an undrivable car.

He eased the knife from his belt and palmed the handle, hiding the blade under his long right sleeve. Then he rolled out from under the car.

"P-please don't harm me," he stammered. "I've done nothing."

The instant he said that, he realized his mistake. Ray Caldwell would probably phrase a plea for mercy as: "C'mon, dude! I ain't done nothing." Which meant that he still hadn't fully acclimated. But that was the least of his problems right now.

CHAPTER 4

THE MAN WAS tall and thick. He was wearing jeans with a huge belt buckle and a tee shirt with the sleeves ripped out. Ray Caldwell noticed the chains across the heels of his boots. Pointless for combat or even walking. Similar to the ancient warriors who clung to the belief that colorful emblems on their shields would protect them better.

"I've done nothing!" The man mocked him. "What the hell does that mean, boy? You trying to be Shultz from *Hogan's Heroes* with that *done nothing* shit."

Ray Caldwell never looked up. Never raised his eyes above the man's belt. Using proper grammar to say, "I've done nothing" was an error. The man noticed the out-of-place diction for someone of Ray Caldwell's time and station but dismissed it as simply humorous. That was a bigger error.

"Where's my shit, Ray?"

"I dunno."

"Don't bullshit me." There was no more humor in the man's voice. "I ain't gonna hurt you. Just give it back, and everything's cool."

Whoever this man was, he knew Ray Caldwell well enough to know he just might be stupid enough to believe that.

"I don't know. C'mon, man. I didn't do nothing."

"You're pissing me off, boy." A heavy hand grabbed the back of Ray Caldwell's skinny neck and drove his face into the dirt. "You're gonna give me back my shit, or I'm gonna feed you a dirt sandwich."

"Dunno!"

Ray Caldwell took a big gulp of air and closed his eyes while his face got pressed into the hard ground. He couldn't breathe, and his nose was bleeding. But minor distractions didn't bother him. All the while the man was ranting and raving at him as if he could respond.

Half a minute passed. Then Ray's head was jerked upward. The man was down on one knee next to him, his face inches from his ear. "One more time, where's my—"

Ray Caldwell stabbed him in the eye, a diversionary strike, and finished him with an upward slash between the legs. He struck with surgical precision. The big man toppled with a defeated whimper of death.

"Don't move!"

The woman had gotten out of the truck; she was pointing a gun at him.

CHAPTER 5

RAY CALDWELL DIDN'T TWITCH. The man lying dead on the ground had made one error. This woman with the gun had made another. The right move for her would have been to drive the truck away as fast as possible.

Yelling "don't move" was also a bad decision for her. That told him she didn't want to shoot. And now, she hesitated. Another mistake. That told him that she *really* didn't want to shoot him. Not that he cared. He still had to disarm her one way or another.

"Drop the knife and lie down on your stomach," she said.

Ray Caldwell surveyed his mind and his surroundings. This trio of trailers was situated at the top of a hill with pine-scented woods spreading out below with no paved road in sight. And this time of year when they shot animals for the hell of it, distant gunfire under a light-blue Carolina sky was unlikely to draw much attention.

"Hey! I'm talking to you, asshole."

Ray Caldwell responded with a blank stare.

"I won't tell you again."

She would, though.

The woman held the pistol out in front of her in a two-handed grip. She was in a shooter's stance with her feet too far apart. Her chest was heaving as if straining under a heavy weight. From ten feet away, he could see the flare in her nostrils and the fear in her brown eyes. The eyes of a sheep trying to stare down a wolf.

And Ray Caldwell's vision was even better than reported. He could identify the Beretta M9 in her hand. The fifteen-round clip on semi-automatic would more than make up for any lack of stopping power. He could also see that she didn't have her finger on the trigger. Not yet, anyway.

"I mean it," she said. "I'll blow you away."

Soon, it would be an easy throw of the knife, a mere flick of the wrist, and she'd never get a chance to pull the trigger. But not yet. Not enough time had passed since becoming Ray Caldwell for full brain-to-muscle synch-up to occur.

That left him with several options: one, throw the knife and dive out of the way; even if he didn't bury the blade in her, a knife spinning at her would affect her aim. Two, pretend to obey her commands and lure her in closer.

He decided on option number three. Locking Ray Caldwell's eyes onto hers, he focused his gaze deep down into her innermost soul. Yes, the eyes belonged to a dimwitted human, but they projected memories from a world more savage than she could ever imagine. Still, there was no logical reason why she couldn't just shoot him. He was going to give her one.

"Give me the gun," he said. "I don't want to have to kill you too."

A tremor went through her. A soft breeze played with her feathery 80s hair.

Ray Caldwell stepped forward. "It's not worth it," he said.

CHAPTER 6

THE GIRL'S name was Rita. Girl, not woman, because she turned out to be only nineteen years old, even though she looked much older. Ray Caldwell tied her up with interwoven strips of clothing from her male companion, whom she called Meathook, even though his driver's license called him Aaron. He secured her hands behind her back and fashioned a slipknot around her neck.

She didn't hand Ray the gun. But she did let him take it from her. Then she started to cry.

He didn't care about that, except to note that she'd be easy to break. One thing of interest: the faint scent of her perfume was overpowered by the tang of sweat and fear. This wasn't the female who had recently been in Ray Caldwell's trailer.

At any rate, the unreality of the situation had shocked this girl into helplessness. Big, bad Meathook bleeding out on the ground, compliments of a scrawny, dimwitted loser like Ray Caldwell just could not happen. Yet there he was, lying there with his balls cut off. And that same guy, staring her down, walking forward with total assurance that she posed no threat ... She just shut down.

Meathook had a wad of cash in his front pocket, at least two thousand in twenties and hundreds. The keys to the truck had been in his pocket the whole time. Rita's reason for not high-tailing it out of there. Still, running would have been better than trying to face down Ray Caldwell. That was a losing proposition. But nobody knew that. Not yet.

He almost asked, *What did you want with the guy who lives in this trailer?* Couldn't do that. He *was* that guy. It just took getting used to.

Instead he said, "So tell me, Rita, what did I do to piss Meathook off?"

"I don't know."

"Sure, you do." He gave her ribs a gentle prod with the side of the knife.

"You took his stuff," she said. "Ten grand worth of shit." She sniffled and looked at the ground. "Or you know who did. At least that's what Meathook thought."

Ray Caldwell paused to let her wonder what came next. None of this had any bearing on his mission. Except—he now had a knife, a gun, plenty of money, and a truck. What he needed from the girl, Rita, was to find out if anybody else would be coming after him (since he was, after all, Ray Caldwell now), and see what else Meathook had that he could use. He'd probably have to kill her, but she needed to think she could survive this encounter.

"Anybody else coming after me when Meathook doesn't come home?"

"Please. I don't know."

"Sure, you do. Who does he work for?"

Tears rolled down Rita's cheeks. "Meathook and me ... I just hang with him. You know. I'm not involved."

"You just watched Meathook get himself killed. Now you're pissing me off. You're involved."

Rita started breathing heavy, almost panting. "You're crazy," she said. "They'll find you."

"Who's they?"

"Meathook's suppliers. I don't know who they are. But they're bad people."

"And what exactly do these bad people supply?"

"You know as well as I do," Rita said.

Ray grabbed a handful of hair and twisted. "Guns, dope, what? Tell me."

"Coke," she squeaked. "Other stuff too. But mainly blow."

"And that's what he thought I took. Ten grand worth of his blow?"

"He was totally convinced," Rita said. "Why else would he ...?"

Bother to have any dealings with a nobody like Ray Caldwell. He wouldn't. Had Ray Caldwell done something contrary to his profile? He shouldn't have had the guts or initiative to even consider ripping off a dude like Meathook. And the unknown girl in his trailer ... Another loose end. Only, how important?

He'd become Ray Caldwell about an hour ago. And one hour was as far back as Ray Caldwell's memory went. He was in Ray Caldwell's mind, so he knew all about snorting coke. The burning in the nostrils, the drip down the back of the throat, the excited perma-grin that came with the loose tongue and numb ecstasy of suddenly feeling awesome.

He could also drive a car, use a phone, read a map, understand money (even though Ray Caldwell had trouble with arithmetic). All of the life skills that Ray Caldwell possessed remained intact. They weren't much, but they were a starting point. He'd quickly fill the gaps—had already done so at Meathook's expense.

But big things had happened during the past day or so, things that shouldn't have happened in the life of Ray Caldwell.

Whether those happenings affected his mission was unclear at this point.

Here was a major decision: take out Rita and continue his mission as planned or look into recent events in Ray Caldwell's life and tie off any loose ends.

He approached Rita from behind. "Look straight ahead," he said. "Check out that cloud way out there beyond the trees, the puffy one that looks like a sheep ..." Silently, he eased Meathook's pistol out of his belt. It would be over in an instant. She'd never feel it.

Then he saw it in the distance. A hint of dust from an approaching vehicle.

Ray Caldwell really did have awesome vision.

CHAPTER 7

ALREADY, Ray Caldwell, in the short hour of his new existence, had experienced way too many surprises. So he decided that dealing with whoever was driving the approaching vehicle would be a bad thing.

"In the truck." He prodded Rita's spine with the tip of the knife. "Move."

Rita moved. With her hands tied behind her back and a noose around her neck, he had to help her climb up to the passenger seat of Meathook's truck. The driver's seat was too far back for Ray Caldwell, but he didn't have time for adjustments.

He shifted into four-wheel drive and drove behind the trailer of his furthest neighbor. The big wheels crunched across a patch of rough ground. He could barely see over the dashboard with his foot on the gas. The truck was nearly as tall as the trailer, but it wouldn't be visible to anyone approaching from the road. Meathook's body, however, was out in the open for anyone to see.

Ray killed the engine and waited. The backside of the trailer was dingy corrugated metal that might have been white in its early existence. A pair of small windows had curtains across them. He glanced over at Rita. She was looking out the truck's passenger side window, but there was nothing for her to see. Just a propane drum with lines running to the trailer and strip of gravely dirt with a few stray weeds. This tiny excuse for a neighborhood was a blight, an ugly spot on a piece of ground that could have been a nice stand of forest.

Not that I care, he reminded himself. He was tempted to wipe this place out of existence. But, again, he reminded himself that he didn't give a shit one way or another. Besides, this was his starting point. Nothing else. His mission lay onward.

He rolled down his window and Rita's so that he could hear the approaching vehicle pulling up. Rita glared at him, then stared straight ahead. He should have gagged her. But he'd been prying information out of her before this sudden change in plans.

A curtain moved from within the trailer. Then a face appeared in the window. A child's face staring at the grownups in the big black truck.

Ray Caldwell's trailer had a phone. Stood to reason this trailer had one too. Yes. There it was: a black wire running from a wooden pole to the side of the trailer. He hadn't noticed it before because it wasn't important—and because squeezing into Ray Caldwell's tight skull also squashed his powers of observation.

It had sure as hell become important now. Could a child use a phone to call somebody? Not while he was staring out the window.

Ray Caldwell smiled and waved. The child, probably a boy based on his short hair, didn't respond or react. He just kept staring at them.

No, he was staring at Rita.

Rita sitting straight up like a lollipop with her hands behind her. Maybe the kid thought the cloth noose around her neck was a strange scarf. Maybe it was good that Ray hadn't gagged her after all.

He could hear the tires of the approaching vehicle now. It was driving right up to this very trailer.

Decision time.

A flash of white-hot pain swept over him as he assessed the situation, processing every detail with a speed and accuracy that shook Ray Caldwell's skull. The whole thing took a couple of seconds, but Ray Caldwell's feeble brain didn't process that much shit in a year.

He rolled up the windows so that Rita couldn't yell and locked her door so she couldn't get out. (He'd caught a break having a truck with electric windows and locks in the 1980s.) He put the keys in his pocket, even though she wouldn't be able to work her hands free any time soon.

Then he pulled out the knife, keeping it below the dashboard so the child in the window wouldn't see it. Rita turned white and trembled as if her life's blood was getting drained. "Don't even think about moving," he said.

The truck was loaded. Not only was there a police scanner mounted under the console, but a C.B. radio as well. Actually, no. This radio was a high-end job; it wasn't limited to Citizen's Band channels. Not that it mattered. Ray turned the radio off and cut the microphone cord. He left the police scanner on.

He could hear tires rolling to a stop in front of the trailer. Easing his door open, Ray Caldwell got out and dropped to his knees. The trailer was up on blocks, so he had to look under it and get an idea of what he was dealing with here. He could see the grille of a compact car. Somebody wearing walking shoes and jeans stepped out.

One person. He could handle that.

Ray Caldwell's eyes were awesome, but his hands weren't as steady as they needed to be. Full brain-to-muscle synch-up would take another couple of hours. If he was going to be here in this idiot's being for days or weeks—which he wasn't—he'd train some solidity into those frail limbs. In the meantime, shooting the shins of whoever had driven up had a fair chance of success. Fair, not guaranteed. And doing that meant shooting the kid in the window, and probably Rita as well.

Not that he didn't have total leeway to make these judgment calls—but racking up a body count of people having nothing to do with his mission would invoke a massive hunt for Ray Caldwell. And then there was the noise that a gunshot would make. Not good either.

Instead, he drew his gun and crept around to the front of the trailer. Fast and silent, he peered around the edge and saw a clean-shaven dude in his thirties wearing a green uniform shirt with a tree logo. He was unlocking the trailer door.

And Ray Caldwell would go in right behind him.

Just then, a horn blared. Long and loud. From behind the trailer.

Rita. She was laying on the truck's horn.

CHAPTER 8

"RAY! WHAT THE HELL?"

The guy who'd driven up to the trailer was yelling at Ray. His words were drowned out by the truck's horn. So Ray Caldwell read his lips. This guy, whoever he was, knew him. And he was staring with amazement at the gun in Ray's hand.

Ray beckoned. And the guy followed him behind the trailer.

Rita was in the driver's seat; she was folded up like a pretzel with both feet on the horn. Ray pulled her out of the truck by the hair and dumped her on the ground. Everything went suddenly quiet when the horn noise ceased.

The new arrival started to rant. "Oh my God, Ray. Are you nuts? Hey! What happened to your face?"

Ray had forgotten the dirt and dried-up blood from Meathook face-planting him.

"He's really screwed up, Cory," Rita said. "It's going to go bad for both of you."

"And it's going to go even worse for you if I have to shut you up," Ray said.

Rita fell silent.

"Is that Meathook's truck?" Cory asked.

Ray Caldwell didn't answer.

"He's gonna kill us!" Cory wailed.

This Cory was average height, average build. Probably could have kicked Ray's ass a couple of hours ago. Now … he had the look of someone who'd opened the wrong door and just wanted to slam it shut and run. Rita had wasted her efforts blowing the horn if he was the only help she could get. He was too terrified to even function at the moment.

"What are you doing here?" Ray asked.

"That bitch left Justin here by himself," Cory said.

"What bitch?" Ray gestured at Rita. "Her?"

"What's wrong with you, man? You know damn well who I mean."

"Where is she now?"

"Out being a bitch. Hell, I don't know. I just need to get my boy and go."

"And do what?" Rita yelled. "Go where? You know they'll find you."

"Ray!" Cory was near tears. "What did you tell her?"

"I told her to shut up," Ray said.

Killing them both and then driving away seemed the most expedient course of action. But the obvious move wasn't always the best one. *Look for a better plan. Seek to optimize your position.* Those lessons had been drilled into him over and over till they'd become part of his makeup.

Meanwhile, Cory had arrived at his own decision. He turned and sprinted around the trailer. Ray Caldwell followed and watched him go inside. He was going in there to get the kid. Justin. And neither of them was going to call anybody because Cory was scared shitless.

Ray Caldwell pieced it together. Rita saying, *It's going to go bad for both of you,* meant that fellow masterminds Cory and Ray ripped off the wrong dude. And the blowback landed at Ray's doorstep shortly after the transfer to his puny brain occurred.

Which sucked for Meathook. Half an hour sooner, and he would have had his way with a very different Ray Caldwell.

There'd been no sign of high-ticket dope in Ray Caldwell's trailer. Sure, there were other hiding places. But Ray Caldwell was the kind of guy who'd hide top secret, life-or-death merchandise in his sock drawer. So Cory had the stolen blow stashed away somewhere.

He also didn't live here. This trailer belonged to his wife or girlfriend—*that bitch*, as he called her. She lived here with Justin, the male child. And she'd left him by himself. Which was alright for household pets. But you weren't supposed to do that with children.

Therefore, the logical conclusion was that Cory had come to get Justin out of here and show *that bitch* who was boss, never dreaming what he'd encounter when he got here. Not smart. But if this Cory had half a brain, he never would have ripped off somebody like Meathook in the first place. And he certainly wouldn't have teamed up with a guy who lived right across from his son and ex-wife-or-girlfriend—much less an idiot like Ray Caldwell.

There were now four players in the game. Rita, Cory, the child, and the alleged bitch who'd left him alone. Best to simplify the situation.

CHAPTER 9

CORY HAD ARRIVED in a yellow Ford Escort. Ray Caldwell used the knife to slash all four tires, then he popped the hood. Cory emerged from the trailer as Ray was sawing his way through the radiator belt. He had a small gray duffle bag on his shoulder and was leading a young male child by the hand. His mouth fell open when he saw what Ray was doing.

Ray Caldwell ignored him. What was Cory going to do—stop him? He finished cutting through the belt, then he went in the trailer and cut the phone line.

Meanwhile, outside, Rita was yelling at Cory to untie her. The urgent whine of her voice penetrated the trailer's thin walls as if they were a mere optical illusion. "He's going crazy, Cory. He's going to get both of you killed. And they'll go after your son too—don't think they won't."

Untying Rita was a waste of time. Cory would be better off running for the woods or arranging an ambush for Ray when he came out. Or finding something to use as a weapon. Escaping in the truck wasn't a bad idea either. It wouldn't work because Ray Caldwell wasn't careless enough to leave the keys in it. In the end, Rita couldn't help Cory any more than Cory could help her.

They were two overmatched victims, not to be underestimated, but not resourceful enough to pose any real danger.

The only question was how to leave things here.

Rita was still yelling at Cory, imploring him to be smart and untie her for his own good. He could see Cory through the trailer's front window; his feet were glued to the ground, his eyes wide and confused, his fate sealed by his total inaction.

Taking a quick detour to the bedroom and bathroom, Ray found a bottle of perfume in the medicine cabinet and sprayed it into the air. It was sweeter and lighter than the overpowering smell in his trailer. He found a photo of a woman posing with the male child. She looked to be in her twenties and had a kind face, at least on the surface. Blue-green eyes and soft blonde curls. Based on her glowing smile in the picture, she didn't look like somebody who would leave a child unattended. Ray committed her face to memory. (High cheekbones. Ski-slope nose.) Their paths would probably never cross, but just in case.

The phone was hooked to an answer machine with a flashing number indicating three messages. He unplugged it and took it with him. Again, probably not important, but just in case.

When he got outside, Cory had made a decision; he was working on untying Rita. He looked up when Ray approached. "We've gotta let her go, man. That's the only way. Rita can stop them from killing us. It's already gone way too far!" That idiot actually believed that you could unring a bell, alter the past, go back and fix something gone wrong. (Actually, you could, but not in this case, and certainly not by untying Rita.) Anyhow, this guy was an associate of Ray Caldwell, which pretty much said it all.

Cory stood up, his arms spread wide as if he was making a grand gesture. "You've screwed up, man. Big time. All we can do now is keep things from getting wor—"

Ray Caldwell punched him in the throat. Not hard enough to kill him, but a sharp, focused strike at an upward angle so as to not collapse his windpipe. Cory wallowed in the dirt, coughing and gagging, flailing for breath. Rita had gone silent again.

Ray wondered if he'd hit him too hard, then decided that it didn't matter. He did a quick inventory of the truck. No holster for the Beretta. Pure stupidity to have a gun with no good way to carry it. But he found a shotgun behind the driver's seat. That was good. And in the rear storage compartment next to a toolkit was a heavy eight-foot chain. Perfect.

PART TWO
JOY RIDE

CHAPTER 10

HE DROVE over to Ray Caldwell's car. Not that he planned on changing vehicles. Not yet, anyhow. Despite the short time interval, Meathook somehow seemed deader than before; the dirt around him had darkened with his blood, and a column of tiny ants was marching in and out of his thick beard. A human waste-heap going back to nature.

Meanwhile, across the way, Cory had made it up to his hands and knees. He'd recover from being hit in the throat, but for his softness and stupidity, there was no hope.

Ray put the Impala in neutral and chained the car's rear axle to the truck's towing hitch. Then he drove up the dirt road with the Impala in tow. Slow and easy at first, because stopping would cause a rear-end collision. He didn't plan on stopping.

Rocks crunched under the truck's big tires as Ray kept to the center of the narrow road, kicking up a cloud of reddish-brown dust even at his low speed. The road was barely wide enough for two cars to pass one another. There was no shoulder on either side. To his left was a line of chest-high barbwire fencing that bordered an overgrown field. To his right, thick woods with unruly bushes and vines. Very good. No off-road driving into this place.

He'd driven almost a mile when he spotted a black patch of paved road in the distance. The time had come. During the past ninety minutes, the essence of his being had been seeping into Ray Caldwell. How far along? Just one way to find out.

He sped up and veered way over to the right. Then, at the precise moment the car he was pulling threatened to whip around him ... hard left. The truck almost flipped. But his instincts were spot-on as he banked hard—back towards the middle of the road.

Ray felt the towing chain snap. The Impala flipped and rolled.

He stopped the truck and got out. Squinting through the dust he'd kicked up, he couldn't suppress a glow of satisfaction. He had a knack for handling ancient vehicles (chariots, buggies, tanks, you name it). And he'd nailed this maneuver. The Impala had landed upside down across the road. Nobody was driving beyond this point until it was moved out of the way. And, as an added bonus, the towing chain had broken off of the truck's trailer hitch, saving him the effort of removing it.

Lucky and good. An unbeatable combination. Ray Caldwell wasn't such a loser anymore. Hell, he'd never been this lucky in his entire pathetic life.

Giving the Impala a final satisfied look, he drove away. This truck was a fine piece of machinery for this day and age. He also had weapons, money, radios, and a nice head start. He turned left on the paved road and decided that his mission was going well.

"Hi Ray!"

A high-pitched shout from the back seat. Ray damn near veered head-on into an approaching car in the other lane.

It was the male child from the trailer park named Justin.

CHAPTER 11

THE MALE CHILD had wild blue eyes—shimmering, radiant blue that didn't look real for a human. Standing on the rear floor-board, he was just tall enough to smile at Ray over the seat back.

Ray bit down on the rage that was boiling inside him. Smacking that grin off the boy's face would only create tears and bloodshed before it was time for tears and bloodshed. This wasn't personal. He'd lost track of the kid, written him off, decided he didn't matter.

A blunder. A fixable blunder, but a blunder nonetheless.

Those jackasses he'd left at the trailer were a hopeless cluster-fuck for the police to untangle, assuming they contacted the police at all, given their illegal lifestyles. But a missing child ... that was a different matter altogether. Cory might be short on guts and brains, but he loved this male child he'd probably sired. A major weakness in itself, as was any personal attachment.

"Where we going?"

The male child's voice drilled into his eardrums, causing bright spots of pain in Ray's skull. "Hey. Not so loud," he said. "We're both right here in the same truck."

The male child, Justin, responded with a giggle and dove into the front seat. "Can I drive?"

"Maybe later," Ray said. "If you're good."

He was just spouting lines from immersion feeds he'd watched on 1980s American culture. He didn't know a damn thing about dealing with child humans, male or female. They couldn't live on their own or care for themselves. He knew that much. Their survival skills had to be developed over time. Something that had never happened for anybody in that trailer park.

So this Justin male child didn't stand much of a chance of making it in this world (or any other). Now he was bouncing around in the passenger seat, chanting, "I wanna drive. I wanna drive."

Ray opened his door, intending to fling him out into the middle of the road, then stopped abruptly. Something had fetched himself up short—probably the situational training he'd had. At least that's what he assumed, because he was approaching an intersection with a red light and lots of other cars. A child flung from a truck would definitely attract attention.

Besides, he needed a map. For starters. Some food wouldn't hurt either, based on the gnawing in his gut. It had probably been a while since the last time Ray Caldwell had eaten solid food.

He pulled into a crowded fast food joint, vaguely disgusted by the prospect of processed food saturated in grease. Not important. He was here for the kid's outdoor play area; it had a slide, plastic tunnels, and bars to swing on. Enough to keep this male child Justin occupied. With luck, he wouldn't even notice Ray Caldwell leaving without him.

"Why we stopping here, Ray?"

The damn child was inquisitive.

"Aren't you hungry?"

"The food here's yucky. You said so yourself."

"Well, I've gotta eat something." That was true. He was starting to feel shaky and lightheaded. Just a small meal to tide him over while he transitioned to the next phase of his mission.

"I want Chuck E. Cheese," the male child protested.

Whatever the hell that was. "Sure," Ray said. "I'll get you one of those."

"No, Ray! Stop teasing."

Ray Caldwell wheeled into a parking space. "Get out," he ordered.

The male child locked his blue-eyed gaze on him. Didn't say a word. Didn't make a move. Just stared.

There was lots of traffic, a constant stream of vehicles driving in and out of the parking lot. A lot of them were waiting in line at the drive-through. But many were parking and going inside. He could shove the boy out right here and be long gone before anybody noticed.

Should he consider heisting one of the parked vehicles or performing an outright carjacking? Probably not. It would take some time for police to make it back to the trailer and put out an alert for the truck he was driving. At least two hours. Probably longer.

And he had a police radio in his truck. He switched it on and turned up the volume. The 911 dispatcher was reporting a domestic assault in the North Hills area—not that Ray knew where that was. He still needed a map. Car 32 was pulling someone over for speeding and calling in the car's plate number. Meanwhile, car 11 was responding to the assault call.

None of these procedures were quick. They had to call in a street address or plate number ... and wait. Just sit there while they looked up background info. No computers in cars. No worldwide web. No data cloud. No real time interconnectivity with satellites orbiting the planet. And certainly no presence of the seekers. You'd need to jump a whole century into the future for that.

So if a police cruiser started following him, he'd have plenty of time, if not plenty of options.

"You're not Ray!"

The male child's screeching voice hurt like icepicks driven into his ears. He turned the police scanner down. "What the hell—"

"You're not Ray. You're not, YOU'RE NOT ..."

Ray tried to hit him but failed. Fully intended to crack him right across the bridge of the nose. To shut him up by giving him something to scream about. But nothing happened.

"YOU'RE NOT ..."

Normally, he acted on reflex. He hadn't thought about castrating Meathook; he just waited for an opening and took it. Same thing with punching Cory in the throat. And slinging that old Chevy Impala across the dirt road at the end of a towing chain felt natural as breathing. Yet, when he'd tried to smack this screeching brat, his arm hung helpless.

Could there be some strange glitch in the transfer? Some part of his own consciousness that hadn't totally gelled with Ray? Highly unlikely. A transfer wasn't about gelling. It was about taking over completely. Becoming Ray Caldwell.

"YOU'RE NOT!" The male child paused for breath. He was beet red, his face covered by snot and tears. Ray watched him sucking wind from working himself into such a frenzy. Now would be an outstanding time for them to part ways.

Again—he went to hit him. This time, just a slap across the face to snap him out of hyperventilating. It would only sting a little and probably do him good.

Couldn't do that either. His hand lay useless by his side.

Turning in his seat, he placed his hands on the male child's shoulders and positioned him so that they were face-to-face. The kid was crying softy. His initial outburst had dissolved into despair and fatigue.

Ray shook him gently (noting that he had no problem at all doing that), and said: "Look at me, Justin."

The kid looked down. The crying got a little louder, the sobs moved to a higher octave.

He (gently!) pulled the boy's head up, forcing eye contact between them.

"Justin! Why ..."

The boy wriggled away and opened the passenger door. Perfect. Now all he had to do was ... nothing. Just let him get out of the truck and run away. Then drive off.

Instead, he ran after him, cursing his inability to do otherwise.

CHAPTER 12

RAY CALDWELL'S head swooned the moment he jumped out of the car. His body needed food, and the smell of cooking meat made his stomach lurch. He'd parked in a space that abutted a white sidewalk that led into this food place.

Justin ran down the sidewalk. Ray walked briskly but didn't hurry. He'd just follow the boy inside and feed both their faces. They'd both feel better once they ate. His head would be clear. And the boy would stop freaking out. He could hope, anyhow.

Then Justin darted away from the building. Between two parked cars.

Ray sprinted. That was automatic.

A trio of laughing teenagers in a blue convertible with its top down careened into the parking lot way too fast. And the stupid kid ran right out in front of it.

Ray Caldwell grabbed the boy and dove. Felt the nearness of the oncoming car, the hot air from the engine whooshing past. It hadn't even slowed down. Meanwhile, the parking lot asphalt had done a number on the right side of his body. His shoulder throbbed from the impact. The sleeve of his flannel shirt was ripped at the elbow, and his skin with it. He'd also scraped the side of his knee. The knife was sheathed on his left side so that he could reach across his body for it—much better for slashing that way. It might have cut into him if he'd landed on that side.

That's when Ray realized that he'd sacrificed his body to shield Justin's fall. Not that the little shit appreciated it. He was yelling and kicking, trying to wriggle away. He should have let those idiots run him over. Everybody here would have been focused on the accident—child killed by irresponsible teens. And he'd be off and away, moving on to the next phase of his mission. But his body had betrayed him once again.

Patience shot, he jerked Justin to his feet and shook him. (Funny—he could do that, but couldn't harm him, nor let harm befall him.) "What the hell are you doing?" he yelled. "You almost got yourself killed!"

Justin's lower lip quivered as he sought a reply, then he burst into a fresh explosion of tears. Ray limped across the parking lot with him, keeping a firm grip on the boy's right arm.

"We're going inside to get something to eat, and you're going to behave yourself."

"No!"

"Or else I'm going to saw your fingers off and feed them to you."

That shut him up. He stopped to lock the truck, glancing inside to make sure the guns were out of sight. Then he led Justin inside. Man, he was starving. This body he was in was no prize—he didn't care what happened to it—but he'd still have to be careful not to gorge himself on the greasy food here.

"Order anything you want," he told Justin.

"A fun box toy," Justin said. "But I can't decide."

Ray glanced at the menu choices on the wall behind the counter. Apparently, a fun box meal would net Justin the plastic toy of his choice.

"Get two. I can afford it."

That brought a look of pure shock to the boy's face. "Did you do something bad?" he asked.

"What do you care? I'm not Ray."

CHAPTER 13

IN THEIR BOOTH, Ray's hands trembled. The aroma was overpowering. He wanted food so bad, he couldn't eat. He carefully put a fry in his mouth and almost dropped it. Then he took a bite of his burger and washed it down with a huge gulp of dark, sugary soda. An energy spike washed over his body, the surge to his brain almost electric, as he swallowed one bite, then another. Before he knew it, he'd devoured his burger and fries and then started on the caramel sundae.

Justin hadn't touched his food. He was playing with a pair of plastic figurines—a hamburger with limbs and something that resembled a pile of shit with eyes. "You better eat something," he said, wondering why he cared.

"Okay."

But the boy never looked up. He'd agreed to follow a suggestion, but ...

"Look. I'll eat one of those boxes of fun and you eat the other," Ray said.

Ray grabbed one of the open boxes and dug into the tiny food portions. Justin still hadn't looked up.

"You can eat or lose those toys," Ray said.

That worked. Justin started eating. (Again, why did he care?)

Ray went for a refill. There were a few people lined up for food like livestock. And a girl wearing a paper hat was wiping off tables, voluntarily cleaning up messes made by others. Incomprehensible that humans did that of their own free will!

At any rate, he'd fed this famished body and felt much sharper, much more attuned to his surroundings. He heard them laugh, saw them sitting in a booth. Three teenagers. From the car that had almost run them over. Two males and a female. Grown-up children that weren't yet fully developed. They'd almost killed Justin, a helpless male child, and didn't care.

He glanced at the blood under his ripped sleeve and focused on the rage coursing through his veins. The sharp blade of the hunting knife grew hot against his leg as his fingers itched for the handle. Calmly averting his gaze, Ray refilled his soda and returned to their table. He longed for one of those clueless kids to get in his way, to threaten the mission ... then his retribution would be completely justified.

But they almost ran us over, he seethed. Surely that was reason enough.

No. He'd willingly put himself at risk. Far better to have let them run the boy over. They'd be in handcuffs right now. And he would have driven off, free of all appendages. Distractions and misdirection worked wonders.

At the very least, he ought to drive off and leave Justin sitting here.

"I'll be right back," he said. "Gotta take a whiz."

CHAPTER 14

JUSTIN WAS TOO obsessed with those stupid toys to notice him leaving. In fact, Ray made it all the way to the door ...

But that damn weakness!

He stood in the doorway and watched the mid-afternoon sunshine beaming in through the plate-glass windows; the welcome darkness of sunset wasn't far away. Yes! Darkness was nature's cloaking device, a shroud of safety and seclusion.

But, try as he might, he couldn't will himself to walk outside, couldn't bring himself to leave the boy alone. Had to return to the table and tell him to get his ass in gear, that they had to get going. As they returned to the truck, he almost took Justin by the hand out of an abundance of caution—what the hell brought that on?

He took a quick glance around, alert for danger. Aside from his unexplainable weakness, everything seemed cool for now.

In the truck, Ray listened to a few transmissions on the police scanner just to be sure. And things weren't so cool anymore.

Stolen vehicle report. Dodge Ramcharger. Black.

How? There wasn't enough time for anybody to get to the trailer, or for Cory and Rita to get to a phone.

Suspect Ray Caldwell. Gray eyes. Slight build. Mullet hairstyle.

Damn! There were *three* trailers in that pathetic excuse for a neighborhood. He'd cut the phone lines in *two* of them. Since the police radio made no mention of a homicide, Ray guessed the cops hadn't physically arrived at the scene to see Meathook's body firsthand. They wouldn't crank up a full-scale manhunt based on a phone call. Not yet, anyhow. But they would be on the lookout for a black truck driven by someone who looked like him.

Update. Dodge Ramcharger. License plate FAT-2095. Registered to Aaron Bitner.

Rita must have given them Meathook's real name; from there, they'd been able to look up his info. Things weren't very computerized in this period of human existence. No widespread networks. Very basic communication devices. People didn't have phones they could carry around with them. But, apparently, the authorities could access digital info or maybe printed documents from their command center and dispatch their findings via radio.

As he listened to the transmissions, Ray's knuckles turned white from his ever-tightening grip on the steering wheel. How in the hell could he have neglected to cut off the phone in the third trailer? And an even bigger gaffe on his part: he should have eliminated Cory and Rita altogether, or at least left them tied up in the trunk of a car. And left Justin back there with them ... things would be a whole lot better right now if he'd done any of those things.

Weakness ...

Weakness!

Weakness like he'd never experienced before.

But how? What could have gone so wrong with this particular transfer? Research algorithms screened out the smart and strong-willed as potential hosts. In Ray Caldwell's case, there wasn't much to go on, mainly because he'd never done anything, as in anything at all. Of the billions of humans that had lived and died over the millennia, very few had noteworthy accomplishments. But Ray Caldwell was just a big blank nothing.

Until now. Suddenly, he'd become a person of interest both inside and outside the law. And it was about to get a whole lot hotter.

Surveillance cameras existed in the 1980s. But not at most businesses. He could get away clean with some quick action and misdirection, and conduct a test in the process.

Sorting through the glovebox and console, Ray found a pack of cigarettes, a lighter, and another "Shelly's Gentlemen's Club" matchbook. Not that Ray Caldwell and Meathook frequenting the same scummy establishment mattered now.

"You wait right here," he told Justin. "It's dangerous out there."

"Are you in trouble?" the boy asked.

"We both are," Ray said. "But not for long. Now don't you move. Okay? Promise me."

Justin nodded consent; his blue eyes seemed like giant pools capable of drowning an unsuspecting victim. Ray cursed under his breath. He was failing so far. Wasting time trying to reason with a male child that absolutely did not matter.

He walked to the back of the truck and got two screwdrivers out of the toolbox. Then he strode quickly across the parking lot to the bright blue sports car that the teenagers were driving.

It was a Ford Mustang with a stick shift. Fast. Maneuverable. A better plan emerged. He could get the guns from the truck and hotwire this car, leaving Justin here for the police to find.

But he wasn't going to do that.

Again—weakness! Failure!

There wasn't time for this shit. If he was going to go with an inferior plan out of weakness, he ought to at least execute it with some degree of precision.

A stream of cars flowed in and out of the parking lot. People looking for parking spaces or trying to pull out. The Mustang was parked with its rear facing the building. Unscrewing the license plate would take too long and be too visible. Did he have time to search out a vehicle parked on the outer perimeter that had backed into its space? Ray decided he didn't. A plate swap would have to wait.

Ray gazed across the parking lot and spotted Justin's head through the back window of the truck. The boy was keeping his word, staying put, waiting for him to return. Probably playing with those plastic toys.

He sat on the pavement between the Mustang and the car parked next to it and went to work. First he used the hunting knife to cut off his ripped shirt sleeve. The skin underneath it was a jumble of bleeding scrapes. He'd need to clean himself up once he got to a safe stopping point. But, for now, onward.

Next he wrapped his cut-off sleeve around the lighter, laid it on the pavement, and stomped with his heel; the lighter shattered, saturating the flannel with lighter fluid. He slid on his butt to the rear of the Mustang and removed the gas cap.

Now for the fun part. He used the matchbook to light a cigarette, resisting the urge to inhale deeply. Still, he couldn't help but savor the taste of burnt tar on the tip of his tongue. Nasty habit. But pretty awesome before it cooked your lungs into a biological wilderness.

He tore both rows of matches out of the matchbook and wound them around the butt of the lit cigarette. From there, he slid the cigarette back into the pack, wrapped the butane-soaked flannel cloth around it, and shoved his creation into the Mustang's gas filler hole.

It was hard not to run. But he managed a casual walk back to the truck despite his pounding heart.

CHAPTER 15

It wasn't the danger of a pending explosion that scared him ...

Ray Caldwell's terror came from the possibility that he'd change his mind and go back to the Mustang, that he'd yank his makeshift time bomb out of the gas filler before the cigarette burned down. That the weakness within him would stop him dead in his tracks before he got the hell out of here.

He was waiting for it. That threatening thought. *What if those teenagers make it to their car before ... ?* And he'd care!

Panic dogged his every step as if the black pavement was about to turn into hot lava and devour him one charred remnant at a time. That damn truck, just across the parking lot, seemed miles away. Again, he wanted to run, compliments of a fresh surge of adrenaline. But you couldn't outrun weakness, couldn't outdistance failure. Besides, he needed to appear casual.

His hands shook as he pulled the truck door open and climbed into the driver's seat. Salvation! He'd made it.

"What's wrong?" Justin asked. The sweat pouring off him probably tipped him off.

"Not now. We've got to get out of here."

But as soon as he cranked up the truck, a fat woman in a

green Ford Escort stopped behind him. Just stopped. Literally parked herself perpendicular to his rear bumper and sat there staring into space—at what?

Ray realized that she was waiting for a car several spaces down from him to pull out. Couldn't park on the other side of the lot and walk an extra few yards. That would be way beyond her weekly exercise quota. (Although, in this case, given what was about to happen, sloth might just prolong her life.)

One thing was clear: he needed to get the hell out of here. And fast.

But the driver of the car she was waiting on didn't seem to be anywhere near ready to leave. In fact, it was a male helping his wife or girlfriend adjust a car seat. Ray Caldwell really did have awesome vision.

He took a deep breath, a full breath, a cleansing sigh of relief. The weakness had left him. He didn't care what happened to any of them. Didn't care at all. In fact, if that porker blocking him in parked right beside the Mustang, it would tickle him pink. And if those teenagers came out and made it to their car in time to get barbecued, even better.

That being true, he ought to be able to kick Justin out and leave him here. *Damn and double-damn!* Somehow, the mere thought of abandoning Justin ignited a fresh bloom of panic.

Blowing his horn to get her attention, Ray jumped out of the truck and signaled for the fat woman to roll down her window. "I'm leaving now," he called. "You can have my space."

The woman pursed her lips and muttered something under her breath. Two other cars had pulled in behind her, so she couldn't back up now. Her answer: roll her window back up and settle in until the space she wanted opened up. Not caring about the person she'd blocked in or the logjam behind her.

Mission or no mission, if the situation had been different, as in not driving a stolen vehicle that the police were looking for and no imminent explosion, Ray would have kicked in her window and stabbed her. He had no feelings, no concern, no empathy, no qualms at all about what happened to her or any other humans he'd encountered so far. With one exception: a male child named Justin.

He got back in the truck and kept his voice even. "Get in your seat and buckle up," he said. The boy was standing on the passenger-side floorboard, moving those plastic toys around on the dashboard. "C'mon. Now."

"Why?"

Because I told you! Ray thought. Then he said, "We're about to go fast. Real fast. Remember back there on the dirt road? Well, that was nothing. Now put those guys in the glovebox so they won't get hurt."

Justin's blue eyes widened in protest. But he did it. He stowed those silly toys in the glovebox and Ray helped him buckle himself into his seat. Then he shifted into reverse.

They didn't have much time.

CHAPTER 16

ANOTHER MINUTE FLEW by way too fast, and the fat woman's car still hadn't moved. In fact, three other drivers had gotten tired of waiting and gone around her. And the parking space she was waiting on wasn't opening up any time soon. In fact, that male driver wasn't even behind the wheel anymore. He was rooting around for something in the back seat.

Another twenty seconds ...

Justin started getting antsy. "Can I get my toys out?" he asked.

"Just give it another minute."

Ray reminded himself to loosen his grip on the wheel. He'd involuntarily braced himself for an explosion that should have already happened. Well, it wasn't foolproof. The cigarette could have burned out before its bright orange ember kissed the white match heads. And the matches could have been duds. A dive like Shelly's wouldn't spend big money on free matchbooks for their patrons. There was even a chance that the rag wouldn't ignite, despite being soaked in lighter fluid.

I wouldn't bet on any of that, Ray thought. *Damn sure wouldn't be sitting in that Mustang right now.*

The fat woman inched forward—slowly, but at least moving. She made it a couple of feet before stopping again, still blocking Ray. Two more cars pulled in behind her. One of them paused a moment, then went around her. Smart driver.

"Don't move," Ray told Justin. "And don't even think about getting those toys out of the glovebox."

He got out of the truck and ran over to the fat woman's car. "Hey, lady!" he yelled.

She gave Ray a sideways glance and ignored him.

Ray pounded on the roof of her car. "Hey, c'mon! Move up so I can get out."

This time, the fat bitch rolled down her window. She had the pouty expression of a fat cat that didn't want to be bothered. Ray noticed her flabby arms and wondered who in this particular day and age would wear a sleeveless dress with a body like hers. He never saw the pepper spray in her right hand till she pointed it right at his face.

CHAPTER 17

IT ALL HAPPENED IN AN INSTANT. Ray Caldwell stared into the tiny nozzle of the pepper sprayer and knew he was about to be blinded for a good long while. Game over. Mission aborted. He'd wind up in custody, locked away in a 1980s jail cell.

He let his body go limp as he threw up his hands and turned his face away. He landed hard on the pavement, acquiring still more scrapes and bruises on his right side. As an added bonus, some of the spray landed on the back of his left hand like an angry wasp.

And that wasn't all. The fat bitch was getting out of the car, apparently not yet satisfied.

Now she decides to move! Ray swore to himself.

Again, his reflexes sprang into action. The moment her left leg touched the ground, he jumped up and hurled himself against her car door. Metal on bone. Always a painful proposition.

The fat bitch bellowed like a wounded buffalo. Ray didn't wait. He knew she'd attracted attention. He knew people were watching, maybe writing down his tag number. He knew he had to get away before she sprayed him again.

And he knew there were bigger things coming real soon.

Ray raced back to the truck and made sure the doors were locked before looking in the rearview mirror. The fat bitch was hanging on her car door, one flabby arm hooked through the rolled-down window. People were starting to notice. Three of them rooted to the sidewalk. Two more standing next to their cars.

Justin had listened to him, though. He hadn't snagged those toys from the glovebox. No monkey business with a running vehicle like putting it in gear. He was just sitting there waiting for Ray with his seatbelt fastened and that gaze of blue-eyed earnestness.

"Hold on tight," Ray said. "It's time to go."

Again, he shifted into reverse—but, this time, he stomped on the gas.

The green Ford was parked with its back half-blocking Ray's truck. The fat woman still had her car door open; she was sitting sideways in the driver's seat with her feet sticking out of the car. She was hunched over her injured right leg.

Ray Caldwell took all of this in by rote. He shot out of his parking spot, wheeling hard to his left. The heavy rear bumper of the Ramcharger slammed into the top half of the Ford's rear quarter panel, popping its trunk open in the process.

At the moment of impact, he straightened his trajectory. That spun the Chevy's rear end away from him. Ray kept right on backing up. He sideswiped the front of a white car that had pulled up behind the Chevy. But whatever. It was time to go.

People would damn sure notice now. There was the smell of burning rubber, the crunch of metal on metal, the roar of the truck's big engine, the thick bellowing of that troublesome fat bitch. He whipped around the perimeter of the parking lot and made for the nearest exit.

A burgundy van shot through a yellow light as Ray was about to pull out. Screw him. That asshole could stop or swap paint. That's what brakes were for.

The driver of the van laid on the horn, then shot around him. Which took some doing, because Ray wasn't driving slow. Then the van driver slammed on his brakes. Ray started to pass him, but the van swerved to block him. Their speed was down to nothing now. They were crawling.

Slamming on his brakes, Ray parked his truck right in the middle of the busy road with cars moving around them like confused ants. He grabbed the shotgun from behind the seat—he wanted them to see that he was armed!—and came out firing. His first shot shattered the van's rear window. And yeah, assholes were getting out of the van. Three of them.

He had one more barrel to fire. The shells were in the truck, as was the Beretta. He could shoot one of them if they rushed him, then there was the knife.

One of the trio ducked back into the van on the passenger side. Going for a weapon of his own, Ray guessed. He backed up slowly, keeping the shotgun trained on them, and got back in the truck.

"Police are coming," Justin said. The words were all wrong for his innocent-sounding child's voice. But the radio confirmed it. *All units. Hit-and-run. In the vicinity of 651 Strickland Road. Suspect seen driving the stolen Dodge Ramcharger. License number FAT-2095.*

Unbelievable. In a time before camera phones and real-time communication, he'd managed to make it thirty yards before the police showed up. Sure enough, he could see the blue lights behind him coming fast. They'd be here in a matter of seconds.

On top of that, this traffic disturbance he was causing was pretty conspicuous. He was on a four-lane road with a median down the middle and sidewalks on either side. Nobody was driving around him; traffic in the opposite lanes had slowed to a crawl, even though there was nothing preventing them from moving. Drivers were like dumb livestock. Anything out of the ordinary, they all had to stop and gawk.

And those three assholes were coming at him. Construction workers. Two of them had hammers. One had a handgun. Fool! You didn't hold a pistol down at your side; you pointed at your target.

Ray stomped the gas. No need for him and Justin to scrunch down. There'd be no time for this moron to raise his weapon, much less fire it. He wasn't going real fast when he hit him, but a human body didn't stand a chance against a ton of metal.

The asshole's gun fired twice before he landed on his back. A reflex action. He was just shooting pavement. Nothing to worry about.

And those other two just stood there, mouths hanging open. They were used to scaring people, having them back down, simply because they were crazy enough to take things to any level necessary. Ray wasn't crazier or meaner; he just didn't care.

Except where it came to Justin. That was his weakness. His liability. But he could work around that. He had to. Hell, it wasn't like he had a choice. And not just Justin—this whole damn mission! It was supposed to have been a steady progression of unobtrusive actions ...

Screw it, he told himself. *Drive!*

One small problem. Ahead of him, coming from the opposite direction, a police car had crossed over the median. It was coming straight at him.

CHAPTER 18

I HAVE the location in sight. But there's a disturbance up ahead. Under 200 yards and closing.

Ray didn't need the radio to tell him that. He could hear the siren and see the flashing lights just fine. Two of the assholes from the van just stood there, hammers in their hands, not knowing what the hell to do now. Of course, neither did he.

Once the cop spotted his black Dodge Ramcharger ... It wasn't likely that Ray would be able to shoot him before he radioed his findings. Which would bring all kinds of heat down on him.

"We're getting out," he told Justin. "Stick right by my side. Police are going to ask you some questions. You tell them you're my boy. You are, right?"

Justin nodded and climbed out the passenger door. Ray tucked the Beretta in his waistband and confirmed that his shirt-tail concealed both the gun and the hunting knife. His arm was bleeding; his face was still a mess. This was going to be a hard sell.

The police car screeched to a halt in front of the van. A uniformed cop got out. He was tall and athletic with dark hair and a mustache. Ray couldn't help admiring his imposing black gear. He wore mirrored sunglasses, and the setting sun reflected off his black shoes. Also his black belt held a shiny nightstick, holstered gun, radio, and mace canister.

Ray took hold of Justin's hand and led him towards the approaching cop.

"Officer! Thank God you're here." Ray's voice cracked. He gasped for breath, stammered and stumbled over his words ... all by design. "This truck rear-ended my van. With my little boy in it! And now they're trying to kill us."

"What's your name?"

"Dodson," Ray said. "Jim Dodson. This is my boy, Elton."

"I'll need to see your driver's license, Mr. Dodson."

"They took my wallet," Ray said. "Then they shot out my rear window! What kind of maniacs would do a thing like that?"

"Please take your son over to the sidewalk and wait," the cop, whose nameplate identified him as Officer Brewer, said.

Ray did as he was told. This could work. He had several things going for him. Maybe because Rita didn't care, or maybe because Cory didn't want to be blamed for showing up at the trailer and losing Justin, there'd been nothing in the police transmissions about a missing or kidnapped child. So a man with his kid didn't fit the description of the suspected truck thief. There was also the blood on Ray's face and arm.

And then those idiots ...

Brewer was shouting for them to drop the hammers. Morons! They were still holding on to weapons right in front of an amped-up cop.

Of course, Ray's story wouldn't hold up. Brewer wasn't going to let him drive away in the van while he arrested the asshole trio for truck theft. All he could do was wait for an opening to present itself.

Anyhow, Brewer had the two assholes spread-eagle across the hood of his car. The third guy was still down. Brewer knelt down to check on him while he radioed for an ambulance, Ray assumed. And probably calling for backup as well.

He was headed their way now. Ray resisted the urge to draw the Beretta and start firing, even though that might be his best option. His new body would be no match for Brewer unless he caught him off guard. But his instincts told him to wait—for what, he didn't know. But he met Brewer's stern gaze with an expression of relief and gratitude.

"I can't tell you how glad I am you showed up—"

"Sir. I'm going to have you and your son wait in the back of my car."

"What! Am I under arrest?"

"We need to clear some things up," Brewer said.

Immobilizing without alarming. That's what he was doing.

"Please raise your arms and turn around," Brewer said.

"Officer. I don't understand."

"Sir! Raise your arms and turn around. I'm not asking."

This was bad. Brewer was going to pat him down, and the first thing he'd find was the gun. At that point, Ray Caldwell would be kissing concrete.

He took a step back.

Brewer reached him in one long stride. "Hands up. Turn around."

Ray pretended to trip and fall, skinning himself—again!—on the sidewalk in the process. He rolled onto his back.

"Roll over onto your stomach," Brewer said. He nudged Ray's leg with one of his shiny black shoes. "Over! I won't tell you again."

Ray rolled and reached for the knife, fully intending to fling it at Brewer's face.

"No! Don't hurt my dad." Justin had a grip on Brewer's pants leg.

When the police officer reached down to peel him off, the kid sank his teeth into his right hand. Brewer swore under his breath, then yelled. He was trying to be gentle—Justin was just a kid, after all—but he had locked onto the fleshy part of his hand like a snapping turtle.

Ray hopped to his feet.

If Brewer hurt Justin ...

Knife or gun, noise or not, mission be damned ...

If that cop treated Justin even a tiny bit rough, he was dead.

CHAPTER 19

EVERYTHING WAS UNRAVELING ALL AT ONCE. MORE police cars were coming, mostly from the direction Ray had just come. They'd likely converge on that burger joint parking lot, but at least a couple more would join Brewer here.

Another police car was approaching from the opposite direction. But, unlike Brewer, this one lacked the initiative to jump the median and drive headlong into oncoming traffic. So it was jammed up, working its way through the cluster of gawking drivers. (Amazing how police in this era could be so crippled. A few memorable acts of violence, and people would be driving across the sidewalk and beyond to get out of the way.)

And providing the backdrop for it all: the setting sun. Ray loved sunsets. They represented closure, the end of something. In this case, however, the fiery explosion of color sinking into the vast beyond signified his own demise.

But not Justin. If nothing else went right, that small male child was coming out of this unscathed. A weakness that had undoubtedly become Ray's own sunset. But if that's what took him down, he'd succumb to it on his own terms.

Hand on the Beretta in his waistband, Ray watched Police

Officer Brewer jerk his right hand free from Justin's teeth. *Treat that child even the slightest bit rough and you're done,* Ray decided. But Justin was fine. He was pretty worked up, though, having himself a full-on tantrum. Fortunately, the blood on his chin was Brewer's. The only reason Ray hadn't started shooting … yet.

In the meantime, the two assholes no longer had their hands on the hood of Brewer's car. They were evaluating the situation, probably contemplating some dumbassery.

Brewer unclipped his mace from his belt. His mirrored shades flashed in rage as he stared Ray down. "Hands up. Turn around," he said between clenched teeth. "Last chance."

Justin ran up and tried to kick him. Brewer reached down and grabbed his arm. Ray went for his gun. And …

BOOM!

The explosion was heart-stopping, loud enough to make your feet unsteady. A plume of flame surfaced in the distance. That was big. The Mustang must have had about half a tank of gas. A full tank wouldn't have had enough oxygen for a combustion like that one. A near-empty tank wouldn't have had enough fuel.

Yeah, that was epic. And there was a decent chance for the flames to spread to unfortunate cars parked near the Mustang. A chain reaction. That would be cool.

Ray Caldwell took all of that in but kept his eyes locked on Brewer. Hand on the Beretta, ready to fire at a moment's notice.

Obviously startled, Brewer actually flinched. Only for a moment. Before his face hardened into a decisive mask. Then he sprinted to his cruiser, actually pushing one of the idiots from the van out of his way in the process. In mere moments, his siren was blaring and he was flying up the road—still against oncoming traffic!—to the scene of the explosion.

Ray took Justin by the hand. "Let's get the hell out of here," he said.

CHAPTER 20

Justin was still sniffling when they climbed back into the Ramcharger. He didn't seem hurt, just mad and upset. First thing, he popped open the glovebox and grabbed those plastic toys. Well, that was a good thing. Something to distract him, to keep him calm while Ray handled business.

Ray felt a bit more at ease himself, the cab of the truck safe and familiar, a metal fortress of sorts. The police radio was spewing chatter about the explosion. Everything urgent and critical, as if nothing else mattered. One good thing: there was no further mention of Ray Caldwell and his stolen vehicle. At least for now. It seemed that the police were scurrying around like frantic ants whose mound had gotten kicked. Except for the squad car on the other side of the median; it seemed content to remain stuck in the glut of stalled traffic.

Meanwhile, the asshole idiots had decided not to stick around; they were helping their fallen comrade into the van. Ray started his own engine and decided to wait. That cop ahead ... sitting there ... it bothered him.

A fresh explosion rocked the fast food joint's parking lot. But Ray didn't move. Amid car horns, sirens, radio chatter, and explosions, he just sat there, watching the darkening sunset, a true harbinger of finality. Just sat and waited.

The van pulled away. Ray didn't follow.

Sure enough, the waiting cop car U-turned across the median and fell in behind it. Ray decided to follow at a distance and look for a turnoff.

That's when he noticed the red temperature light on his dashboard. A warning that his truck was overheating. And, yeah, he didn't even have to get out to see the steam pouring out of the Ramcharger's front grille.

Ray cursed himself out loud. "Remember those bullets, dumbass? You know—the ones that asshole fired into the pavement when you ran into him. That harmless gunfire you didn't need to worry about?"

Damn! One of them must have ricocheted up and hit the radiator.

CHAPTER 21

FOR RAY CALDWELL, the black Dodge Ramcharger had proved reliable as a small tank. Now, with steam pouring from its front grille, it was a stationary target with a huge bullseye.

About two hundred yards ahead, the police car had pulled the van over. Cars were starting to drive around Ray's stalled truck, some blowing their horns, a couple of drivers holding up middle fingers. Ray knew what that meant, but insults were pointless unless you wanted to provoke a reaction.

Nobody on the other side of the median was going anywhere. Not with the traffic jam up ahead of them.

The right move would be to hop out and leave Justin behind. The boy was engrossed in those toys, oblivious to all of this shit around him. Ray couldn't help but wonder if all 1980s human children were so detached from turbulence going on around them. Not that it mattered at all. A better question was: why did he care?

"C'mon," he told Justin. "We're getting out again. Bring your toys with you."

Then he reconsidered.

"Never mind. Stay put."

How far would they get on foot with dozens of eyes on them? The Ramcharger was overheating and not drivable—if you'd paid money for it and didn't want to permanently cook the engine. But if you'd stolen it and didn't give a shit ... why not cause a matching pileup on this side of the median?

As Ray shifted into gear, a driver in a silver roadster laid on the horn and stuck his middle finger up through the open sunroof. Good a choice as any.

Ray swerved into his backside as he went by, spinning him around like a top. The next car coming couldn't react in time. It ran into the spinning roadster with a sickening crunch of metal on metal.

Fuck yeah! Ray kept driving. Across the sidewalk, across a grassy area in front of a series of tall, uniform buildings. Steam thick as fog billowed across his windshield as he rolled to a halt behind a tall fence that surrounded some painted rectangles with netting stretched across them. The Ramcharger was done. But it was out of immediate sight, and he'd left another mess behind for the cops to sort through.

"Okay," he said. "Now we're getting out."

CHAPTER 22

ALL OF THE buildings had the same gray paneling on the outside walls. Gray boxes, all about forty feet tall, with windows on three floors. There were stairs connecting each level under a covered breezeway.

Housing units. Ray would have recognized them as such even without mission prep.

Getting out of the truck, he left the shotgun behind (too visible), opting for the Beretta and the knife. But he took a minute to root through the toolbox in the back of the Ramcharger. His efforts were rewarded with a small carrying case the size of a tackle box. He threw in a few select tools: a flashlight, a razor knife, a hammer, two screwdrivers (flat and Philips), pliers, wire cutters, and (based strictly on intuition) a metal tape measure.

"Let's go, Justin," he said. "We can't be here long."

Already the shadows of the tall housing units were lengthening as the setting sun sinking ever further beneath the horizon marked precious minutes slipping away. It was way too easy to track them here. Behind all those windows were eyes. People with phones.

Ray's first thought was to cut the phone lines and find a unit to break into, preferably one with somebody home to coerce into hiding them. But that wouldn't work; they needed more distance. Once they got here, the cops would stay for a long time.

They moved between buildings through a covered breezeway into a parking lot. Ray guessed the layout. There were several clusters of tall housing buildings, each with its own set of marked parking spaces. All of them were connected by a service road that bled into the main thoroughfare they'd just escaped.

Cars were arriving and parking. Ray watched people wearing various forms of clothing getting out. Nobody looked his way. A couple of them glanced at their watches. A young couple was engrossed in conversation, oblivious to their surroundings.

Nobody seemed alarmed or on high alert. If anything, they were just annoyed at the stalled traffic delaying their return home. All of them seemed pretty anxious to get into their housing boxes.

It wouldn't be hard to break into one of their cars and hotwire it. But there was too much activity in the parking lot and around the surrounding buildings. One thing was sure: they couldn't keep standing here waiting to be picked up.

A headache had started, right between the eyes and pressing down against the bridge of his nose. Ray Caldwell's skull was too tight, no question. But this pain was caused by tension and fatigue on his frail human body—that and standing here motionless with a full understanding of his dire situation and nary a clue where to go from here.

"Where are we going?" Justin asked.

Ray looked down at him and shook his head. "No idea," he said. *Nope. Not a fucking clue.*

"Are we going to call a cab?" Justin asked.

"What?"

"That's what Mom and Cory do sometimes when they can't drive."

There was the answer. Too far to walk. No vehicle. Being hunted. Can't steal a car. So get someone else to drive you. You could do that one of two ways: force them. Or just pay them money. Which he had.

"We need a phone," he said.

One hell of an understatement. No number to dial, nor a phone to dial it. And that's where he was going to have to force the issue. But how? With whom?

"C'mon," he said.

They couldn't walk behind the buildings where they'd abandoned the Ramcharger. They were going to have to act like they belonged here. Maybe they could take a leisurely walk to the edge of the property and just keep moving. As long as nobody paid attention, they had at least a piss poor shot at it.

Suddenly, Justin ran up to an older woman getting out of her car. Just ran right up to her. "Can we use your phone?" he asked.

CHAPTER 23

Out of all the cars pulling into the parking lot, Justin had to pick this one. The woman had iron-gray hair and suspicious eyes. Not gaudy with jewelry, wearing slacks and a plain blouse, she seemed smarter than most humans, at least from a survival standpoint. Ray could tell by her stiff posture and accusing stare that she trusted very few people. Not even a little boy.

Something else: she had a dark cross-body purse on her left hip. Perfect for a concealed firearm. And a quick draw. Just a simple matter of reaching her right hand across her body.

"Let's not bother this nice lady," Ray said. Then to her: "We're fine. I just need to get a cab." He smiled at her, and she didn't smile back. Well, no shit. Here he was, all dirty and skinned up. That got her guard up. Forget about feeling sorry for him. This woman really was smarter than most humans he'd encountered.

The woman shut her car door and pushed a button on a fob. She'd pulled up in a tan station wagon with alarm decals on the window in a time before car alarms had become an industry standard. She'd had an aftermarket system installed because she knew damn well that she lived in a hostile world.

Justin, the male child that Ray's weakness wouldn't let him detach from, had just walked them into a pickle. They could try to bullshit a sharp, distrusting bitch or try to get the hell away from her fast, which would definitely get her on the horn with the cops.

"Oh. No bother," she said in a raspy voice. "Where are you trying to go?"

Well played, but her voice sounded just a shade too pleasant; it didn't match her stare. Ray knew she wasn't offering help; she was fishing for information.

"His grandma's house," Ray said. "My wife ... things aren't good right now. So I need to get him away from here."

"I'm Martha King," the woman said. "Do you live here in these apartments?"

Ray's right hand itched. This Martha King was checking out his bloody face and ripped sleeve and likely drawing some conclusions that wouldn't bode well for him. But he didn't go for his gun. He'd defer that for now.

"No, ma'am," Ray said. "We were visiting some of my wife's work friends. She's a waitress. They live a couple of buildings down from here." He paused as if working up to confiding in her. "Things got out of hand. I had to get Justin away from that."

"I see," Martha said. "And where does Grandma live?"

"2908 Quail Hollow Drive," Justin said, his child's voice strong in high-pitched recitation. "Raleigh, North Carolina."

Martha King almost smiled.

"I'm John Smith," Ray said. "And you've met my son, Justin. The plan is to get him over to his grandmother's for the night while I head back over here and try to talk my wife into going home."

Martha King reached into her purse—with her right hand!—and produced cigarettes and a lighter. Ray tensed but remained placid on the surface. No giveaways.

"How did you get over here in the first place?" she asked.

"Rode over in my wife's car. She has the keys."

"You know how much cabs cost nowadays?" Martha said. "There's no need for you to waste good money on a ride across town. How about I drive Justin where he's going? That way, you can go deal with your wife."

She was bluffing. Trying to draw him out. Or maybe not. Martha King might really have an honest desire to help a male child in need. In a way, she was giving him an opportunity. An out. Having her drive Justin to some bullshit destination would leave him unencumbered and get her out of his business. But that damn weakness wasn't going to let him detach from the boy ... One thing was sure: he was wasting way too much time standing here trying to talk his way out of this impromptu interrogation.

Thing is, she had him. What could he say? Didn't want Justin riding with strangers, maybe. But he'd already told her that he planned on putting Justin in a cab by himself.

He really didn't want to have to fight his way out of this mess. Not that he cared about what he did to Martha King. (Which was a bonus! If he had any qualms about taking out an elderly woman, he was destined to fail.) But one press on that fob in her hand was all it would take for her car alarm to start blaring. And a smart woman like her was armed—had to be. So better to not underestimate her.

"I couldn't ask you to drive him all the way to Quail Hollow," Ray said.

"Glad to do it." She had a triumphant gleam in her eye when she said that, as if she knew he was bluffing and was calling him on it.

"No, really ..."

"Yes, really! I insist."

Ray pretended to ponder for a moment. "Well, okay. I can't tell you how much I appreciate this. Justin, this nice lady's going to drive you—"

"No!" Justin's high-pitched scream penetrated his inner ear. "You're not leaving me."

"It'll be alright, baby," Martha King said.

"No!" Justin was sobbing now. "Not going with you ... Not a baby!"

Ray offered a helpless shrug. "Know what—this was a bad idea. I guess we're both taking a cab now."

"Twice the money," Martha King said. "With you having to take a cab back here again."

"Oh, well. Sometimes you save money, sometimes you don't."

"Well, I can at least call the cab for you."

"Would you?"

"You wait outside my door—can't be too careful, nowadays —and I'll have them come out here."

No, she wouldn't. Ray knew that for a fact. This woman didn't get nosey just for the hell of it. She pried out nuggets of information. Did they live here? How did they get here? Where were they going? Why didn't Ray have his own transportation? And not a single question about why Ray was carrying a toolbox around. Really?

She was a snake. They were her prey. She didn't have all the details, but she saw through Ray's sham. Martha King wanted to keep them around and get police involved. Twenty years after this time period, she would have hit the emergency button on her cell phone already.

What she didn't know was she'd picked the wrong prey to fuck with. Again, he'd rather not go there. But if she didn't back off, Martha King was going to find out the hard way.

CHAPTER 24

CARS WERE STILL PULLING into the parking lot, but fewer than before. They all had their headlights on as the shadows vanished into darkness. The curtain was falling on another day on Planet Earth in a 1985 city in the eastern region of the United States.

He'd spent several hours being Ray Caldwell, nearly half of this day in the body of a weakling and an imbecile. Now a dumpy old woman with a soft body and hard eyes was staring him down through a haze of cigarette smoke.

Setting down the toolbox, Ray knelt down and patted Justin's cheek. "It's alright," he said. "I'm not sending you off alone." He was using the boy as a prop to distract Martha King and deflect her penetrating gaze. Maybe the sight of an upset child and concerned dad would convince her to move on.

All bullshit. He'd knelt down out of pure instinct because he really cared about a meaningless male child. Weakness! Ravaged by weakness!

And he was running out of time. Police were coming. Probably here already. And this old bat would damn sure point them in the right direction.

"You got a tissue?" he said.

Before Martha King could respond (probably to grill him about that too), a car door slammed. A harmless-looking male with a briefcase called over to her. "Hey, Martha. Police have the entrance blocked. What's going on?" She *was* the right person to ask.

"How'd you get in?" Ray called back.

The man walked toward them. "They're only stopping people from leaving," he said. But he was talking to Martha. She had all the answers as far as he was concerned.

She looked down at Ray; something like a smirk flitted across her face. "That means your wife's not going to be leaving anytime soon," she said.

"Not in her current condition," Ray agreed. "But now I've got to go warn her so that she doesn't try anything stupid." He got up and took Justin by the hand. "Besides, like you said, nobody's leaving here anytime soon."

The businessman approached, his face a question mark of curiosity. "Chuck, this is John Smith and his son, Justin," Martha King said. "He's having wife and car problems."

"Ouch!" Chuck said. He offered a sympathetic chuckle.

Ray sized him up. Middle aged, average height, and soft without a mean streak. Definitely prey in the food chain of human existence. Martha King was made of sterner stuff. She didn't look like much on the surface, but she had venom.

Worse still, Ray noticed something else.

"Looks like they're coming around back too," Chuck observed.

Yeah. The police had found the Ramcharger, not that that was a difficult feat. And Martha King hadn't taken her eyes off of him. She was still staring him down with the look a snake gives a cornered rabbit. Ray saw her right hand sliding across her body and into her purse. That's when he knew he had to act.

He had an advantage. She'd pasted on what humans called a poker face, devoid of any telltale expression. So she couldn't actually look down. She'd have to extract the gun, or whatever weapon she was going after, by feel. And that would slow her down. Hopefully enough.

Rushing forward, Ray slashed with his knife. Her purse landed on the pavement with a loud metallic clunk. Yeah, she was carrying alright. But Ray had cut the purse strap before she could extract the weapon. He kicked the purse under her car. Then he kicked Chuck square in the nuts.

"Help! Police!"

Martha King started running towards the flashing blue lights behind the building. Running was overstating it. She was actually struggling to maintain a brisk walk. And her smoker's voice wasn't strong enough to attract attention. At any rate, she was leaving this Chuck person to fend for himself.

"You can do better than that," Ray called after her.

Then to Justin: "Run over to that next building. I'll catch up with you. Go!"

Justin didn't hesitate. He was moving a hell of a lot faster than Martha King. Still, she'd almost turned the corner. She'd be conversing with the cops any minute now.

Ray kicked the side of her car. Hard. Driving his heel into it. The alarm was excruciatingly loud and produced the desired effect. Martha King stopped and looked back.

Ray grabbed his toolbox and ran like hell.

PART THREE
CAUGHT WITH HIS PANTS DOWN

CHAPTER 25

NIGHTFALL HAD COME. No more lengthening shadows or setting sun. Only darkness. The end of daylight. Somehow, this transition between sunset and nightfall had occurred while Ray had been verbally fencing with Martha King. It wasn't an event or a sudden change like opening or closing a book. No. This transition had happened gradually, but inevitably, bit by bit, little by slowly, until it was just over. Before Ray realized it had happened.

As he ran after Justin, Ray saw that electric lights had popped on everywhere, illuminating breezeways, sidewalks, and parking areas. He grabbed Justin's hand and rushed him around the corner of the nearest building. At least out of sight from the parking lot they'd just fled.

There would be no driving out of here. Not tonight. Not for him. And calling a cab—was there any other transportation option in this time period?—wouldn't work either. Even the distraction he'd engineered was working against him. Between the explosion at a crowded public eating place and his altercation with those assholes in the van, the local authorities would be relentless in their search for him. And now, that nosey old bitch would confirm they were looking in the right place.

They couldn't stay here. Couldn't hide outside in the bushes or behind a dumpster. Couldn't sneak out of this place by car or on foot. That left one option. They had to hole up inside an apartment. Sure, just knock on somebody's door and ask to be invited inside. Something like that. Only without asking.

That plan was way too flawed for Ray's liking. Someone could scream, make a quick phone call, even have a gun of their own. Or be big enough to knock Ray on his ass. Or he could be seen forcing his way inside. And once there, he was pretty much trapped. Way too easy to surround one of these buildings.

But he didn't have a better idea. So they walked straight up to the first door on the bottom floor of the closest building. A cloud of insects swirled around the light above the entryway. But Ray's day was over, his light source gone.

"Stay behind me," he said. "If anything happens to me, run back the way we came. Find the flashing blue lights." It was the best he could do.

Ray knocked on the door. Waited a few seconds, then knocked again. Harder and louder. There was nobody home. Probably. He tried the door and found it locked. Picking the deadbolt wouldn't be hard if he had the tools. But hammers and screwdrivers weren't going to get the job done—not without leaving obvious marks on the doorframe. Same problem with forced entry through a window.

A door opened behind him. The neighbor. A stout young man wearing tan khakis and a golf shirt. "They moved out last week," he said.

Justin walked right up to him. "We're looking for my mom," he said.

This was the second time in a row the boy had done that. But, in this case, he couldn't have created a better distraction. For a brief moment, the young man's attention shifted to the little boy standing in front of him, before he had a chance to notice the seedy-looking man with the ripped shirt and bloody face.

Which gave Ray the opening he needed.

The guy in the doorway was average height and build, maybe a little on the chubby side. Probably not fast. But he could be an even match for Ray Caldwell in a fair fight. Not that a fair fight was going to happen.

By the time he looked up from Justin's blue-eyed gaze, Ray had the Beretta pointed at his nose. "Back up," he said. The man obeyed, stumbling over the threshold but catching himself. Ray almost pulled the trigger.

"Shut the door and lock it," he told Justin.

Just like that. They were inside an apartment.

CHAPTER 26

THE APARTMENT HAD a living area with a TV and an adjoining kitchen. A hallway led back to bedrooms and baths, Ray assumed. The place was neat and didn't smell. There were flowers in a vase on a dining room table with a bright wooden finish. There was a recliner facing the TV, but also a couch with too many flowered cushions to sit comfortably. This guy had a woman living here with him.

Right on cue, a female voice called from down the hallway, "What's going on?"

"Don't answer," Ray said and shoved the gun at the guy's nose.

No need. The unfortunate man of the house was flushed and sweaty, quivering like a frightened sparrow. Words didn't come easy under those conditions. What the hell could he say anyhow? *Hey honey. I just let a bad guy into our home. He's got a gun. Hope you don't mind.*

Ray heard the padding of feet; an angular woman came down the hallway in a pink tee shirt, sweatpants, and flip-flops. Her long face was a question mark of uncertainty. "What's going on—oh, hey sweetie!" She'd spotted Justin.

Then she noticed Ray. Saw the gun. Opened her mouth to scream.

"Go sit down," Ray said.

"You can't do this. Joe! This man ..." She glared at Ray. "You need to leave."

She was coming unglued. Her nostrils flared; her face had exploded in blotches of red panic. Totally unable to accept or process this sudden stroke of bad fortune in her life, she couldn't think clearly. This woman was going to try something foolish and desperate.

"You put that gun down right now before somebody gets hurt!" she said.

Yeah, Ray thought. *Telling a man with a gun to put the gun down because you say so. That oughta work great.*

"I mean it," she said.

Her words were just too ridiculous. A guy that looked like Ray Caldwell, beat up and bloody, pointing a gun at your man's face ... and you respond with verbal ultimatums? Maybe seeing Justin had thrown her. A small, innocent-looking male child was way out of place in a situation like this one. That could have dislodged something in her psyche. She obviously wasn't processing the facts about her situation with any semblance of reality.

And now the woman was slinging open her kitchen drawers. Going for a weapon.

Sure enough, she emerged with a gleaming butcher knife.

That's when Ray realized he was screwed.

Damn that weakness! It was spreading, growing stronger. He could kill both of these strangers in cold blood and then raid their icebox for a late dinner. No problem. But not in front of Justin. For no reason that he was able to ascertain, he couldn't let this male child witness the spattering of brains and guts.

"Please don't make me blow this guy's head off," Ray said. "I don't want the boy to see that."

CHAPTER 27

EVERYTHING WENT STILL. The woman's mouth became a frozen snarl. The sweat on the man's face quit dripping and just sat there in some bizarre suspended animation. And Justin stared up at Ray with unconditional trust in his unblinking blue eyes.

All of this in a split second that felt like an eternity.

The woman set the butcher knife on the counter. Without taking his eye off of Joe (the man of the house with the gun barrel pressed against his nose), Ray grabbed the knife and flung it across the kitchen, sticking it in the wall next to a bulletin board with a calendar covered in sticky notes. The woman let out a stifled squeak when he did that. And Joe had a dark stain on his crotch now.

Mission accomplished. So far. Keep them too scared to fight back, yet not desperate enough to react.

Once again, decision time. Hole up in this apartment and wait things out or try to get out of here altogether. Staying was easier (no shit). But if the police did a door-to-door search, he was screwed. And escaping by car or on foot would be walking right into their net.

The phone rang. Loud and obnoxious *Brrriiing!* It sounded

more like an alarm than a notification, another 20th century thing. One ring. Then another. Joe looked ready to pass out. After four rings, their recorded message kicked on. Her voice, of course. She wore the pants in this household. *Mandy and Joe are unable to take your call right now ...* At the beep, a female friend left a message for Mandy about tennis tomorrow.

Easy for her to say. Tomorrow was still a long way off. More for some than for others.

"Okay. We're all going to sit down right here in this main room," Ray said.

"Would you like something to drink?" Mandy asked.

The bitch was smart. She probably wouldn't try spiking his drink with him watching, but he'd damn sure leave his fingerprints on the glass. Not that Ray Caldwell being here was going to be any big secret at this point.

"Coke, please," Justin said.

"Alright, sweetie."

"Not so fast," Ray said. "We'll sit in your living room around your TV. Justin will get whatever he wants out of the fridge."

Ray put Joe and Mandy on the couch, and he took a straight-backed chair and positioned it in front of the door. Joe looked flushed and embarrassed, clearly wanting to change his pants. Mandy looked pissed off at the situation. Her eyes reminded Ray of a cornered snake looking for an opening. He wasn't going to give her one.

Justin was resourceful. Probably a byproduct of those loser trailer park parents he'd been unlucky enough to get. He came out of the kitchen with chips and sandwiches for himself and Ray, replete with plates and napkins.

Eating with one hand (while holding the gun in the other), Ray scarfed down the sandwich and chased it with sweet fizzy liquid from a can. He barely tasted the food, but it woke up his empty stomach and cleared his fuzzy head. He hadn't realized how hungry he'd been.

"I've gotta use the bathroom," Justin announced.

"I'll show him," Mandy said.

"No, you won't. He can find it."

When Justin left the room, Mandy asked, "Why us?"

"Joe here opened the door."

"Then why don't you take whatever you want and leave?"

This woman was taking what came, dealing with her (and Joe's) suck-ass situation. She wasn't about to try anything stupid. But she wasn't going to miss an opportunity either.

"Actually, what *do* you want?" For her to be grilling him was beyond ridiculous. Yet she was glaring at Ray, her eyes demanding an answer.

And her question was a good one: what *did* he want? A car and safe passage out of here to continue his mission. Without Justin in tow. Better still, he wanted a do-over; he wanted to have driven away in Meathook's truck without Justin stowing away, and he wanted to have left Rita and Cory unable to make a call by any means necessary. But those weren't wants; those were regrets. And regrets were useless with only now and the future in front of him.

"Seriously," Mandy said. "You've invaded our home and involved your little boy. There has to be a reason. Unless you're just some sicko."

"Mandy ..." Joe said. "Don't."

"Don't what? Provoke him? He's already holding us hostage."

"If you were to step outside, you'd see police all over this complex," Ray said. "They're after me. I'm prepared to do whatever is necessary to get out of here. And I mean anything. Nothing is out of bounds. So shut the hell up and use your imagination."

Mandy's glare melted. She was avoiding eye contact now. They'd be easier to control from here on out. Sometimes, telling the truth was more effective than a good bluff.

CHAPTER 28

HE WASN'T KIDDING when he said he'd do anything necessary. Violence didn't bother him. But he didn't get off on it either. It was just a means to an end. A *necessary* means because it had been part of every mission he'd undertaken or knew about.

He wasn't afraid to put himself in harm's way either. Not at all. Granted, if Ray Caldwell got killed before his mission was completed, he'd simply vacate his persona. It was an automatic process: the death of a host always triggered a reverse transfer. So one might say he had nothing to fear. But that wasn't true at all. Natural survival instincts kicked in. After all, the whole idea of a transfer was to become a new version of the host persona. As such, self-preservation and fear of bodily harm came with the territory. That's why those of his kind were the fixers, the elite, the unstoppable.

And yet, I am completely stopped, he thought. Ridiculously stopped. He should have been well on his way to acquiring his target. Instead, he was hiding out in this apartment. All he'd done was cause a big disturbance and attract a lot of attention, all the while making zero progress towards his end goal.

The mere thought of it was exhausting. His eyelids became

bricks, a condition that could transform a blink into a full-on nap. The stiff, wooden chair back actually became comfortable. He didn't realize he was dozing off until Justin's scream jarred him awake.

Mandy was standing over him, reaching for the gun.

"You really want to do this?" he said.

She did.

Practically landing in his lap, she grabbed the Beretta that was resting on his leg. But not before Ray had the knife out of his belt. "Just let go," he said.

"Gun against a knife," Mandy said.

"I'll stab your eyeball before you can pick that thing up and point it."

She let go.

"And don't even think of going for my nuts," Ray said.

Mandy strode across the room—*her* living room—like a jilted queen. Then Justin ran up and tried to kick her. With surprising strength, she grabbed the boy and spun around, facing Ray.

Time to quit fucking around.

He was already wide awake and pissed off as hell. Standing up, gun in hand, pausing to regain his cool, he walked over to her, reminding himself not to go too far. Not yet, anyhow. But something went through him when she grabbed Justin. He wanted to carve her up one painful piece at a time.

"Put that gun away," she said. "You won't risk shooting me now."

"You're right," he said.

Then he rushed forward and stuck her with the butt of the pistol. Right between the eyes. Not hard enough to knock her out. But her grip sure as hell loosened. Justin wriggled free and scurried to safety behind Ray. He moved in close enough to smell the sour tang of sweat through her lavender body wash. He whipped out the knife and pressed the blade behind her left ear. "On the floor," he said.

"Please ... no!"

"Face down or I'll lop it off. Three ... two ..."

Mandy dropped to her knees, then onto her stomach. Sobbing now. No longer outraged but broken. Not even frustrated at Joe anymore for taking no action besides wetting himself. He was still sitting on the couch as if waiting for a bad dream to just end all by itself.

Ray pressed the knife against the side of her neck. "Don't even twitch," he said. Then to Joe: "Stand up. Now!"

Joe stood, his face flushed, unsteady on his feet. Stood to reason that Mandy would grab herself a good-natured doormat like this guy.

"Drop your pants," Ray said.

Joe complied.

"Now kick them over and sit back down."

Removing the belt from Joe's trousers, Ray tied Mandy's hands behind her back. Then he bent her right leg at the knee and secured it tight around the ankle. He had enough leftover belt for both feet, and securing both legs would prevent any kind of movement, but he didn't really like this adult female. If she did manage to get up, he'd hear her thumping around and kick that one leg out from under her. Just for the hell of it.

CHAPTER 29

RAY CALDWELL NEVER QUESTIONED THINGS. It had always been that way. From his earliest childhood memories, life had been fired at him from point-blank range and he reacted. End of story. And now that his psyche had been hijacked by a warrior from the future who didn't give a shit, that was truer than ever.

Evaluate, decide, and act. Never second-guess. If you made an error, you corrected it down the line.

They'd made it through the meat of the night, to the point where daylight was approaching but darkness hadn't yet abated. The sweet spot. Ray looked at the boy asleep on the couch, the shrew hogtied on the carpet, her hapless husband sitting in a kitchen chair without his pants.

It was time to act.

First, he woke Justin, gently shaking him out of slumber, and then he had the boy leave the room. A kid didn't need to see what came next.

He glared at Joe. "Okay, sport. Time to lose the underwear."

Joe stepped out of his boxers, his golf shirt barely covering what manhood he had left.

"Okay, Joe. You need to follow my instructions to a tee or else I'm going to practice plastic surgery on Mandy. Understand?"

"Ya-yes," Joe stammered.

"Walk out that door and head for the road. Don't stop and talk to anybody. You keep walking no matter what."

"Not like this."

"I mean now!" Ray said. He was still on his knees next to Mandy. He nicked the back of her head with the point of the knife. A superficial wound that would stop bleeding in a minute or two. But head wounds always looked worse than they really were. Ray jerked her head to give Joe a good look at her blood-soaked hair. "Get going. Or I start cutting. I won't tell you again!"

"Just go, damn you!" Mandy moaned.

Joe walked out of the apartment like someone in a trance. Exactly the effect Ray was going for. He got up and shut the door behind him. Then he opened his toolbox. He didn't have much time.

He extended the metal tape measure and locked it at the three-foot mark. Then he cut an angled piece out of the end so that it resembled a hook of sorts.

He bolted the door and engaged the chain lock. Then he wedged the back of the chair he'd been sitting in under the door-knob. Just to slow them down a little. He blindfolded Mandy with a bandana from her dresser drawer. He placed another bandana around her mouth but left it loose enough for her to work free. Her cries for help were part of the plan.

He called to Justin in a loud voice that she couldn't help but overhear. "Go in the back bedroom and shut the door and lock it."

Immediately after that, he turned on the stereo, loud enough to disturb the neighbors. They'd be complaining in a little while. And he did lock the bedroom door after opening the outside window. All for show. But Mandy wouldn't know that, not with the loud music muffling his real instructions to Justin.

It all came down to distractions. Joe getting spotted by the police; them having to figure out what in the hell was going on with him. Pretty soon, there'd be an investigation of his apartment with Mandy working free of her gag and screaming her head off. Add to that the loud music and neighbor complaints. The blocked door. A woman in danger. They'd move slowly. Too slow. That's what came from being overly cautious. It was like trying to win in chess without sacrificing pawns.

But success for Ray was far from a sure thing ...

They went out the sliding glass door. Just walked right out onto the ground-level patio with the tiny grill on the stone floor and flowerpots on the wooden railing. Careful to disturb nothing, Ray hefted Justin over the railing and joined him on the other side.

Justin carried a lunch bag from the kitchen. Ray had instructed him to make a couple more sandwiches and grab more sodas to go. He'd also instructed him to use the bathroom (wouldn't have that luxury for a while). The boy had pulled that off in the five minutes Ray had allotted. Cool kid.

Ray dropped to his knees and faced him. "If the cops show up, if there's any kind of disturbance, walk right over to them," he said. "Don't worry. They won't hurt you."

"I'm not leaving you, Ray."

Ray felt a pang of something unfamiliar tug at his chest. A tightening in his throat and tears welling in his eyes. He shook it off. "It's all part of the plan," he said. "It'll help me get away. But I'll come back for you. I promise."

What a crock of shit. There'd be no coming back. Not now, not ever.

Plan A stupidly involved escaping with the boy in tow. But if (probably when) that didn't pan out, Plan B entailed getting Justin clear of the inevitable shootout. And in that case, if Ray did manage to get away clean, he'd be forced to do it solo. A workaround for that damn weakness infesting him.

They walked across the grass and sidewalk to the parking lot. In plain sight. All by themselves at the moment. Ray picked out a long white Cadillac. This was an era where anti-theft technology was still in its infancy. He slid the metal tape measure that he'd modified between the driver's side window and doorframe and used the hooked end to pop the lock.

But he wasn't stealing this car, because he'd never be able to drive it out of here. Instead he found the button to open the trunk. "You sure you can do this?"

No point asking. Justin was already climbing into the open trunk. Ray shut the car door and locked it. Then he got in the trunk himself and unscrewed the interior light bulb before pulling the lid shut.

Only for a little while, Ray told himself. That's why he'd waited till it was almost dawn.

CHAPTER 30

THE CADILLAC'S trunk was large and roomy when it came to hauling your shit around. But it was still claustrophobic as hell for someone trapped inside. Car trunks also weren't airtight, but that didn't mean an abundance of fresh air either. It was also pitch black inside the trunk. Not even a sliver of light.

Around fifteen years from now, they'd require a glow-in-the-dark pull cord to be installed in the trunk of every new car to ensure that it could be opened from the inside. A reaction to a high-profile news story about a woman getting abducted. Kinda silly, when you thought about it. It would be piss poor planning to abduct someone and not tie them up, or at least cut the damn cord first.

This being 1985, the car had no pull cord. But Ray did have a flashlight and tools he would use to pop the latch from the inside when the time came.

Fortunately, it was September and the sun had set. Otherwise it would be like an oven in here. As it was, Ray found himself drenched in sweat. He turned on the flashlight, knowing it couldn't be seen from the outside. Justin seemed surprisingly calm. He was just lying there, stretched out cool as could be, as if they were camping in a tent in the woods just for the fun of it. Ray hoped the boy's calm would last. He was somewhat more cramped, but he managed to lie on his side and angle his body into a position he could at least tolerate.

A good twenty minutes crawled past. At least that was Ray's best guess. Twenty minutes that felt like a whole damn year. He would have preferred leaving the trunk lid cracked. With the light disabled, he'd be able to see what was happening and get some fresh air as an added bonus. But he couldn't risk it.

Finally, he heard police radios. They walked past the car, obviously searching the surrounding area near Joe and Mandy's apartment. Ray liked his chances. After all, what fugitive would intentionally lock himself in the trunk of a car?

A few more minutes passed. Ray thought he heard Mandy's voice ripping harsh words through the night air. Yeah, definitely her. Loud and animated. And her apartment was a good forty yards away. Here was another advantage he had over the police of this era. They were forced to waste gobs of time going over the blow-by-blow saga of how Joe wound up walking around with no pants with Mandy bound and gagged in their apartment. Just in case one of them shared important info consciously or unconsciously.

Sure. Of course. Their intel would be invaluable. The cops would be better off propping up Meathook's dead body and questioning him.

He wasn't going to get caught, at least not tonight. And being locked in the trunk of a car really wasn't much of a problem for him. Already, he was jammed inside of Ray Caldwell's puny little skull. And any claustrophobia had been trained out of him long ago.

His main worry was Justin. A male child. He might start freaking out and making noise. And strangely (fucking weakness!) Ray found himself worrying about the boy being traumatized when his mission should have been his chief concern—hell, his *only* concern.

"Hey, buddy," Ray whispered. "You alright?"

But Justin didn't respond. He was just lying next to Ray, breathing softly in a steady rhythm. Ignoring a twinge, the closest thing to panic for him, Ray leaned in close and checked the boy's pulse. Justin was fine. Not traumatized. Not freaking out one bit. In fact, he felt perfectly safe. The boy was sound asleep.

CHAPTER 31

RAY CALDWELL never replayed events in his head. He didn't have the brain for it. His new hijacker persona never did either except to plan ahead and learn from mistakes. Never had there been any regrets or second thoughts. Morals were for the weak, conscience for the feeble-minded. Besides, there wasn't any question of right or wrong, only whether the mission had been completed or not.

But no calm came to him in the trunk of the Cadillac. During the next half hour, Ray Caldwell sank deep in thought, replaying —yes, replaying!—everything. Particularly where Justin was concerned. Such a strange male child, perceptive beyond his years.

YOU'RE NOT RAY!

He'd figured that out early on. Granted, anybody with half a brain could see that Ray Caldwell wasn't Ray Caldwell. Interestingly, though, at the fast food place, after the boy had pitched a full-on tantrum, he seemed perfectly content to latch on to him, even knowing full well that he, in fact, was not Ray. Furthermore, he wound up physically assaulting grownups on Ray's behalf. Quite the transition from hostile and frightened to unconditional trust.

Ray had almost slipped into his resting phase, a light sleep where he remained completely aware of his surroundings. Then he was awakened by a dog barking right outside at the rear of the car. The noise woke Justin. And he woke up frightened and disoriented. Ray covered his mouth before he could scream.

"It's okay," he whispered. "We'll be out of here before you know it."

Justin nodded affirmation, and Ray took his hand away from the boy's mouth.

Meanwhile, the dog was still barking up a storm. This was bad. Probably not a police dog. Most likely, one of the residents here was just out for a morning walk. (The fact that morning had arrived was encouraging in itself.) The dog had picked up a human scent and couldn't see any other humans around, so it was freaking out.

The owner, a male judging by the voice, yelled for the dog to shut up and come along. "Come on. Now. I don't have time for this shit!" He was too obsessed with the running of his own little life to even question what his dog might have seen or smelled just a few feet away. Heads down. Herd mentality. That's why humans reminded Ray of cattle.

Ray whispered to Justin, "Won't be long."

He hoped he was right about that. They'd been in here for close to an hour by Ray's estimation. Once the sun got overhead, this sealed compartment would get way too hot for them.

His decision was made. It *wouldn't* be much longer. He'd told Justin the truth. Another half-hour and he was popping the trunk and taking his chances on another plan. What that plan was ... he had no idea. But he'd think of something. He always had before.

No sooner had Ray made this decision than the Cadillac's owner got in and started the engine. He was going to drive out of here past any police checkpoints with them safely stowed away. Of course, a lot of things could go wrong. This man (or woman) could be leaving for a long trip somewhere. Or they could break down on the side of the road. But they were probably just driving to work in a reliable vehicle.

Then the trunk popped open.

Just like that. Everything had gone to shit.

With lightning-fast reflexes, Ray made a grab and stopped the trunk lid from flying all the way up. "Don't look outside," he told Justin. "Put your fingers in your ears and look away."

He drew the Beretta. He heard the car door open. When the driver came around, he was going to switch places with him. Owner in the trunk, stowaway behind the wheel.

Then a woman's voice called from somewhere across the parking lot. "Donald! You left your briefcase in the den."

New plan, Ray decided. If this Donald-male human looked in the trunk, he was going to blow him away. He was probably caught anyway at that point ... But Donnie Boy just slammed the trunk shut without looking and backed the car out of his parking space.

CHAPTER 32

THE CADILLAC MADE a right turn into the hum of traffic and picked up speed. With a big engine and plenty of shock absorption, it was designed for a smooth, comfortable ride. But Donnie Boy kept speeding up and stopping in a herky-jerky rhythm that meant he was constantly running up on other driver's asses and having to slam on the brakes.

They'd been in the trunk way too long, and Ray didn't like Justin getting jostled like that. *Real soon,* he thought, *I've gotta get him someplace safe.* That was a change. For the first time ever, his mission had taken a back seat to something else. Weakness. No two ways about it. And he didn't care. That meant Ray had to get away from the boy before he totally lost his edge.

Several start-and-stops later, the Cadillac made a sharp turn, then coasted to a stop. Donald killed the engine. Ray heard his car door slam. Getting out of the trunk right now wasn't a good idea, but Ray decided that he didn't care. Focusing his flashlight, he jammed a screwdriver into the latch and popped the trunk lid.

Bright sunlight blinded him. Amid the chirping of birds and

the hum of traffic on a nearby roadway, he heard the scrape of footsteps walking away.

Squinting through watering eyes, he saw that they were in a middle-class neighborhood with green lawns and tall shade trees. Donald hadn't noticed his open trunk. He'd parked in front of a white two-story house. He'd already made it up the cement walkway to the front porch; he was practically running. Ray studied him from behind, noting his wide shoulders and the bright suspenders holding up his business slacks.

Donald entered the house without knocking. The man had himself a key.

Ray got out of the trunk on unsteady legs that were threatening to cramp up on him. No choice. This was a different scene than the one at Joe and Mandy's. For one thing, it was daylight. For another, the police hadn't blocked off this neighborhood, and Ray wanted to keep it that way.

"I've gotta pee!" Justin whined.

Ray lifted the boy out of the trunk. "Run around the side of the house," he said.

"It hurts bad."

Ray pointed out the greenery on the left side of the house. "Think about a hot fudge sundae," he said. "You make it past that bush over there, you've got yourself another batch of fun box toys."

Justin scuttled across the lawn and disappeared behind a huge boxwood. Ray got the toolbox out of the trunk. He had his knife sheathed against his right leg and the Beretta stuck in the back of his pants, hidden under his sweat-soaked flannel shirt.

He softly shut the trunk and surveyed his surroundings in more detail. Nobody was outside, maybe because kids had already left for school and their parents for work. That could change at any moment. Someone going for a walk or running errands.

They were in a cul-de-sac that was long enough to create the illusion that it might lead somewhere. He memorized the street name and also the name and number on the mailbox. Lane at 5501 Woodlawn Avenue. Ray Caldwell really did have awesome vision.

Then he caught up with Justin around the side of the house. The boy was pissing up a storm, enough to fertilize that boxwood for the rest of the season. Ray guessed he'd sweated most of his out already.

At any rate, they were hidden from immediate view. And Ray had a pretty good idea why Donald had driven here instead of going to work.

"Let's try something," he said. The house stood on a brick foundation that was waist-high; there was a picture window just above them. Ray hoisted Justin up on his shoulders and felt a hint of pride that the boy knew to barely peep over the bottom of the sill and to cup his hands on the sides of his head to kill the glare and reflection.

"See anything?" Ray asked.

"Heavy makeout session," Justin said.

That sounded right for the mid 80s. "Hooking up" was an expression that wouldn't be around till the next century. Ray lowered the boy to the ground. "Did you see where they were?" he asked.

"Kitchen table."

"Not eating or talking?"

Justin huffed in exasperation. "Heavy makeout session," he said.

"Okay, got it," Ray said.

"They were rolling around. Same as you and Mama sometimes—"

"I know, Justin." Ray gently cupped the boy's face in his hand. "I know."

Only he didn't know. But that was for later. Right now was a different story.

Right now, he needed to steal Donald's car while he was too distracted to notice. No mobile phones in this decade, so he'd cut the phone line. That way, Donald would have to go to a neighbor's house to call. And he probably wouldn't want anybody knowing he was here. That would slow him down considerably.

Then Ray got a better idea.

CHAPTER 33

THERE WAS a red Honda Accord parked in the driveway. Ray passed on that choice. Instead, he hotwired the Cadillac and drove to a convenience store just a quarter mile away. He and Justin took the edge off of their hunger with Gatorade, bread, and peanut butter. Not a good breakfast. But carbs, protein, and electrolytes would get the job done.

He was standing in front of a payphone thumbing through the thick phone book. A momentary twinge of worry tugged at him. This Lane who lived on Woodlawn might have an unlisted number. But he found the listing. Pam and William Lane. Even better.

As a preliminary step, he'd gotten Donald Bradford's name and address off the Cadillac's registration slip and used that to get his phone number. An ensuing phone call had him talking to Donald's wife, Ellen. (He'd posed as a friend in town on business.) He'd also purchased a map of Raleigh and zeroed in on this part of the city.

Now he dropped a quarter into the phone's coin slot and dialed up the Lane household. Five rings. Then a recorded message. A man's voice explained that Pam and Bill were unable

LONG DAY FOR RAY 105

to come to the phone right now. Ray wasn't surprised. Answering machines in homes were still fairly new, but not uncommon. He also wasn't surprised that nobody picked up. Thirty seconds to hotwire the Cadillac. Ten minutes to drive to this store. Another couple of minutes to get change for the payphone. Pam and Donnie Boy were definitely unable to come to the phone right now.

Ray heard the beep and started talking. "This call is for Donald and Pam. We've been watching you. At this moment, we know you're right in the middle of a serious game of hide the salami. You really want to stop what you're doing and pick up."

He waited a few seconds, then hung up and called back. This time he said, "I'm leaving a callback number. You have five minutes. That'll give you time to get dressed."

"Who is this?" The woman was loud, the tremor in her voice bordering on panic.

"Put Donald on the phone," Ray said.

"What do you want?"

"I want to talk to Donnie Boy."

"You have no right! How dare you?" Pam slammed down the phone.

Ray let things cook for a minute, then called back.

"Hello!" Pam answered on the first ring.

"Put Donald on now. Or I'm calling Bill," Ray said. "By the way, we've got photos."

What followed was a few seconds of bickering in the background. Then Donald picked up the phone. "Who are you?" he said. "And what the hell do you want?" He had the harsh voice of a pompous ass who was used to getting his way through bullying.

"Look out the front window," Ray said.

The line went silent. Ray heard Donald's roar before he picked up the phone again. "What did you do with my car?"

"We're borrowing it for a few days," Ray said.

"What?" Donald hyperventilated for a few seconds. "You're in deep shit," he said. "You better hope the police find you before I do."

"Shut up and listen," Ray said.

"No! I'm through dealing with you. I'm hanging up and calling the police."

"And tell them what?" Ray said. "That your ride got stolen while you were over here banging Pam when you were supposed to be at work?"

Donald said nothing, but Ray could actually feel him seething on the other end of the phone.

"How's that going to fly with Ellen?" Ray asked.

"I'm going to find you!" Donald said. "So help me God ..."

"No," Ray said. "What you're going to do is tell Ellen your car threw a rod on your way to work this morning. So you're getting a rental for a few days. You don't want her or Bill finding out who the real rod thrower is."

"You can't do this."

"Already done," Ray said. "Play it cool for a few days and you'll get your car back. Or you can choose to be a stupid asshole. But I don't think you'll do that, will you, Donald?"

Donald slammed down the phone.

Ray hung up and got Justin back in the car. Either his risk had paid off and bought him a couple of days with a car that nobody was looking for or Donald was calling the police.

That's why Ray had chosen this location, and why he'd studied the map. The store where they were parked was on a main road. From the parking lot, he could see the turn into Pam Lane's neighborhood. The map told him that there was no back entrance. If anyone was coming or going to her house, they'd have to come this way.

Ray doubted that Donald would call the police, but it didn't hurt to make sure. It would take about twenty minutes for a police car to show up at Pam's house. If that happened, Ray would see it.

There were other possibilities. Donald could call a cab or have Pam drop him wherever he worked. He could go in for a while and then pretend to be surprised that his car wasn't in the parking lot. But Ray thought he was too shaken up to pull that off.

Besides, Ray hadn't been bluffing. He fully intended to enlighten Bill and Ellen if Donald pulled any shit on him. Donald didn't want that. Pam didn't either. She'd be riding his ass, insisting that he just go along with whatever he'd been asked to do.

Fifteen minutes passed. Ray was feeling pretty good about things, but he'd give it a little while longer just to be sure.

Then a police cruiser turned into the parking lot.

CHAPTER 34

THE POLICE CAR pulled into the convenience store parking lot and slowed to a crawl. Ray wished he still had the police scanner to enable him to run off of info instead of instinct. Thanks to his battle cool kicking in automatically, his heartbeat throttled itself down to match the squad car's deliberate approach.

Justin had sunk down out of immediate sight in the Cadillac's front seat. That invoked another twinge of inexplicable pride in Ray. Again, the boy made the right move without being told. He recalled what Justin had told him. *Heavy makeout sessions. Rolling around. Same as you and Mama sometimes ...* No, not likely. That boy was smart as a tack; Ray Caldwell had a weak mind—wouldn't have been chosen as a subject otherwise.

At any rate, if that cop car pulled up behind the Cadillac, Ray would disappear behind the back of the store. The lone cop in the driver's seat would spot the boy and start asking questions. He'd see that the car had been hotwired and call it in. Protocol and fact-finding always got in the way of direct action.

But the cop pulled into a parking spot, then got out and went into the store. No interest in them whatsoever. He was just grabbing himself a coffee and maybe something to eat.

Ray got back in the car. "Might as well go get that sundae," he said.

"For breakfast?" Justin asked.

"Yes, sir. For breakfast," Ray said.

He was wasting time taking a male child to a fast food restaurant instead of handling his assignment. And he knew why. He didn't want to admit it or even think about it, but it was a fact. He was stalling for time. Stalling because he knew what came next. He was going to have to find somebody to take Justin off his hands.

He'd start with the boy's mother. Only he couldn't drive back to the trailer park. Even if he could, he didn't want Justin going back there. But he hadn't been sent here to rescue a boy. Besides, he didn't know anything about childcare in this or any other time period.

Ray felt a tug in his gut, sensing the danger before he saw it (and his vision was awesome). The guy behind the counter was talking to the cop. Their conversation didn't look casual. Not two guys who knew each other shooting the shit. The clerk kept casting agitated glances in Ray's direction. Talking fast. Trying way too hard not to point.

How?

There were very few security cameras in public places and no real-time satellite footage. But they did have news stations. His picture and Justin's would have made for one hell of a story last night. And maybe even this morning. (Of course, it wasn't like there was a TV in the Cadillac's trunk for Ray to have seen that.) He'd also stood right in front of the clerk, buying stuff and getting change. Everything had seemed cool at that point ...

Wasn't so cool now. The cop was staring and he was on his radio. If he was smart, he was calling for backup. If he was picturing himself as a hero, he was about to make a grave error in judgment. His mistake was tipping Ray off. He should have pretended to walk down the aisles browsing for chips and beef jerky while calling this in.

Ray told Justin to fasten his seatbelt as he backed out of his parking space.

"We're not getting a sundae," Justin said.

"No," Ray said. "And not getting a fun box either."

CHAPTER 35

SQUINTING INTO THE MORNING SUN, Ray drove slow and easy out of the parking lot. The road was four lanes separated by a concrete median about ten inches tall. His only option was to turn right, but a parade of traffic streamed past him.

Ray told Justin to buckle his seatbelt and glanced in the rearview mirror. No reason to do anything crazy. There was still a chance that the cop was just having a casual conversation with a convenience store clerk. No such luck. The cop came out of the store and never bothered to get in his car. He made a beeline across the parking lot—headed straight towards them. Ray noticed that he had his right hand on his gun as he approached.

And still the traffic continued unabated. One car after another.

And another.

Damn this luck! That was a new kind of reaction, the kind that Ray never had. Normally, he was a machine, moving with uncanny fluidity from one action to the next.

The cop was right at their rear bumper now. Hand still on his gun. The right move was to hop out of the car and pump three quick rounds into his chest. In the meantime, the Cadillac would roll out into oncoming traffic and cause a crash. Probably a significant pileup. From there, take the cop's radio and anything else he could use and get out of there—either on foot or in a stolen or hijacked vehicle.

The boy ... well, he didn't matter.

Sure, he did.

In the meantime, it was still one continuous wave of cars on their side of the road. The other side of the median was clear.

Rotten, horrible luck, Ray thought. Then he stomped on the gas. Tires squealing, he rammed the Cadillac between two passing vehicles. The impact stunned him for a moment. But he jerked the wheel in the right direction a split second before the familiar thud that accompanies every wreck.

He bounced the Cadillac over the median, drove the wrong way up that side of the road, and took a hard left *back* into the neighborhood they'd just left. Then he screamed around the turn to Pam Lane's street. *Be there,* he said to himself. Sure as shit, her red Accord was still parked in her driveway. Exactly what he needed for his new escape plan.

Ray slammed on the brakes, bringing the car to a screeching halt. And himself.

Something wasn't right. Well, no shit. He was running from police in a dinged-up car. In plain sight of a cop who could see which way he went! It wouldn't take much detective work for them to figure out where to look first.

But that wasn't it at all. Ray's internal alarm had been triggered by a larger and further-reaching pattern than this isolated shit storm he was in right now. He was smack in the middle of his third straight car chase; if he carried out his new plan, he would embark on a fourth. A recurring series of events destined to spiral into a death trap.

He had to force a different outcome lest he be trapped in an infinite loop that tightened during every iteration. The universe did indeed flow in repetitive patterns of cause and effect, much like the winds and tides.

Ray touched Justin's arm. "Grab the toolbox and run around to the back of that house," he said. The boy moved without question. "Wait," Ray said. "Don't forget your fun box toys." *Wouldn't want the boy to do without a plastic shit mound with eyes,* he thought.

The second Justin was out of the car, Ray backed into the yard across the street and then floored it. He dove out the driver's side door onto the thick grass in Pam's yard right before the Cadillac crashed into the Accord.

Ray got up and ran after Justin. From the corner of his eye, he caught a glimpse of Donald's loud suspenders in the window. He'd probably shocked the hell out of him. Well, the bastard had his ride back after all.

He saw Justin sitting on the back step of the house behind Pam's, just waiting for him. Ray ran over. At the bottom of the steps, an eight-foot slab of concrete served as a patio. There was a grill, two lawn chairs, and a chest-high Japanese maple in a white five-gallon ceramic urn. "Really ought to plant that in the ground," Ray said.

Time was running out. They wouldn't be able to outrun the police. Ray tried the back door and found it locked. If they made it out of this, he was getting proper lock picking tools. The top half of the door was glass with a frilly white curtain pulled across it on the inside. Breaking in would be like putting up a sign.

Ray tilted the maple's urn. Finally, some luck that wasn't bad. There was a key under it.

Justin's face was tight and distraught. "In *here*?" His voice cracked a little. The boy had sense enough to know this was a dumbass move of the highest magnitude.

"You got a better idea?" Ray said. He unlocked the door and

led Justin inside, then absently slid the key into his right pants pocket.

Yeah, this was stupid as all hell. Hiding out in the house right behind the one with the wrecked cars in the driveway. Not even knowing if the people that lived here were home.

He'd broken free, though. Busted that damn pattern of car chases wide open.

It just might be crazy enough to work.

CHAPTER 36

So MUCH COULD GO WRONG. If the owners were home, if the house had an alarm system, if anybody saw them go inside, if the cops decided to start knocking on doors ...

They were standing in a bright kitchen with sunlight streaming in through a box window over a white porcelain sink. The adjoining dining room featured a table with a lace covering (also white) surrounded by six ornate wooden chairs.

He got Justin out of there, down a corridor that connected the kitchen to a den and a foyer with a set of carpeted stairs that probably led to second-floor bedrooms. The den had closed blinds on the windows and frilly curtains that were just for looks. He sat Justin down on a couch and told the boy to stay put and not touch anything. No TV. Not a sound.

Drawing his gun, Ray went upstairs and checked the four bedrooms, the master bath, and a laundry room. From the bedroom decor, it wasn't hard to guess that a family of four—boy, girl, and two parents—lived here.

He moved fast. But he also opened closet doors and checked underneath beds. Nobody home. In fact, the mom had left an iron plugged in, a fire waiting to happen. Ray decided to leave it that way.

No sign of a house alarm. Those weren't real common yet in middle-class America, and there was no internet or drone surveillance to worry about. And the family that lived here had left in a hurry this morning. So Mom was busting her ass to get to work. Hopefully. Or she might be taking the kids to school and coming right back. But then, why bother ironing her clothes? They probably had a few hours.

And if they came back? Another hostage situation meant another pattern swirling up from the depths of misfortune. Ray wasn't going to let that happen. They'd need to be out of here way before anybody got home. How? They couldn't set out on foot.

Ray found a piece of mail and got the address. He thought about calling a cab. The police wouldn't be chasing the Cadillac anymore. They'd be grilling Donald and Pam and would know they were hiding something. They'd keep at them till one of them cracked and confessed to the fling they'd been having. Donald might even tell them about Ray's phone call to him. None of that mattered when it came to catching Ray, but working through all of that would take time.

In the meantime, they'd be patrolling this neighborhood. A cab rolling up to a house might attract attention. And the cab driver might recognize Ray from the news. Couldn't take that chance.

What now?

Ray walked into the den. Justin was sitting on the couch doing something with those plastic figurines. "What's your mama's name?" he asked.

"Jill Bailey."

Ray found a phonebook on the kitchen counter right under a phone hanging on the wall. He thought he might have to use the map to find the trailer park's address. But there was only one Jill

Bailey in the book. Ray punched in the number and let it ring ten times before hanging up.

He walked back into the den. "Is your mama at work?" he asked.

Justin looked up from his figurines and shook his head. "Not this early," he said.

"Do you know where she'd be if she wasn't home?"

Justin stared up at Ray with those wild blue eyes and shook his head again. And just like that, Ray was pissed before he knew what happened. Rage shot through him like a sudden shock, then he realized he was grinding his teeth. How many days was that boy left alone out there in that remote trailer park not knowing where his mama was or when she was coming home? That soft-shelled loser, Cory, might have been around to watch over the boy. But Ray wasn't going to ask. Didn't want to know. He was already too fired up without adding more fuel to his rage. That was just feeding his damn weakness all the more. This male child's welfare was none of his business. *Your mission,* he scolded himself. *Remember that?*

"I know her pager number," Justin said.

"She has a pager?"

Ray called Jill's pager from the kitchen phone. When prompted, he left a brief voice message. "Call me back at this number."

This was an era before mobile communication devices were commonplace. Especially handheld ones. Forget about embedded neuro transceivers. Mostly, it was people with mission-critical jobs who were strapped to a pager. Ray had never met Justin's mama—at least not in his current conscious-ness—but he had a strong hunch she didn't fit that bill. If Jill Bailey carried a pager, it was for sketchy activities.

Then the phone rang. Ray thought for a second and had Justin answer it. "If it's not your mama, tell them it's a wrong number," Ray said.

Anybody besides Jill would be calling for the family that lived here. They'd be way less freaked out hearing a child's voice at the other end of the line.

"Hello?" Justin said.

Then he handed the phone to Ray.

CHAPTER 37

RAY HEARD her shouting even before he took the phone from Justin. "Where the hell are you? You scared the hell out of me! You know that?"

She was having a complete meltdown. From the sound of her ragged voice, Ray guessed it didn't take much for that to happen. He waited till she stopped to take a breath.

"This is Ray," he said.

Tense breathing on the other end of the line. "Oh, Ray ... You really fucked up. Everybody's looking for you."

"Shut up and listen," Ray said.

"You're not Ray." Her voice was almost steady, as if that sudden realization buoyed her somehow.

"Justin's going to tell you who I am."

He held the phone in front of Justin's face and nodded at the boy.

"Ray Caldwell," Justin said.

"You know my voice," Ray said. "You heard it from your son. So you know it's me."

"Ray Caldwell could never have done what you did," Jill said.

"Either way, you've got Justin to think about. And you're going to do like I tell you."

Jill argued and protested every step of the way. At one point, Ray almost hung up and devised another plan. Seeing this thing through meant reuniting the boy with a loser who was probably unfit to care for a goldfish. But that was still preferable to Justin being around a guy whose mind and body had been taken over by a ruthless warrior on a deadly mission, a dude who would soon die. No future there.

Finally, she listened. Ray gave her the address where they were hiding. She was to come alone. Park in the driveway. Wait. That simple. He didn't trust her for a skinny minute. But she was the only option that he had.

If nothing else, he'd get the boy away safe. What happened to him was way less important. In fact, it really didn't matter at all. He was only borrowing this body anyhow. And yet ... he didn't want to leave the boy unattended. The weakness was propagating. Bad enough it had influenced his actions here. Now, he dreaded the inevitable reverse transfer where he'd return to his own world and leave Ray Caldwell to die.

They settled in and waited. Ray asked Justin what kind of car his mama drove. Justin said red. That would have to do.

CHAPTER 38

TEN MINUTES PASSED. Ray thought about letting Justin watch TV since it probably wouldn't make any difference at this point. More weakness. *Probably* didn't cut it in his business. There was always a chance that he wouldn't be able to hear somebody approaching the house over the TV noise. So you eliminate that chance. It really was that simple.

Ray sat in a chair across from Justin, facing the window. At the twenty-minute mark, he'd chilled himself into a state of total calm. Relaxed, cool, and in complete control. Zero energy expenditure on worry or stress. Absolutely no distracting himself with anything in this house he'd broken into. He wouldn't be here much longer, and he hadn't come here to steal anything.

He recalled Jill's photo that he'd seen in the trailer. Fresh face, healthy skin. Her picture didn't look the way she sounded over the phone. Justin had been with her in the photo. Ray compared that memory to the boy sitting on the couch. This was about a year later. At least. Jill had gone downhill. Or maybe she'd gone through a healthy patch. At some point, she'd met Cory. Justin's dad. A pathetic excuse. Duh! He'd been in cahoots with Ray

Caldwell, hadn't he? Becoming a loser of that magnitude took some doing.

Clearing those thoughts from his head, Ray calmed himself again and settled in to wait out those final minutes. In 1985, Raleigh was still in the early stages of a growth spurt. But getting from one part of the city to another could take well over forty minutes, depending on proximity and traffic.

An hour passed, and Ray needed a new plan. He knelt in front of Justin. "Your mama's not coming," he said. "You know how to get back to that house where you peed in the bushes?"

"She'll be here," Justin said.

"It's been an hour."

"It takes her a long time to do things," Justin said.

"What things?"

"Everything."

Ray sat down. He'd give it a little while longer, a few more minutes. Then he was going to have Justin walk over to the Donald and Pam house and turn himself in to the police. He'd light out in the opposite direction. Nothing about that idea sat right with him. But he didn't have a better idea, and there was no sense in dragging things out.

A car pulled into the driveway. Lightning fast, Ray shot across the room to the front window. "Get ready to move," he said.

His plan was in place. He was ready to react. Everything a go. Except ...

The car in the driveway wasn't red. And the woman behind the wheel wasn't Justin's mama.

PART FOUR
JILL GOES DOWNHILL

CHAPTER 39

THE ROOM CRACKLED WITH TENSION. That always happened when something was about to go down. The air became electric, the oxygen molecules agitated in anticipation. Nothing to do with Ray's mental state. His breathing and heart rate remained calm and steady. This was a real thing; the world had always ebbed and flowed in sync with its inhabitants.

Keeping an eye on the blue car in the driveway, Ray remained still and calm while his mind blitzed through available options. Hide, go out the back door, shoot, stab, tie her up ... none of those.

She was getting out. An overweight woman with a big helmet of dark hair and shoulder pads. No looker in any century, but a total eyesore in this decade. The best move was to slow her down. And there was a chain lock on the front door. Ray latched the door from the inside and waited.

Justin had pretty much sized up the situation. "What are we going to do?" he asked.

"Keep away from the windows and stay quiet," Ray said. Beyond that ... he was keeping his options open to the end. Buying another minute or two.

The deadbolt clicked. The front door swung inward and caught on the chain. Then exasperation from outside. The woman huffed in exasperation. "You've got to be kidding me!"

Ray watched her walk across the front yard on her way to the back door. He had about thirty seconds to decide what to do next. He counted to ten, told Justin to keep watching the front, then headed to the kitchen. Just in time. The back doorknob was turning.

Justin called out to him, "Mama's here."

CHAPTER 40

THIS THING COULD PLAY out several different ways with only a matter of seconds between one outcome and another. Through the frilly white curtain on the back door window, Ray could see the vague silhouette of the female homeowner approaching the back patio. One moment, he was readying himself to disable her when she entered, then Justin had called out to him that his mama had arrived.

He told Justin what to do. "Go! Get in the car. Don't wait on me. Tell your mama to leave."

"I can't get out," Justin whined.

Can't get out! What the hell did that mean?

And the heavyset female had started up the steps.

Ray glanced into the dining room. Those ridiculous wooden chairs were useless to him. Their backs were all curves and swirls—no straight edges. Jamming one of them under the door-knob would be a waste of time.

He'd have to disable the lady of the house when she entered

...

Then he noticed the lock on the back door. A key was

required to lock and unlock it from the inside. Of course. That prevented a burglar from breaking the window and unlocking the door by reaching in and flipping a lever. At that moment, Ray felt (more than remembered) the key in his pocket. He locked the deadbolt and broke the key off in the lock. That would buy another minute. Maybe.

Running to the front door, he understood what Justin meant by *can't get out*. He'd latched the chain on the front door, and the boy couldn't reach that high. He opened the door for him.

"Get in the car and tell your mama to leave," he said.

"Not without you."

"It's all good," Ray said. "I'm going to meet the two of you tonight. I promise. But you've got to leave now." With zero understanding of what impulse was driving him, he gave the boy a quick hug and shooed him out the door. "Hurry!" he said. Then he locked the door to prevent Justin from coming back inside.

Inexplicably, the woman was knocking on the back door now. The back door to her own house! How the human race had survived all these centuries was anybody's guess.

"Brian? Sara? Is anybody there?" She rapped on the glass again.

Nobody home, Ray thought. *Except the guy who broke in here to evade the police.*

He looked out the front window and cursed. A red Camaro was parked in the driveway with a woman behind the wheel. He spotted Justin's head in the back seat. They hadn't left!

Ray checked the back door again. The woman's outline in the curtain was gone. Sure as shit, she was coming back around to the front of the house.

Reacting without thought, he sprinted out the front door with his tools and weapons in tow. He pounded on the roof of the car. "Go, go, go! Get the hell out of here. What the hell are you waiting for?"

An unkempt woman, presumably Jill, rolled down her window. Her voice had a raspy drawl, as if she was recovering from laryngitis. "We're not leaving without you," she said.

CHAPTER 41

JILL BAILEY DIDN'T LOOK like her picture. Her hair was a stringy mess. Justin's blue eyes were wild in a way that suggested uninhibited depth. Her eyes were simply feral. Ray noted her dilated pupils and decided that her mind was in overload.

He stared at Jill, this woman he didn't know, in disbelief. He glared at Justin, furious with the boy for ignoring his instructions. If they'd been on a sinking ship, instead of this quiet neighborhood with the pretty houses, Ray would have thrown both of them into a lifeboat against their will. As it was, he had no choice but to get in the damn car.

Snatching the passenger door open, he barked out instructions. "Justin! Front seat. Now!" He set the boy in the bucket seat next to his mama and dove into the back.

"Now drive!" he shouted. "What the hell are you waiting for?"

As Jill backed into the street, the big woman rounded the corner. Her face went slack with panic when she saw her front door hanging open. She hurried into her house—again, how the hell humans survived was a mystery to Ray—and never noticed the red Camaro. At least Ray hoped not.

"What the hell was that?" Ray demanded.

"I couldn't leave without you," Jill said. "Justin wouldn't let me."

Ray turned his attention to Justin. "I thought I told you to leave," he said.

Justin stared back at him, a mask of stubborn decisiveness setting his face in stone. "You remember your toolbox?" he asked.

This is one strange male child, Ray thought. But he almost smiled. "Wouldn't leave without it," he said.

Then he addressed Jill. "Okay. You're going to drive us out of here. I'll be scrunched down behind you. You'll have to drive past some police."

"I've got eyes, Ray. I saw them when I drove in here."

"Fine. Play it cool. Follow all traffic laws. Don't give them a reason to look at you."

Ray dropped to his knees and heard an actual crunch. This car was a bigger mess than its driver. Beer tabs all over the carpet. Fast food bags on the seats and floor. This was like hiding in a dumpster.

With shaking hands, Jill drove out of the neighborhood without incident. A little while later, she stopped at a red light. "Any idea where you think we can go?" she asked.

CHAPTER 42

As with many stoplights in Raleigh, the one they were sitting at was long as hell. Ray listened to the smooth purr of the Camaro's powerful engine. That model could hit 140 miles per hour. The stick shift vibrated in Jill's shaky grip, as if the car was psyching itself up for a mighty surge off the starting line.

Jill was wearing a light gray pajama top, long-sleeved with a floral pattern of soft pink all over it. No bra. Her jeans were ripped, and they had a dirty tint to them; this was no distressed style fashion. She'd been wearing the same pair for a while. No shoes either, at least not real ones. She was wearing fuzzy slippers with no heels. Also pink. The thought of those feet working the gas and clutch pedals made Ray nervous.

She lit a cigarette, and he noticed the overflowing ashtray. Any new car smell was long gone. She'd smoked this sucker out a long time ago.

"At least crack a window," Ray said.

"Don't tell me what to do."

Ray leaned forward and rolled her window down a couple of inches. Justin did the same on his side. Jill huffed and exhaled a stream of smoke out her window.

Slow suicide, Ray thought. Not that she'd listen if he told her.

"Your car could use a wash and wax," he said.

"What the hell are you talking about?" Jill said.

"No reflection off the hood at all," Ray said. "The finish is starting to fade."

Jill turned in her seat, her face twisted in disbelief. "After everything you've done, you want to talk to me about a carwash?"

"Light's green," Ray said. "Drive."

"Where?"

"Out of Raleigh. Head north on 85."

"They're all looking for you," Jill said. "You think of that? Your face is all over the news. They'll catch us."

A barrage of car horns cranked up behind them. "Why don't you start by driving through this light?" Ray suggested.

Jill drove a quarter of a mile and caught the next light that had just turned red. She took a final drag on her cigarette and snuffed it out as if it had offended her. Ray looked around at the partly cloudy sky, at the bank thermometer that said it was sixty-five degrees at 1:10 PM.

He waited for the light to turn green and double-checked the rearview mirror. A black Buick was tailing them. Not right on their ass, but several cars back. They were in the far right lane of a four-lane road with a median. When the light changed, Ray told Jill to make a left turn, forcing her to cut across two lanes of traffic.

"Could have told me earlier," Jill snapped. Without bothering to signal, she squalled across oncoming traffic, invoking a fresh outburst of honking horns.

That told Ray all he needed to know. The black Buick was still behind them.

CHAPTER 43

JILL DROVE down a steep hill to a busy intersection with a huge shopping mall. Ray consulted his map and determined that they were in Crabtree Valley. The corner of Creedmore and Glenwood. The mall itself easily spanned two hundred yards. One long interconnected mass of brick and mortar with bold letters touting the names of the various stores that resided there. In every direction the heavily congested roads sloped upward. Yeah. Crabtree was a true valley, a funnel for traffic and money, as well as flooding during a heavy rain.

"What are you doing looking at a map?" Jill demanded. "You know where you are."

"Do I?" Ray said.

The light still hadn't changed. The Buick was still behind them.

Ray focused on the map. A left turn would take them past the mall, heading south on Glenwood. At least two more stoplights involved. After that, a cloverleaf drivers to exit Glenwood and take highway 440 in several different directions. Ray's interest, however, lay in the offramp just beyond the cloverleaf where 440 traffic spilled into Glenwood.

The light changed. Jill turned left.

"Use the right lane," Ray said. "But don't get all the way over. You want to go straight for a ways."

"I know a place," Jill said. "A house right here in Raleigh. Nobody will ever find you there."

Ray said nothing.

"Think about it, Ray. A safe hiding place. Beats driving around. Besides, where would we go? We can't get a hotel. Not with you being hunted."

She'd just driven through the first green light. The one after that was turning yellow. Jill sped up.

"No, stop!" Ray grabbed her shoulder from behind.

"Ray! What the hell?"

"Right where we want to be," Ray said. "First car at the light." He glanced behind him in the rearview mirror. The black Buick was the second car behind him now. Ray spotted two guys, the driver and a passenger.

"Justin, come on back here. Jill, passenger seat. Now!"

Ray hopped out of the car. Jill slid across the console into the passenger seat, losing one of her fuzzy slippers in the process. Justin dove into the back seat, his blue eyes flashing, beaming from ear to ear. *This is all a game to him*, Ray thought. *He has no idea what's at stake. Hasn't known anything this whole time. Just likes being with me and this strung-out woman. Why that is ... well, that's beyond me.*

He got behind the wheel. Their light was still red, but another stoplight had flipped to a green arrow, which allowed mall traffic to exit the parking deck and make a left turn in front of them.

Ray shifted into first, held the gas pedal to the floor, then popped the clutch. The Camaro screamed across the intersection, laying down a line of smoking rubber. He missed an oncoming car by inches.

Jill screamed louder than the car's tires as Ray shifted into second, then grabbed another gear. He checked the rearview mirror. If the driver of the Buick was even halfway sane, Ray could merge onto 440—any exit off the cloverleaf would do—and be long gone. If he was crazy, Ray would have to crank things up.

The dude was crazy. In a roar of smoke and squealing tires, he pushed the white Honda Civic in front of him through the red light and right into an oncoming station wagon that was leaving the mall. Then he swung around the backside of the carnage he'd created, scraping off a nice swatch of paint in the process.

He was crazy, alright.

Ray processed all that while weaving through cars in front of him. A chase down Glenwood was a fool's game. He was bound to get walled in by traffic at some point. And a speed run down 440 wasn't much better, not the way drivers changed lanes without looking. His answer: something way more dangerous and unexpected.

Tearing past the cloverleaf, Ray hit the offramp in the wrong direction. Straight into oncoming traffic at a sixty-mile-an-hour clip. He kept to the right, scraping the guardrail as he squeezed past a tan pickup truck. Then, as the ramp looped around, the lane narrowed.

If traffic had been stalled, the Camaro would have been trapped. But traffic was slowing down to merge off of 440; that left a little space—very little!—between two cars. Ray wove between them, veering left, then right. He'd reached the top of the exit. He was about to hit highway 440 wide open.

Going the wrong way!

Ray turned hard left and hit the brakes. The Camaro skidded into a 180-degree fishtail. Well, almost 180. Without a pause, he merged into northbound traffic and tamped his speed down to the legal limit. The black Buick was nowhere in sight.

Jill punched him in the shoulder. Hard. "Jesus, Ray! Are you trying to get us all killed?"

"You knew we were being followed the whole time," Ray said.

"Followed?" Jill said. "God, no ... Oh, shit."

"Who sent you?" Ray asked. "When Justin paged you, who sent you to us?"

"Nobody. I swear to God." Then Jill's eyes narrowed. "Hey! I don't need this. You get yourself in a world of shit and involve my son. My son, Ray! Then you expect me to risk my ass helping you. You're a total loser. You know that?"

She paused her rant and fumbled for a cigarette. Ray took the Six Forks exit on the slim chance that the Buick had managed to duplicate his wrong-way-up-an-exit maneuver.

The right thing to do here, the logical next move, was to put Jill and Justin out of the car. Give them a wad of cash and drop them off at a shopping center with food and a payphone. Then forget about them and proceed with his mission.

Really, the correct move was to shove them out of the car in the middle of nowhere. But ... weakness. Once again. Weakness!

Instead, he was about to do something stupid. But that's what Ray Caldwell did.

CHAPTER 44

HE TURNED off Six Forks onto a residential road called Dartmouth that went straight downhill for about a mile. It was a middle-class neighborhood with houses and sidewalks. Two turns later, he wound up on Quail Hollow Drive. A wider road, two-story homes, an established community with large trees in every yard. Even the best kept lawns had a sprinkling of leaves and pine needles.

Ray rolled down his window and didn't feel cold. The sky had brightened into a pale blue, as soft and comfortable as nature was going to get. Without forethought, he turned into a public park and parked the car in a space with a trash can nearby.

Jill waited till he'd shut off the engine to light into him. "You bastard! You know exactly where you're at. What the hell do you mean, playing me like that? You almost had me fooled into believing you weren't yourself."

"Justin!" Ray said. "I've got a job for you. Get all those paper bags out of the car and throw them in that trashcan."

The boy launched into it like he was on fire. Ray removed a few napkins from one of the bags, folded them, and placed them in the glovebox. Then he pulled out the ashtray and emptied it into the trash.

"You can cut the act," Jill said.

"Act?"

"Fucking with my head. Pretending you're really not Ray. Like you're this alter ego who cares about things being neat."

"And doesn't like nasty smells," Ray said.

"I know damn well you never cared anything about cleaning shit up."

"Let's all go for a walk," Ray said. "We need to have a serious talk."

"Serious talk, my ass. You gave yourself away by driving here."

Ray left her standing there and took the keys with him. Jill had no choice but to follow. At least he assumed so. Who could tell how an emotionally charged human female would react?

He walked from the parking lot down a man-made trail, a short distance to a shaded area with benches and picnic tables. From there you could walk to the edge of a one-acre pond. Ray sat on a bench and watched a family of ducks swim by.

They built these places as a respite from everyday life. Here, there was nothing happening, no actions to take, no adversity to meet. You could just sit and think about nothing for a while. A bullshit way to waste time, no doubt. Still, Ray couldn't understand why more people—rank-and-file citizens who sold hours of their lives for money and called it career—weren't out here taking a break from it all.

Jill came striding up, and Ray noticed that she'd found her pink slipper. Justin was with her, his eyes flashing in excitement. "This was always your favorite place," Jill said.

"I'll take your word for it," Ray said. "I just drove here because ... okay, I really don't know why I drove here."

"Well, I do. You're Ray Caldwell. And you're playing some sick mind game with me."

"He's not Ray," Justin said.

"Don't interrupt me," Jill said.

"But he's not."

Jill glared at her son. Then at Ray. "No," she said. "I guess he's not."

"He's new Ray," Justin said.

"That's about the size of it," Ray admitted.

Justin danced around chanting, "New Ray! New Ray!"

"Justin baby, please," Jill said. "I've already got a headache."

"New Ray!"

"You wanna go look at the ducks?" Ray asked.

"Yeah. The ducks!" The boy ran down to the edge of the water.

"We can't leave him alone," Jill said. Her tone was accusing and defeated, as if Ray had added a new responsibility to her ever-growing burden.

"I can see him fine from here," Ray said. "We've got to talk."

They sat on the bench, side-by-side but not looking at each other.

"I know a place," Jill said. "I already told you."

"Right. A house we can go to."

"You got no other choice," Jill said. "Everybody's looking for you."

"Fine. But we can't have Justin there with us."

He looked at Jill and studied her reaction. Her lower lip trembled. She hugged her knees to her chest and stared straight ahead.

She'd been planning to fuck him over. Ray had known it the second she opened her mouth about a safe house for him. Soon before the transfer took place, her man, Cory (a real winner himself) and Ray Caldwell had stolen something from a dope dealer named Meathook. And there were bigger players in the game who wanted their merchandise back. Meathook's girlfriend, Rita, had said as much.

Across centuries, Ray had been involved in illegal markets as both a participant and saboteur, depending on his assignment. Commerce was commerce. Legitimate or not. It was all about supply chain distribution, where goods and services worked their way down the pyramid and money worked its way up. They'd pissed off the next level of the pyramid, the one right above Meathook. But things probably wouldn't progress beyond that. Not for whatever piddly theft Cory and Ray Caldwell (Old Ray, not New Ray) had managed to pull off.

"Oh, God!" Jill said. "It just keeps getting worse."

Ray had it all figured out. These next level players, whoever they were, had gotten to Jill. They'd told her, "You'd better tell us if Ray contacts you if you want to keep breathing," or something to that effect. Maybe she'd known they'd been tailing her. Maybe not. But they'd sure as hell told her where to bring Ray after she picked him up.

Jill was trembling all over. A tear ran down her cheek. Then another. Ray wanted to brush the lock of dirty blonde hair out of her face. This was a woman whose life had become one demon after another. She was too busy fighting off a breakdown to ever stop and understand what was happening to her.

And now it had finally fired across the gap. Her dope-addled mind had finally connected a couple of dots. If she drove Ray straight to the address they'd given her, she'd have Justin in the car. She'd be putting her little boy in a very real situation of adult survival.

"You know of somebody we can leave him with?" Ray asked. "Just for a little while."

"You know I don't."

"I don't know anything—never mind. It only has to be long enough for you to drop me off at this house you've got in mind." Did she realize the obvious, that he knew the deal, that he was fully aware of what awaited him at this so-called "safe" haven? Probably not. But what did it matter?

"I can't call my parents. Daddy won't talk to me. And—"

"Someone who can watch him for a couple of hours. Don't they have nursery schools in this time period?"

"Time period? You're talking foolish now."

"Never mind. Focus. Somebody. Anybody you can trust. Just for a little while."

Jill sniffled and wiped her eyes with her pajama top. "Yeah," she said. Her voice sounded husky and defeated. Any sign of that sexy rasp had been extinguished. "One person."

CHAPTER 45

WHILE THEY WERE STILL at the park, they gave Justin a few minutes on a swing set near the parking lot. Then they got back in the car. Jill drove. Nobody spoke as she navigated her way through late morning traffic.

For fifteen minutes, Ray kept looking at the boy in the back seat. Several times, he opened his mouth to say something. But he couldn't meet those blue eyes. In fact, every time Justin stared up at him, he had to look away. He could feel Jill's tight breathing and see the sadness etched on Justin's face. This was a boy who'd spent way too much time having to bid farewell to anything and anyone he cared about.

Jill turned into a neighborhood called Brentwood, as announced by a big sign at the entrance. Not really an entrance, just a road leading in there. When she stopped at a convenience store and got on the payphone, Justin burst into tears.

"Everything's cool, buddy," Ray said. "No reason to cry."

"I don't want you to go."

So the boy had guessed without them telling him. "Only for a little while," Ray said. Even though he had no idea if that was true or not. Justin bit his lip and looked out the window.

Ray didn't bother asking himself why he cared or why he'd stayed involved with these inconsequential humans for this long. The fact of the matter was, Ray Caldwell had fucked up. And he had to fix it if Justin and Jill were going to have a hope in hell.

Jill came back to the car, looking halfway coherent. Her eyes were more red from crying than bloodshot from a harsh week of partying. She'd tied her hair back in a ponytail and seemed way more alert than she'd been earlier. Ray might have tried to gauge her mental state from her voice, but she never said a word. She just put the Camaro in gear and started driving again.

CHAPTER 46

SHE PULLED up to a ranch house with square windows across the front and a blue minivan parked in a carport. Without saying a word, Jill got out of the car and knocked on a door underneath the carport. Ray felt okay about it, not sensing any threat. But he eased the Beretta from his holster on principle.

A middle-aged woman emerged from the house. She had dark shoulder-length hair and wore jeans and a sweatshirt. Unlike Jill, her clothes were clean and her face was bright and alert. More than that, there was a sense of ease about her. Humans sometimes tried to calm themselves by ignoring reality or eliminating unpleasant circumstances. But this female's peace seemed to come from within. *How would I know that?* Ray thought. *And why would I care?*

But he did care. Simply because he felt safe leaving Justin with her.

She and Jill stood there talking. Judging from their body language, Jill was trying to explain things to this woman—like that was even possible!—and the woman really wasn't interested.

"You know your mama's friend?" Ray asked.

"That's Peggy," Justin said.

"What's she like?"

"Different from you and Mom," Justin said.

"Well, that's a good thing," Ray said.

"No! I don't want you to go!" Justin burst into tears.

Ray took the boy by the shoulders, holding him in a firm, but gentle, grip. "You know I'm not Ray," he said.

"Are too! You're new Ray."

"Listen to me." Ray wiped Justin's eyes with one of the napkins from the glovebox. "You and me are both in trouble. Your mama too. Understand?"

Justin's eyes widened into deep pools of hypnotic blue. He nodded. "You don't tell Peggy anything," Ray said. "She's a nice lady. We don't want her involved."

"But she always knows what to do."

"Not this time. She finds out anything besides what your mama's telling her, those people after us might try to hurt her too. We don't want that."

Or, Ray thought, she might call the authorities the second they dropped Justin off with her. He hoped that Jill wasn't spilling too much, that she had the sense to lie through her teeth in this situation.

"They better leave Peggy alone!" Justin said.

Ray cursed himself for a fool. His objective was to calm the male child, not stir him up. But Justin nodded, somber and aware. This was a child with an old man's spirit, a boy who'd seen too much in his five years of life and somehow made peace with it all.

"Don't worry about Peggy. She can take care of herself. Just hang out with her for a while. Does she have any kids?"

"Yeah." Justin wrinkled his nose. "A girl."

"Just be ..." Ray was at a total loss here. "Be well and good," he said.

"What are you and Mama going to do?"

"I've got this," Ray said. "Trust me. Nobody's gonna be coming for us when I get done."

That made him smile. Those wild blue eyes were alight with trust and admiration, and sunlight suddenly beamed through the car's windshield like a spotlight on the two of them, actors on a stage with no script to guide them.

Justin leaned forward and kissed Ray on the cheek. Then he slid something into his hand and got out of the car. He ran to the carport and gave Peggy a hug. She'd squatted down to his level.

Ray watched through blurred vision. On instinct, he used the napkin in his hand to sop up the water that was pooling in his eyes. Apparently, cleaning out the car hadn't eliminated all of the irritants from the air inside it. He'd drive with the window down for a while longer.

He studied the object Justin had placed in his hand, turned it over with his fingers, and had to wipe his eyes again. It was the toy from that burger joint. That plastic turd with eyes.

CHAPTER 47

JILL DROVE HALFWAY up the block and stopped. Taking a deep breath, she wiped her eyes and lit another cigarette. Ray cracked a window and stared straight ahead at ... nothing really. This was just another safe neighborhood that gave its residents a false sense of security. It was quiet, clean, not a lowlife anywhere in sight. The kind of place you'd want to live for comfort and security with nothing to worry about except what to cook for dinner and whether it would rain on a Saturday.

"Where to now?" Ray asked.

She put the Camaro in gear and took off. "You're going to the bus station," she said. "We've gotta get you out of town."

"What about you?"

Jill sighed. "Back home sooner or later. Might have to hide out for a while."

"What about that house you said we could go to?"

Jill turned to stone, her face enameled in an impenetrable coat of irate armor. "Don't fucking talk to me!" she said. "Can you do that?" She made a left turn without looking, and a car blasted its horn.

"Maybe I should drive," Ray said.

"Goddamn you. Shut the hell up!"

Ray looked out the window and wondered how things got so whacked out. Justin was in a safe place, for now anyway. So his concern for the boy, however weak and senseless it might be, had been factored out of the equation. Therefore, the right move, the next indicated action, was to get rid of Jill and take her car. That didn't mean hurting or killing her, necessarily, unless she became a direct threat to his mission. But jerking her out of the car and stranding her on the side of the road was totally in play.

Only ...

He couldn't do it. Any more than he could fail to protect Justin. There was something about the two of them. Something interconnected. Mother and son. A family bond. Their bloodline. Ray Caldwell's bane.

Ray spotted the sign for a sandwich shop that sold foot long subs. "Pull in here," he said. "I've gotta eat. And we need to talk."

For a moment, Ray thought he was going to have to force Jill to turn into the parking lot. But she flipped on a turn signal and parked near the entrance of an eating place called Pete's Subs and Suds. Through the plate glass window, Ray could see several tables and booths occupied by people inside eating their lunch.

"Who's Peggy?" he asked.

"Thought you wanted to eat," Jill said. She reached for her door handle, but Ray placed a firm hand on her wrist. He could feel the slick sweat on her skin, fear and raw nerves maybe coupled with withdrawal from something.

"I need to know who's keeping Justin," he said. "I just do."

Jill made eye contact. Her lower lip quivered. Ray thought she was going to shake apart. "It doesn't make sense," she said. "I'm looking at Ray Caldwell and seeing someone else staring back at me. I mean, I know it's you. But ... your eyes. Same color. Same size. But they belong to another man. Tell me I'm just imagining things, making shit up in my head. Tell me it's really you I'm looking at."

"You wouldn't believe me," Ray said.

Jill gripped the steering wheel with both hands as if it was tethering her to reality, as if losing her grip on it meant floating away into La La Land.

"Tell me about Peggy," Ray said.

CHAPTER 48

IT DIDN'T TAKE LONG. Once Jill got going, the words spilled out of her in waves. An unseen force compelled her to talk faster than any high-tech truth serum Ray had witnessed. Peggy had been her AA sponsor during several stints of clean time that didn't take. That was after drugs and alcohol took her nursing license.

On a laughable side note: she'd been assigned a pager while she was on call with a hospital. They never asked for it back after they fired her. And it still worked. Apparently, they were paying some company to keep a bunch of pagers activated and never noticed one extra. At any rate, she'd made Justin memorize the number so that he could get in touch with her at any time. Risk mitigation for the irresponsible mom.

She'd married Cory three years earlier hoping for some stability in her life. And Justin's. But all he did was clean up her messes like a codependent janitor in the aftermath of a shit storm. The more she screwed up, and the more he tried to fix things, the more she wound up hating him. As a result, she was trapped in a loveless marriage with a weak man who was trying to make a project out of her. She had no love or respect for him at all.

"What about Justin's daddy?" Ray asked.

Jill looked at him as if he had two heads, as if he'd just sprouted an extra appendage and didn't know it. "You did *not* just ask me that," she said.

"What are you trying to tell me?" Ray asked.

"Tell you?"

"Yeah. Spell it out for me."

"If you're that stupid, you really are Ray Caldwell," Jill said.

"Wait a minute, you're saying ..." Ray watched Jill take a drag off her cigarette, her nostrils flaring as she exhaled. A nervous twinge rippled through him like coarse fingernails across a blackboard.

It all made sense now. In addition to having near zero impact on history and no accomplishments of any kind, an ideal transfer host had few personal relationships and no family ties. Because Jill hid it from him, and because Ray Caldwell was a stone idiot, no historical records credited him with fathering any children. Hence, the pile of shit this mission had become. A theory formed in Ray's head, one that had never been tested: a host *might possibly* retain parental instincts for his (or her) offspring after being taken over by a transfer. Perhaps, perhaps ...

Except in this case ...

"Something still doesn't add up," Ray said. "You're an attractive female."

"What did you just call me?" Jill said.

"Attractive. Pleasing to the eye. Sexually appealing. And you seem to have a modicum of intelligence when you're not strung out."

"Thanks," Jill said. "I think."

"So how does Ray Caldwell become the father of your child?"

Jill stamped out her cigarette and glared daggers as she spit out the words. "Because you've got a freaking cannon between your legs," she said.

"Seriously?" Ray said.

"Jesus! You really *aren't* Ray, are you? What the hell did you do with the real Ray—never mind. I don't wanna know. Justin loved when you were a loser, and he loves you like you are now. Whatever that is."

"Let me understand: you engaged Ray Caldwell in coitus simply because—"

"Fuck, man! Do I have to draw you a picture? You could be a major porn star if you weren't so goddamn stupid." She leaned in, her face inches from his. Her nails were digging into his left leg like a predator.

Her voice was soft, raspier, sensuous as hell. "You had more women visiting your trailer than you could shake a stick at," she said. "They'd make sure they were out of there before the sun came up. Every last one of them had to get herself a piece of Ray Caldwell, but they couldn't let anybody know they'd been with a loser like him. Hell, all that perfume smell drowned out every other smell in that nasty trailer."

Ray felt gooseflesh all over his body, followed by a throbbing pulsation in his groin. Jill's hand on his leg had become a burning ember. He'd done orgies in ancient Rome to get close to a centurion who needed to go away. But this thing here with Jill would only complicate matters. He couldn't pursue it.

"Where does Cory figure into all of this?" he asked.

Jill huffed and slammed herself back in the driver's seat, sitting ramrod straight and staring at anything but Ray. "You had to bring him up, didn't you?"

"Yes, I did. He helped—New Ray is what Justin calls me—he helped Old Ray steal something from some bad people. If you know what it is or where they hid it ..."

For a moment her face melted into perplexion, then her eyes narrowed. "I don't know, Ray. I don't know anything. Whatever you and Cory did to piss those people off ... you're both in some deep shit."

Those people. Ray pondered for a moment. Jill was in the dark about all of this. But maybe she knew more than she realized. "What did Cory tell you?" he asked.

"Not a damn thing. He was gone when I got home," Jill said.

"Was anybody there at all?"

"Just the cops taping off your trailer as a crime scene."

"About *those people.* What are you not telling me?"

Jill looked down at her knees. "Some of them caught up with me before I ever got home," she said. "Gave me a number to call if I knew where to find you."

"And you called that number before picking us up this morning," Ray said.

"I had to."

"I know you did," Ray said. "And you were supposed to take me to a certain house."

"They said to call them when I was on my way there with you. So they'd be ready."

"Let's eat first," Ray said. "Then you're gonna make that call."

CHAPTER 49

JILL TURNED onto a road called Boxelder. Ray had expected somewhere remote and tawdry. But this was an expensive neighborhood with large two-story houses spaced far apart on generous plots of land. He guessed that dope money had paid for whichever fancy house Jill pulled up to.

She drove about a quarter of a mile deep into the subdivision. Vehicles were parked along the side of the road. Carpentry crews framing up two new houses on adjacent lots. She turned into a side street, then up a winding driveway that was only wide enough for one vehicle. The driveway snaked uphill through a tall stand of pine trees. With one sappy brown trunk crowded against another, and their intertwined branches heavy with green needles, the tress wove an obstructive tapestry that totally obscured what lay ahead. Elevation and camouflage. Excellent natural defenses.

Ray rolled down his window. He could hear the pop of nail guns and the whine of saws from the construction sites below. Otherwise, nothing. No distant music. No backyard conversations. Even the birds had gone quiet. Their surroundings tense with anticipation of what came next.

He'd debated showing up here alone and surprising those "bad people you didn't want to mess with." Dirtbags one level above Meathook on the food chain. That's all they were. Cockroaches to stomp out.

Instead, he'd directed Jill to make the phone call and let them know they were coming. Why? So they'd know she hadn't screwed them over, that she'd done her part. A precaution in case they wound up getting the best of Ray. Hedging his bets and giving up the element of surprise in the process. His weakness coming to the forefront yet again.

The driveway flattened out at the top of the hill and spread out at least thirty feet. A massive white work truck with commercial plates and a camper shell was parked next to a tan El Camino (more of a long car than a truck from the look of it). No fences. A big brick house with white trim was staring them down. The front porch was too small for a house that size. Not the garage door; it was white aluminum, and wide enough to accommodate three vehicles. Two dormer windows told Ray there was a bonus room above the garage.

The lawn was immaculate, as were the waist-high boxwoods under the first-floor windows. Ray noticed that the walkway was edged to perfection. All for show. There were no small plants, not a flower anywhere in sight. The owner wasn't about personal taste. Just wanted to put up a clean facade.

During the drive over here, Ray had kept his eyes peeled for more cars tailing them. They hadn't been followed.

But the people waiting for them knew they were here. There were cameras. Big clunky boxes with lenses sticking out of them. Ray spotted one on the porch, another over the garage. A couple more in trees. In this day and age, the footage *might* be saved to a hard drive. But probably not. These people didn't want themselves recorded. Still, the feed would be monitored on a TV screen inside, so they saw them coming.

Right on cue, the garage door opened. Ray looked at the vehicles parked in the driveway instead of the garage and wondered what was waiting for them inside. Jill slowed to a near stop, but Ray nudged her and said, "Keep going. You do exactly as you were told."

She drove forward, keeping to the left side of the garage. That's because there was nowhere else to park in there.

Ray had about two seconds to assess things. To the right, there was a long workbench and pegboard on the wall filled with hand tools. To the left were shelves for larger items. Trash bags, detergent, cleaning fluid. Also a chainsaw. Directly in front of them, three brick steps led to a closed door. Ray also noted the gas water heater. It wouldn't take much to blow this place to hell. But he wasn't here for that.

Then his two seconds were up. They were almost inside with the garage door closing behind them.

Ray hit the stick shift and knocked the car out of gear. Then he yanked up on the parking brake. The Camaro coasted to a stop with its front wheels barely past the garage entryway.

The garage door closed. With no safety feature in the 1980s, it crunched down on the hood of the car. A solid thunk, an ugly scar on the paint job, but the engine kept running. The Camaro was probably still drivable.

That told Ray the camera above the garage couldn't see anything right below it. They assumed Jill had driven all the way into whatever trap they had waiting. He got out right as the door at the top of the steps was opening.

Two rough-looking dudes wearing jeans and heavy boots entered the garage, one behind another.

"Jill! Listen to me. Get down on the floor of the car. Close your eyes and cover your ears." Then he let the assholes see him scoot out from under the garage door.

And focused ... *I'm defending Justin's mama*, he thought. And repeated it out loud. "Defending Jill." The only way to ensure that he'd be able to get around his weakness and do what he was about to do.

They walked right up to the garage door and heaved it open. Two weightlifters pressing it overhead. Two dumbasses following a carrot on a stick. Ray put two rounds in both of them. Center-shot one of them, kneecapped the other. The cracking sound of his gun blended nicely with the nearby whine of saws and the popping of nail guns. Nobody would think anything of it.

Ray leaned inside Jill's open window. "Get the hell out of here," he said.

"Jesus, Ray!"

"It's over," he said. "Their ambush didn't work. Now go."

"You forgot your toolbox," she said. "Justin wouldn't want that."

Jill handed it out to Ray. They had a few more seconds. He was out of camera range at the moment. A huge advantage. "Nobody will mess with you after this," he said.

"Oh, Ray."

She backed the Camaro out of the garage and squealed down the driveway out of sight. Something caught in Ray's throat. Letting her go tore at him. Not a cut or a fracture. This pain came from nowhere, as if his body was manufacturing it from deep within.

Fuck it.

Ray ran back into the garage and wove his way around the large table. He made his way to the breaker box in the back corner and flipped all the switches one at a time. When the garage light went out, he flipped that one back on. Then he killed the power to the rest of the house. That would panic anybody who happened to be inside.

When he turned around, the dude he'd kneecapped was

leaning sideways on his good knee. He was supporting himself with his left hand on the concrete floor. Blood seeped from his tattered pants leg.

His right hand was pointing a gun at Ray.

PART FIVE
HOUSE WARMING PARTY

CHAPTER 50

THEY WERE FIFTEEN FEET APART. Ray had screwed up. He'd killed one guy and assumed the other one wouldn't be able to function with a shattered kneecap. This dude had balls of steel or he was on some serious drugs. Probably both. At any rate, Ray had neglected to disarm him.

He had the face of a demon. His eyes shimmered in a wild bloodshot gaze of hatred. The look of somebody who didn't give a shit about anyone or anything. You had to kill him or knock him out cold or he wasn't stopping. Holding himself up and aiming a pistol had to feel like lifting half a ton. But he had Ray dead to rights. All he had to do was pull the trigger.

Ray knew the dude's head was probably spinning, that his vision had to be blurred, that it was taking everything he had to keep his gun steady. Sure enough, the gun dipped downward. But the crazed eyes widened and the gun pointed up at Ray again.

Ray dove across the table and flattened himself on the table-top, giving his opponent a bad angle and making himself a smaller target. Gunfire echoed in the garage as the wounded guy fired three errant shots. Ray drew his own gun, inched forward on his belly ...

His shot nailed the crazy dude's gun hand. A clean hit.

He hopped off the table and snatched up Crazy Dude's gun. Things had changed. He shut the garage door. Now it was just the two of them in here together.

Crazy Dude lay on his side, cradling his ruined gun hand. Since his transference one day ago, Ray had used a knife and fired a shotgun. This was his first time firing the Beretta in this body. And everything worked. Smooth and natural. Ray Caldwell's brain had adapted. As it should. There wasn't enough mental fortitude there for anything besides total compliance. Another mind, one trained in 1980s weaponry, had taken over.

Because *muscle memory* was a bullshit expression. It implied that muscles had actual intelligence, that the brain just said, "Go!" and the body took it from there. Nothing could be further from the truth. Developing a skill—any skill—like playing an instrument, satisfying a lover, carving intricate wood sculptures, or cutting a man's throat—was all about the brain learning to control the body. And it often took a human brain years to fine-tune the instructions that it sent (in the form of electrical impulses) into a harmonious pattern of skill and competence. (Case in point: mastering a golf swing took a really long time or never happened for most people.) In the end, the muscles were just dumb receivers and responders. Sure, muscles got stronger and more adept with practice and/or exercise. But that paled in comparison to the three pounds of gray matter that ran the show.

That's why he was standing over two victims: one dead, the other gravely injured. He looked down into Crazy Dude's eyes. Pure hatred. The wrath was still there. But there was a film of sweat on the man's thick stubble, a flaring of his nostrils every time he took a breath. He didn't have long before death took him. And he was in agony.

"You can save yourself a lot of pain if you tell me what I want to know," Ray said.

"Eat shit!" Crazy Dude spat at Ray's feet. But his voice was weak, and he paid for his gesture with a coughing fit.

"You think you're hurting now, but that's nothing," Ray said. "I can make you beg for death."

Crazy Dude said nothing.

"Why was Meathook after me?" Ray asked.

No response.

"What did I do?"

"You really are an idiot," Crazy Dude said. There was a laugh in his voice. This totally compromised guy was showing contempt. Ray Caldwell had never commanded respect from anyone.

"Who else is in the house?" Ray asked.

Crazy Dude just smiled.

So they were doing this the hard way. Ray went to the pegboard and came back with a hammer, three chisels, and a pair of wire cutters. He laid them out on the floor so that Crazy Dude could have a good look at what was about to happen. "You're going to talk to me," he said.

"Okay, man. You win." Crazy Dude's voice sounded raspy and weak.

"Who else is here?" Ray asked.

Crazy Dude coughed. "Come closer," he whispered. "Can't ... talk."

Ray leaned in. Crazy Dude locked eyes with him, holding him with his gaze. His lips parted as if to say something. But Ray kept looking downward the whole time. At the left hand, the one way this guy could still hurt him. He saw the blade emerge, stepped on Crazy Dude's wrist before he could drive it upward.

"You little shit!" Crazy Dude said. His voice had volume again. "I'm gonna fucking kill you."

"Whatever," Ray said. "I'm done screwing around."

He walked around the table and picked up the chainsaw.

CHAPTER 51

LESS THAN TEN SECONDS. That's how long it took. When Ray came back with the chainsaw, Crazy Dude was on his back staring at the ceiling with blank eyes. The expression of hatred and venom was still etched across his face, but his life had been snuffed out. He was done.

Ray's idea had been to keep one self-proclaimed badass alive and find out why a bunch of alphas had it in for a loser like Ray Caldwell—probably didn't matter, but better to know these things—and more important: find out who else was waiting for him inside the house. So much for that plan. He was going to have to clear out the house one room at a time.

With practiced precision, he went through the pockets of the two dead men. They both had key rings, presumably to those vehicles parked outside and maybe to the house. There were also wallets with cash and several sets of ID. Ray also found vials of blow, a plastic bag full of black capsules, plus some brownish power in a plastic film canister.

The one he'd center-shot had a pack of cigarettes with a "Shelly's Gentlemen's Club" matchbook in the plastic wrapper.

Crazy Dude went one better. He was sporting a black lighter with a naked girl photo on one side and "Shelly's" on the other.

Both men had weapons on them as well. Center-shot guy had a snub-nosed pistol in an ankle holster. Crazy Dude had a diamond-studded switchblade and a pair of brass knuckles. They also had holstered pistols.

Ray laid it all in a pile. No doubt he'd find more of the same in the house. So onward.

Holding the Beretta in front of him, Ray swept through the house one room at a time. The first thing he noticed was the fist-sized mesh wall plates, gray with black buttons, next to the light switches. Ancient stereo speakers? No. This place had itself an intercom system. There was probably a master control panel somewhere. Which meant somebody could be listening to every move he was making. Fine. Let them.

The first floor was easy. Two closets, a master bedroom with an unmade bed. The bathroom door already open. The kitchen and dining room were open space. Nowhere to hide there. That left the den. Ray checked behind a black leather couch and matching recliner. The entertainment center on the opposite wall featured a TV, stereo, and floor speakers that were furniture in themselves. Nowhere to hide there either. He took a look behind a fancy bar built with lacquered wood. Nobody there either. First floor clear.

The second floor was another matter. A shooter could lie in wait at the top of the stairway. Anybody coming up the steps would be easy pickings.

Ray gave the recliner a closer look. It had cup holders in the arm rests and there was an end table next to it with a phone within reach. Next to the phone was a heavy ashtray made of smoked glass, sparkling clean as if it had never been used. The phone's answering machine indicated three messages from unanswered calls. Next to the phone was a chrome box with a speaker and a black button. Some lazy asshole liked being able to kick back and call out to people without moving.

Pressing the black button, Ray did a reasonable imitation of Crazy Dude's raspy voice, injecting a heavy dose of deranged satisfaction into his performance. "Hey! We got him. We got him good!"

Then he listened. Dead silence. No sound of footsteps overhead. So Ray took the first few steps as quietly as possible, then sprinted to the top.

Nobody in the hallway. Ray used his burning lungs and pounding heart from that sudden effort to propel him into the first bedroom. Clear. Same with the other two bedrooms, baths and closets.

The bonus room, the largest room in the house, was also empty of people. No windows except for the two dormers at the front of the house. And those had closed blinds on them. The entire room was lit by track lighting on the ceiling.

Just inside the doorway was a wall panel with buttons labeled by room. Probably the master control for the intercom. On a metal shelving unit against the left wall was a computer monitor. Had to be twenty inches at least. Freaking huge for this time period. It had a monochrome screen divided into four quadrants, each one with a different view of the outside. On the shelf beneath the monitor was a desktop with a keyboard on a sliding tray. And all of that hooked to a computer the size of a sandbag. Here was where they monitored the cameras and stored the video footage—probably just one still photo at a time.

The remaining decor was exercise equipment. A weight bench and at least three hundred pounds of bars and plates. Also a treadmill on a beige mat. The carpet had seen better days; it might have been cream-colored when it was new but had taken on a grayish tone mingled with occasional brown splotches.

Ray heard the phone ring downstairs. He found the button to

the den on the control panel. Very convenient. He heard the phone ring five times before the answering machine picked up.

A man's voice said: "Call me." Then the caller hung up.

Ray went downstairs and played the other three messages on the machine. The first one was somebody looking to score some blow. Real smart of that genius to use his name. The other two were from the same man who'd just called. On every message, his voice was calm, matter of fact. Not a trace of an accent. It was the voice of a guy who got what he wanted without having to raise hell or get excited. Somebody with some juice, in other words.

First message: "Hey, Joe. Know you're busy right now. Call me when you're done." Stupid machine didn't have a time stamp on its messages. But Ray had a pretty strong suspicion it was soon after those two bozos headed to the garage to deal with him.

Second message: "What did you find out? Call me."

Ray cursed a long howling stream of expletives. He'd figured wrong. Not about Jill setting him up for an ambush. That part was obvious. But he'd assumed that the late, not-so-great Meathook and his circle of friends were the only ones he'd have to deal with. Easy enough to walk right in and take their house over. From there, hole up for a few days till the heat died down. Then continue his mission.

But no. Hell no! There was somebody else calling the shots. Telling them what to do. And that somebody wanted Ray Caldwell for something he knew or something he had. Ray Fucking Caldwell! Of all people. Ray Caldwell stole something or knew something that would interest a really bad dude with power and connections.

The historic profilers had blown it. Ray Caldwell was supposed to be a nothing. A nobody. An irrelevant male human whose removal wouldn't leave the slightest void in the temporal plane. But he'd stepped into some deep shit, obviously. How had a record of his inevitable violent death not shown up in at least a couple of lines of newsprint?

Well, for one thing, Meathook would have handled things at the trailer. Then Ray Caldwell would have just disappeared. Nobody calling the police. No family reporting him missing. An insignificant loser never heard from again. And never leaving a void.

Ray went into the kitchen, got a beer out of the refrigerator, made himself a sandwich. He ate fast, barely tasting the ham and cheese. Then he tore the master bedroom apart, emptying closet shelves, pulling out drawers, even flipping the mattress. He found a large brown duffle bag with a shoulder sling. Ray took it to the kitchen and filled it with groceries. Chips, bread, canned goods, peanut butter, soda, coffee. Whatever staples he could carry with him. He threw some plates and silverware in the bag with it. He also threw in a phone book.

Next stop: the garage. He grabbed up the two dead guy's guns, the contents of their wallets, and their keychains. The garage had a lot of useful tools. Given time, he could build himself a really nice arsenal. Instead, he had to find another hiding place. There might be a newly built house in this neighborhood waiting to be sold. Or he might have to risk loading up one of those trucks and driving somewhere.

He heard the phone ringing inside. That big-shot asshole calling again. Ray went back in the den as the answering machine picked up. Same guy. Actually pissed now. "Answer your goddamn phone!"

Ray picked it up. "This is Ray Caldwell," he said. "Come get me." Then he hung up.

Screw running. They'd send a team. At least half a dozen. Maybe more. And Ray would be right here waiting for them. Already, he could see possibilities with the chainsaw and the gas hot water heater. And having Justin in a safe place and Jill in the clear meant NO MORE WEAKNESS! It was going to suck to be them.

Yeah. He'd rid himself of those lowlifes who were after Ray Caldwell for whatever stupid reason. He'd give the police a crime scene that would keep them humping for days on end.

Then he could focus on his mission without getting side-tracked.

The phone rang again. That didn't take long. Ray almost laughed when he picked it up. "What the hell do you want now?" he said.

The asshole was a lot cooler this time.

"We've got your lady friend Jill," he said. "You need to listen."

CHAPTER 52

THE PHONE TREMBLED in Ray's hand. They had Jill.

But how? They hadn't been followed here. Maybe these assholes had set something up outside this subdivision. But nobody in his wildest dreams would imagine Ray Caldwell having even the slightest hope of getting the best of those two in the garage. Furthermore, the messages on the answering machine indicated that the caller had no clue about Ray turning the tables. So there hadn't been time to figure out what had happened here and then chase her down.

"Here's what's gonna happen," the man on the phone said. "You're going to stay right where you are. You got that?"

"Yeah. Got it," Ray said.

"You better. Because Jill's life depends on it."

The man on the phone kept talking. "A car's coming to pick you up. They'll be there in half an hour. They're going to drive you to get the shit you stole from Meathook."

Sure, Ray thought. *And then you'll forget the whole thing.*

"Put Jill on the phone," Ray said.

"No can do."

"Because you're full of shit. You don't have her."

"You willing to bet her life on that?"

Ray didn't respond.

"Half an hour. They'll be there to pick you up. Be out front waiting for them."

The phone went dead. The asshole on the other end had hung up.

Ray grabbed the ashtray off the end table and hurled it through the TV screen. The glass popped and shattered. As did Ray's resolve. He could reason things out all he wanted—timing, circumstances, logistics—all of it added up to those assholes running a stupid bluff. They didn't have Jill. They didn't have leverage. They didn't have shit.

But was Ray willing to bet her life on that? He wasn't.

So half an hour. Which probably meant twenty-five minutes or less. One thing was clear: he couldn't help them find whatever shit Ray Caldwell had stolen from Meathook. It might be floating around in that feeble brain, but he had no way of accessing those memories.

Ray walked outside and stared at the sky. Morning had started out bright and sunny on a baby blue backdrop. Now that afternoon had arrived, everything was overcast and gray. A light breeze tried to stir a couple of brown oak leaves on the driveway but came up short. The distant sound of saws and nail guns had ceased for lunch or an afternoon break. It was a stagnant day, devoid of life. A day for killing. For spilling blood.

The next indicated action for Ray was to drive away now in one of the trucks in the driveway. Complete his mission.

Wasn't going to happen.

That damn weakness was totally unshakable, it seemed.

CHAPTER 53

THE SUN HAD VANISHED. Everything stood perfectly still. The whole world lost a hint of color, its luster masked by the dismal aura of the air and the sky. A black van cruised slowly up the driveway, smooth and purposeful. Its prey was a puny man with a puny brain who'd screwed over the wrong people. Nothing to worry about. But they'd been warned. *Be careful. This moron's gone off the rails. Don't mess around with him.*

Ray Caldwell had been told to expect them in thirty minutes. They'd given him eighteen. The plan was simple. They'd pull up to the house; the passenger would get out and slide the side door to the van open. That moron would only see him and the driver. Then two guys hidden in the back would face-plant Ray Caldwell the second he stepped inside.

From there, it would go really bad for him. Several rolls of plastic were stacked in the very back, along with painting tarps and plastic buckets labeled as cleaning supplies. It might look innocent on the surface, but that shit was there for body disposal.

Nobody spoke. Maybe nerves. Or perhaps it was the thickness of the pines that seemed to be leaning in, ready to snap up the slightest noise on this stagnant afternoon. They rounded the final bend that led up to the house.

"Holy shit!"

The driver slammed on the brakes and froze. He had nowhere to go and no time to process anything before the huge white pickup truck rammed them head-on. The man in the passenger seat yelled, "Everybody out. Now!"

But he stayed where he was while the two in back picked themselves up off the floor and opened the side door. That's when he realized there was nobody driving the truck.

Three quick shots. They mingled with the distant pop of nail guns that had resumed a few minutes earlier. And now the van was rolling backwards. The driver acted as fast as he could. He set the brake. He jammed the gear into park. But the truck was too damn heavy. It pushed them backwards into a cluster of crackling pine trees.

The driver jumped out and tried to run. Another shot ended that.

Which left Rudy Thompson, the leader of this assignment, alone in the passenger seat. He scrunched down and drew his gun. Eased his door open. Planning to slide out of there and use the van for cover. Then, from nowhere, scrawny, stupid Ray Caldwell was right there in the van with him. He'd snuck in through the side door.

Rudy had seen Ray Caldwell around but never paid him any mind. Why should he? The guy was a total loser. But something was different. Ray still had that stupid mullet; in fact, there were better-looking globs of lint on a dirty carpet. But his skin looked somehow more alive, not the gray rotting color of some nothing dude. The eyes, though. Someone else was in Ray's skull and looking out through his eye sockets.

He quickly dismissed that thought as bullshit. Showing no fear, he looked Ray in the eye and said: "You've gotten uglier, boy."

Their instructions were to take Ray alive, rough him up if they needed to, but make him take them to the stolen stash. But he wasn't taking any chances. If he had to shoot this cocksucker out of self-preservation, he was going to do it. He'd have to make up something to tell Gabe, but he wasn't going to die over this shit.

He grinned at Ray and raised his gun. A shot exploded in the van before Rudy could pull the trigger. His right arm hung useless; his pistol clattered to the floorboard. Looking down, he saw that half his hand was missing. Then the pain. A stinging throb. It was like sticking your hand in a blender filled with hornets. He wasn't grinning anymore.

His door opened. Ray pulled him out and dumped him on the ground. This wasn't happening, *couldn't* be happening. This little runt wasn't half his size. Rudy's head swam as the sting in his hand spread up his arm like wildfire. His eyes watered and blurred. He squeezed his eyes shut and tried to get up. His vision cleared but his head was still spinning.

Ray stood over him with a ripped piece of cloth that he must have cut from one of the tarps. "Wrap this around your hand," he said. "We're going for a walk."

"Fuck you!" Rudy said. Then he spat at Ray, hitting his pants leg.

Ray brought out the hunting knife. "I'm real sorry to hear that," he said. He wasn't, really, but it seemed like the right thing to say.

CHAPTER 54

BACK IN THE HOUSE, Ray Caldwell sat in the recliner by the phone in the den. Sipping a scotch and soda that he'd made himself from the bar, he dialed the number Rudy had given him. His original plan had been to herd Rudy up here and have him make the call. But the dude wouldn't have made it that far in his current condition. No problem. He'd talk to Gabe himself.

Gabe answered on the second ring. "What's going on?"

"What's this, Gabe?" Ray said. "No exchange of pleasantries?" He made his voice sound cocky and relaxed. Inside, however, he was shitting bricks over Jill. A cool sweat sprang from his pores, and his heart labored under the lash of unwanted adrenaline.

"Where are you?" Gabe said. "How did you get this number?"

"Bet you didn't know they've been logging every call going in and out of here on that upstairs computer," Ray said. "Took me a while to break the passcode. But, hey! Look at us now. Chatting it up like old friends. Now that I know your name and number." All bullshit. But what did Gabe know?

Ray waited for him to react. Gave it five seconds. "Say something, Gabe. I can hear you breathing."

"You've fucked with the wrong person," Gabe said.

"What can I tell you?" Ray said. "I got tired of waiting. Those guys you were sending for me should've been here thirty minutes ago."

Another pause. Gabe couldn't be sure his guys hadn't arrived yet. At least that's how Ray figured it. No way of knowing. Not in this day and age with no portable phones, much less satellite tracking.

"Listen good," Gabe said. "Your time's up. You can tell me right now where to find what I'm looking for or I can start cutting on your woman."

"Let me talk to her first," Ray said.

"You don't get to call the shots! Start talking or I start cutting. You've got ten seconds."

"I talk to Jill first. She's not alright, you'll never see your shit again."

Ray hung up. He'd meant the exact opposite of what he just said. If Jill wasn't okay, Gabe was going to get an up-close-and-personal look at his own shit after Ray turned him into a one-man suppository.

He'd been listening carefully to Gabe's voice, focusing on accent, inflection, depth, resonance. This asshole on the other end of the phone was a smoker. Probably a big guy with a deep chest from up north. Not New York or New Jersey. Maybe Philadelphia or Delaware. He didn't sound like an old fart, but he was no kid either. Ray put him in his forties.

Some things you had to figure out yourself. It was doubtful he could have gotten those details from Rudy. That dude wasn't firing on all cylinders towards the end of their conversation. He did, however, know where he could find Gabe—a location that also happened to be the address of one Shelly's Gentlemen's Club.

Unfortunately, Rudy had no idea what Ray Caldwell was supposed to have stolen from Meathook. Ray believed him. Rudy had seemed pretty sincere at the time. Maybe he'd ask Gabe. If the asshole decided to call back.

The phone rang.

CHAPTER 55

Ray polished off his scotch and soda and answered the phone on the third ring. Instead of Gabe's deep bellow, he heard Jill's voice.

"Hi, Ray. I'm alright. For now." Her voice was slightly muffled by a burst of static on the line.

Then Gabe came on loud and clear. "You just heard from her. Now start talking."

"Put Jill back on," Ray said.

"I do that, you're not going to like what you hear," Gabe said.

And you're really not going to like where your head's going to wind up, Ray thought to himself. "Tell me something," he said aloud. "Why do you need me?"

"Ray! You're trying my patience."

"I mean, Cory was in on it with me. He's soft as hell. You'd break him down in no time flat. Seems a hell of a lot easier than chasing me all over Raleigh."

"Quit playing dumber than you are," Gabe said. "You're the one who moved the shit to a new hiding place. You caused Cory a lot of pain, by the way. And you're about to do the same to someone else. Or maybe you don't care what happens to her."

Ray would have gladly told Gabe where to find his stolen merchandise if he knew where it was. But he didn't know what had been stolen, or its location. That info resided somewhere in the puny brain he'd occupied; he didn't have access to it.

"I'm gonna count to three," Gabe said. "Then the next sound you hear will be Jill screaming."

That damn weakness wasn't helping either. Ray told himself he was sending Gabe on a wild goose chase as a diversionary tactic. But he was really scared for Jill. Totally unacceptable. But true.

"One ..." Gabe said. "Two ..."

"Alright! I'll tell you," Ray said. "You know where my trailer is off of Strickland Road?"

"Don't hand me that," Gabe said. "We already tore your place apart. It ain't there."

"Of course it's not there, dumbass," Ray said. "You think I'd leave it inside my place?"

"Watch your mouth, asshole! And you'd better not be jerking me around."

"I wouldn't dream of jerking you," Ray said. "Look, you saw the woods behind the place. Right? Well, you have to walk down to the bottom of the hill."

"Are you shitting me?"

"Not at all. At the bottom of that first slope where the ground flattens out, there's three trees within a couple feet of each other. You'll see boards nailed between them. Two-by-fours."

"That's your hiding place?"

"It's my latrine. When my septic got backed up, I wasn't going to have some plumbing company rip me off. So I walked down there and dug myself a shitter."

"Ray! You're trying my patience."

"What? I just told you where to find your shit."

"Funny guy."

"No, wait. Gabe! It's buried underneath the latrine about

three feet down. I wrapped it in plastic and buried it. Nobody would ever think to look there."

"It better be there!" Gabe ended the call.

There was no latrine or shit hole at the bottom of the hill. He'd made the whole thing up just to buy a little bit of time. Too little. But now he knew where Gabe was holed up. He'd need a map to figure out how to get there. And a vehicle. Probably that El Camino in the driveway.

Just then, the window shattered. Two canisters landed on the carpet and exploded softly, filling the den with tear gas.

Gabe had sent reinforcements. How in the hell had they gotten there so fast?

CHAPTER 56

ONE SECOND EARLIER, the den seemed like a safe haven. A place to kick back and enjoy life, to reflect and relish what you had. Settling into that recliner, sipping scotch and soda, it seemed possible for Ray to forget he had a whole lot of shit to deal with. But that oasis was actually a mirage that shattered when the tear gas canisters crashed through the window.

Ray's reaction was instant. Pulling his shirt over his face and eyes, he hit the floor and belly-crawled towards the back of the house. Then the back door crashed open.

He'd cleared most (not all) of the tear gas cloud at that point. So upward. Ray hopped up and sprinted up the stairs. His eyes were watering, his nostrils burning. Hurt like a mother, but he could function. The trick was to keep moving.

As he ran to the bonus room, he listened for the creak of footfalls on the stairs. Nothing yet. Somebody had busted in through the back door and held up, assuming that he'd come coughing and wheezing out of the den and stagger right into his lap.

He checked the bonus room cameras. Two guys out front. Two around back. And at least one inside now. Pressing the intercom button to the den and turning the volume all the way up, he coughed and gagged into the microphone. The down-stairs intruder was standing much closer to the speaker in the den than to Ray in the bonus room. Ray wouldn't be heard upstairs unless he way overshot the mark on the loudness of his voice.

"Oh my God. My eyes! I can't see!"

He heard them calling to him; their voices floated up the stairwell. Two of them. "It's all over, Caldwell," one of them said.

"Might as well come on out," the other said. "We'll help you rinse your eyes out."

"Can't see!" Ray whined.

Two guys in camo pants and mesh shirts had gas masks hanging around their necks. They looked at each other, shrugged, and fitted their masks over their faces and eyes. They were headed into the den to retrieve Ray Caldwell, dumbass extraordinaire, when two shots rang out. They both landed face first. A steady trickle of blood leaked from their masks and seeped into the carpet. A solid stream of blood gushed down their necks and shoulders from the back of their heads where Ray had shot them.

Ray raced back upstairs and heard the front door crash open before he made it to the second floor. He stood still and silent. Voices floated up to him. "Holy shit! He shot them. From behind. Only a coward shoots a man from behind!"

Ray wondered if they'd hear him if he snuck quietly down the hallway to the bonus room. Probably not. They were too busy yelling and giving their position away. But might they be coerced into doing something ridiculously stupid? Like running up the stairs. Then Ray could just take a good angle at the top of the landing and pick them off with ease.

"Hey, scrotum head!" Ray yelled. "Come up and get me."

For a brief instant, Ray questioned whether they'd be that stupid.

They were.

Ray fired twice. Two point-blank direct hits. Then he ran back to the bonus room and checked the camera feeds just in time to see the last two entering the house through the busted back door. Actually, "entering the house" was overstating their intent. "Entering the house" implied going into battle, joining the fray. These two stood and argued for half a minute. Started to leave, then changed their minds. Probably deciding they were more scared of Gabe than Ray Caldwell. A bad decision.

Ray addressed them over the intercom. "You two wussies can get the hell out of here or wind up dead. I've got a bead on both of you. The next step you take had better be in the right direction."

He watched them running away—down the hill with tree branches smacking them along the way. Probably to whatever vehicle they'd arrived in. If they had any sense at all, they'd get the hell out of Raleigh. Run long and tall. Start over somewhere that Gabe wouldn't find them. Ray doubted that they did.

CHAPTER 57

RAY FOUND a thermostat on the second floor and turned the temperature down to sixty degrees with the fan on high. The front and back door were both open, but he could smell the sting of tear gas coming up from the den. It was a burning harshness that floated through the air the way a school of jellyfish floats through the ocean.

With a wet towel over his head, he relieved one of the prone assailants of his gas mask. A lot of the gas had dissipated, but Ray put on the mask and opened windows. He was taking zero chances on having his vision or breathing compromised. Bad enough that the rotten-egg-laced-with-spoiled-pepper taste still lingered in his mouth. It was time to stock up and get the hell out of here. Partly because it was only a matter of time before more of Gabe's stooges or the police showed up, but also because this house had become a boneyard that reeked of death.

None of the new arrivals had any ID on them. But all were carrying cash. They also had some useful weaponry. When Ray got done, he had two pear-shaped tear gas grenades, a set of brass knuckles with a four-inch blade that flipped out on demand, one can of mace, a proper shoulder holster, and more ammo than he needed. At least fifty extra clips by his estimation. But you never had too much ammo. He kept his gas mask as well. He'd hoped one of them had been carrying lock picking tools, but theirs was more of a *knock the door down and kick somebody's ass* kind of operation.

Ray decided to add to the provisions he'd started to gather. He found a black leather gym bag in the closet of the master bedroom. He loaded that with his new weapons. From the kitchen, he took the eight remaining beers. Then he headed to the garage. The first thing he grabbed was the chainsaw—had to have it. He also scored a heavy crowbar, a hacksaw, and a battery-powered drill with a full set of bits. He took his smaller toolbox along because his city map was in it, along with other tools he might need. And because Justin would be disappointed if he didn't.

Then he got the keys to the El Camino that belonged to Crazy Dude's partner. He rifled through El Camino guy's wallet and checked out his driver's license. Not expired. That was something. Assuming it wasn't an alias, his name was Felton Renfro. And the photo on his license showed him with dark hair and a scraggly beard that had never quite filled in above the jawline. Ray hadn't shaved in several days, so the hair and beard were maybe a close enough match with some fixing involved, except ... Felton stood five-eleven, according to his license, and tipped the scales at two hundred and five pounds. Ray Caldwell wasn't a big guy.

Then he looked down at his shoes, comparing their size to the black cowboy boots Felton was wearing. He kicked off his worn-out sneakers and pulled off Felton's boots. Both size thirteen. An exact match. Ray Caldwell did have some big body parts. The heels on the boots elevated him somewhere in the neighborhood of Felton's height if Felton happened to be barefooted. It would have to do.

He loaded everything up in the El Camino's back seat and

turned the key in the ignition. The powerful engine rumbled to life, ready to gorge itself on gas like a stoned pig eating everything in sight.

On the truck's dashboard was a black cowboy hat. Felton must have been worried about messing it up with Ray's blood. So he'd left it out here. Ray put it on. The hat was a tad large for him, but he liked the way it sat down on his head. He checked the glovebox and discovered that Felton had insurance and a current registration. The inspection sticker was also good to go.

The hat was a nice touch. If Ray got stopped and showed them Felton's license, it might work. It just might. That was reason enough to wear that hat. But Ray knew better. He would keep wearing it for as long as he was in this world, until the inevitable reverse transfer killed this host body he occupied. He would wear this hat because he liked it. It was cool.

He drove down the driveway past the wrecked van and white work truck to the bottom of the treeline. Making a left turn, he drove past the two houses under construction. The carpentry crews never gave him a second glance.

CHAPTER 58

AT A KMART, he purchased cheap sunglasses, two pairs of socks, three undershirts, and three pairs of underpants—all white. He also bought a pair of jeans, a flannel shirt, a Duke Blue Devils hoodie, and a plain blue ball cap. In the cosmetics aisle, he picked up a bottle of black hair dye. In sporting goods, he added a pair of binoculars and a digital watch to his haul.

In the same parking lot was a costume store. There he found a shiny black jacket that might have been leather; with its turned-up collar, it seemed more of a costume than a wearable coat. Still, it zipped up and fit his needs exactly. The jacket didn't fall off of him, but it was roomy enough to conceal a shoulder holster with a gun with plenty of space left over. After that purchase, he went back into the Kmart and picked up a red corduroy shirt. The jacket and shirt just went together.

He headed south on a street called Saunders to a town called Garner. Out of Raleigh. Away from anyone who might be driving around looking for Felton's truck. There would be no police report. But Gabe's people would be looking for it.

He found a cheap hotel that took cash towards the edge of the city limits. On principle, he signed the register as Joe Britton from Wilson, N.C. In his room, using Felton's driver's license photo as a guide, he stood in front of the bathroom mirror and combed the black dye into his hair and beard. Not bad at a glance, the biggest difference being Ray Caldwell's lame mullet. His hair was way too thin up top, and, above the ears, it had been shaved down in a hapless effort to look ... who could tell what that moron had been thinking? The hat took care of that. With the hat clamped on his head, all you could see was a mane of black hair across the back of his neck.

Ray put on the shoulder holster with the Beretta in it. He holstered another pistol to his right hip. A smaller 38 to the ankle holster on his right leg. Then he put on the jacket and studied himself in the mirror above the scratched-up dresser. It didn't look like he was carrying. The right and left pockets were large enough to accommodate one tear gas grenade apiece. You wanted some extra room to ensure they wouldn't fall out unexpectedly.

As an added bonus, the jacket had a concealed pocket in the inner lining around the right ribcage area. Ray almost missed it at first. A strip of velcro sealed it from within and made it look like a seam. Maybe some carnival actor had used this coat as an onstage prop to hide streams of colored handkerchiefs (not enough room for a live rabbit). The bladed brass knuckles fit in there nicely, totally undetectable unless you patted the jacket from both the inside and out. Most people conducting a search would run their hands underneath a man's jacket.

Perhaps this would turn out to be Ray's rabbit from a hat trick. Abracadabra!

He hung his jacket in a dusty closet on one of three wire coat hangers. He put the guns and holsters in the black leather gym bag with his other weapons and the rest of his clothes. He slid the gym bag under the bed and out of sight. The Beretta he placed under a pillow where he could grab it faster than he could hit the snooze button on the digital alarm clock on the nightstand.

That's how things were supposed to work out after a transfer. Ray Caldwell, in the wind, untraceable (at least for the time being), and weaponed up. Free to focus on his mission with no outside interference. He could eat, sleep, and tomorrow start gathering info. Forget about Gabe, Jill, and Shelly's jerk-off club because none of that mattered. With his entire focus on the task at hand and his brain fully acclimated in Ray Caldwell's body, he could expect to complete his mission within forty-eight hours. Three days at the absolute most.

And his weakness? That damnable affection for an irrelevant male child and his mother! Well, it no longer mattered. He hadn't been transferred to this time and place as a tourist or a nanny. He was here to get shit done. He was here to serve.

He'd had to contend with totally unexpected obstacles in past assignments. But every last one of them had involved the mechanics of the mission itself. More opponents than antici-pated, inaccurate facts and dates, hard-to-find intel, accidents, injuries, and sometimes plain bad luck. He overcame things. He was a warrior. That's what he did. He completed his assignment, undeterred by anything that got in his way.

He couldn't be bargained with, wouldn't listen to reason, couldn't be bought. He kept moving forward, impervious to pain, immune to fear, unmoved by sympathy for anyone or anything. And altering the future didn't bother him at all. Not even changing events in the past to the point of wiping out his own future existence ... It was the reason why he was one of the chosen ones: he simply didn't give a ripe fuck.

But this weakness ...

There was only one way to look at it. Suppose that, following a transfer, he'd discovered that his designated host was stricken with kidney failure; he would have continued to show up for dialysis while he got his shit together in the way of info and weapons. Then he would have gotten one final treatment to tide him over while he executed the mission. Everything would take longer, no question about that, but he'd get it done. Same as always.

Well, following this particular transfer, he'd discovered that Ray Caldwell was stricken with mental and emotional failure in the form of a feeble mind and an irrational weakness. A weakness so embedded in his very being that no amount of acclimation could purge it from his psyche. With no way to treat it, and no means of wresting it out of himself, it was just there.

Until now. Through no fault of his own—why should he care about fault anyway?—Jill had been kidnapped and there was nothing he could do to guarantee her safety one way or another. Not a thing. Going after Gabe could easily get her hurt or killed that much faster. So the logical course of action was to move on. Complete his mission. Gabe would realize that Jill was no good to him anymore and that would be that. What happened, happened. What came, came. After the reverse transfer, Ray Caldwell wouldn't be around to see it.

When nightfall descended, he ordered a large pizza loaded with meat and onions. Then he sat on the bed with his back propped against the weathered headboard in the silent room. He ignored the blank TV screen and stared straight ahead. The pizza box sat next to him unopened on the bed; his nostrils were filled with the smell of meat and cheese, but he had no appetite. He opened a warm beer, then set it on the nightstand without taking a sip.

He stared straight ahead at his reflection in the mirror above the dresser. His disgust was totally expected. Ray Caldwell was nobody you'd admire or respect. But the bile in his throat and the grinding of his teeth had nothing to do with what he saw staring back at him. It was an inside thing. He hated the person within, the man Ray Caldwell had become. His anger and disdain were directed inward at himself.

For a moment, he considered grabbing the Beretta and eating a bullet. But Ray Caldwell didn't deserve to die like that. Not in a cheap hotel room with his boy in trouble and not doing a damn thing about it. Ray Caldwell had business to attend to.

Suddenly ravenous, he opened the pizza box and wolfed down two slices without a pause, relishing the pleasant burn of greasy food in his gut. He washed it down with a beer and opened another. Tomorrow was going to be a big day.

PART SIX
CRANKING UP SOME SERIOUS HEAT

CHAPTER 59

THE NEARBY RUMBLE of big trucks on the highway woke him from a light sleep at 4:00 AM. For a cheap hotel that took cash, the bed was more comfortable than he'd expected. The sheets were threadbare but clean, the mattress reasonably accommodating.

Last night, Ray had reinforced the doorknob to his room with a wooden chair. He got the Beretta from under his pillow, took it with him to the bathroom, laid it on the sink. Leaving the bathroom door open, Ray undressed and got in the shower.

Above the showerhead in a corner of the ceiling, a moth was encased in a spider's web. Seeking the light, the moth had ventured into a place it couldn't return from. Ray left the bathroom door open and a gap in the shower curtain that allowed him to look out. Probably an abundance of caution. But no way in hell was he getting trapped. Ever.

The water in the shower was hotter than he'd expected. He turned it all the way up to a near scalding temperature that reddened his skin, washing away the blood and stench of the past two days. When he'd finished, the top half of the mirror was barely fogged over; most of the steam had escaped through the open door.

He toweled off, then pulled on his jeans and the flannel shirt. He'd wear the ball cap instead of the cowboy hat this morning. No bright red or black leather till the time came. A warrior didn't don his battle gear till the enemy was within sight. And he didn't want to attract attention in the meantime.

Spreading his city map out on a round table barely big enough for one person's dinner, he located Shelly's Gentlemen's Club. From there, he mapped out the nearest public library. And a place to get breakfast in the interim while he waited for the library to open.

It was now 4:50 AM. Ray attached his ankle holster with the 38 and his shoulder holster with the Beretta. The hunting knife was sheathed against his right leg. He loaded all his stuff in the El Camino and took one last glance around the room. There were five cans of beer left. Whatever. He didn't need them. Then, more on impulse than logic, he wrapped them in one of the pillow-cases and took them along.

CHAPTER 60

DAYLIGHT WAS APPROACHING. But the lights in the parking lot provided more light than the sun at this early hour. Ray turned on the El Camino's headlights and merged onto the highway. He'd memorized the turns and approximate distances to avoid having to study the map while driving. Phones that called out directions were years into the future.

Ray loved this time of day before the sun came up. Most people were still in bed and hardly at their best. The best time to strike! A twinge of excitement surged through him, the anticipation of a bloodletting on the horizon. Ray flipped on a right turn signal and made a smooth, legal turn at a green light. He relaxed his neck and let a slow river of tension flow out of him. Bloodletting would come later. This morning was about reconnaissance. Unless an unexpected opportunity presented itself. You never knew.

He didn't have to look for Shelly's. The sign was set far enough away from the road to prevent the highway lights from muting its glow. Lit up in gold letters ten feet tall, it was unmissable from fifty yards away. The sign looked like the matchbox, but on a larger scale.

Ray drove past it without slowing down. No cars in the large parking lot. Just a cinderblock building with a flat metal roof. The occupancy limit was probably around one hundred when the club was open and the gentlemen were getting off on the dancers. At least Ray assumed that was the setup.

Half a mile up the road, he took the exit. There was a shopping area with a grocery store and gas station on the right and two hotels across the street. It was a typical North Carolina highway exit with roads and businesses at the top of the ramp and thick woods right behind them.

Leaving the truck in the store parking lot would be a risk this early in the morning. There were six cars parked together well away from the entrance. They obviously belonged to employees who were inside stocking shelves or getting produce ready. His truck would stick out.

Time for breakfast.

CHAPTER 61

IT TOOK Ray twenty minutes to find a Waffle House. He sat at the counter and ordered three buttermilk pancakes with a side of bacon. He didn't need coffee. He was already amped up. Big time. But he still drank three cups of their caffeine-laced sludge simply because he got off on it.

On the TV behind the counter, a news blip—no longer a full segment—announced that the dangerous fugitive, Ray Caldwell, was still at large. Wanted for murder, arson, kidnapping, breaking and entering ...

"I can't imagine who would do all that," the waitress said. Her nameplate identified her as Merry Ann. She was young with dark hair tied back in a ponytail and a tired face.

"It's still early," Ray said.

She laughed. "You drink any more of that coffee, you're going to float away." Her voice had a hoarse twang that Ray found alluring as hell.

"Better than driving in my sleep," he said.

The place was quiet. There were only three customers: Ray and two guys in a booth. The two men in the booth wore jeans and work boots. One of them had a down vest and a cap advertising Cat Diesel Power. The other had slicked-back hair and a windbreaker. Ray had sized them up the moment he walked in. They belonged to a big rig parked in a corner of the lot. Truckers taking a break on their way to pick up or drop off a load. Probably not local. No ties to this part of the country. Not a threat.

The morning news on the TV moved on to a prediction of warmer weather and a human interest story. Nothing about the carnage from yesterday afternoon. Which meant nobody had called the police. Gabe *really* didn't want law enforcement involved.

"Where are you headed this morning?" Merry Ann asked.

"Work," Ray said. "I'm a carpenter. Got to get there before eight."

"I'm a waitress," Merry Ann said. "I've gotta be here now."

Ray almost laughed. In fact, he barely caught himself in time. Laughter was bad. Joking and cutting up was the fastest way to lose your edge. He couldn't stop his eyes from lighting up, though. Ray Caldwell's dull gray eyes had a light in them. Not what he wanted.

Merry Ann broke the silence. "What do you build?" she asked.

"Houses. Framing crew. We're up in North Raleigh in a subdivision called Wood Valley."

"You've got a long drive."

"Not if I start early enough," Ray said. "Gotta go where the job is sometimes."

The two men in the booth headed out to their truck. It was just Ray and Merry Ann now. "Did they spell your name right?" he asked.

"Yeah."

"I always thought Mary was spelled M-a-r-y."

"That's not my name," Merry Ann said. Her tone told Ray that she was dead serious about that. He held her steady gaze and didn't look away. She had dark brown eyes with specks of black in them that made that light brown apron-vest she was wearing look tacky as hell. That stupid vest and dumber name-plate were why he hadn't noticed her tight body until now. That getup she had on was an attempt to squash any and all feminine attributes a waitress might possess.

"Well, I'd better get going," Ray said.

"You got a name?" she asked.

"Yeah." He got off his stool and headed for the door.

"You want to share?"

"I'm married," he said.

"Do I look like I care?" Merry Ann disappeared through a door behind the counter.

Ray paused at the booth and tucked two hundred dollars under the edge of one of the trucker's empty plates. Then he headed outside.

CHAPTER 62

7:20 AM.

Still too early to leave his car in the grocery store parking lot. The library wasn't open either. Daylight had arrived in the form of a dirty yellow backdrop across the horizon. Dark cloud cover dusted the poor excuse for a sunrise like a layer of soot.

Ray got back on the highway and drove past Shelly's, this time on the opposite side of the road. Three miles later, he turned around and headed back for a second pass.

Driving by in broad daylight, Ray was able to spot more details. The sign wasn't lit up anymore. The block building was about fifteen feet tall. Maybe forty feet long. Smaller than Ray had originally thought. Several thick black cables about twenty feet long ran from a tall wooden pole to the back of the building. There was a tall antenna mounted on the roof. For what? Cable television had become a thing, and, besides, the club had live entertainment. Still no cars in the parking lot.

Ray kept driving, processing what he'd seen. You could pick up a lot when the sun was out and you knew what to look for. Why the antenna? How did people stay in constant contact from wherever they happened to be in this pre-cell-phone era?

Through the airwaves on radio. Even car phones in the 1980s relied on that. Gabe was able to get that second wave of guys to the house by calling out to them from a radio transmitter.

Ray cursed himself for a fool for not remembering the radio in Meathook's truck. And when he'd set that work truck rolling down the driveway to ram the van like a runaway tank? Yeah. It had the same equipment in there too. A radio and a police scanner. But he'd been in full attack mode, never bothering to notice. This truck he was driving, however, had only an FM radio and a tape player. So not everybody got hooked into Gabe's party line.

At any rate, the absence of cars in the parking lot didn't necessarily mean the building was empty. Gabe could have Jill confined in there; he might have left someone to guard her. Maybe several people to be on the safe side. Or even an ambush, hoping Ray would try to break in.

Ray took the exit and turned around for another pass. Eight o'clock was approaching and the traffic was suddenly thick as hell. He studied Shelly's from the opposite side of the median as he drove past. Not easy to do because of all the idiots on the highway dodging and weaving in front of each other without looking. Then everything stacked up. A wreck or something. Everything totally stopped.

He took advantage of the situation. Traffic wasn't going anywhere, so he pulled into the breakdown lane and turned on his hazard lights. A guy parked on the side of the road during a traffic jam wouldn't attract nearly as much attention as when traffic was flowing. Breaking out the binoculars, he gave Shelly's a good closeup look. Two boxy cameras were mounted on the side of the building. Another on the wooden power pole in the parking lot. The front doors had been painted black and looked to be solid steel. No windows on that side of the building. There was probably a back door, but that was later.

Putting away the binoculars, he eased his way back into stalled traffic and inched forward one car length at a time for another twenty minutes. He turned around at the exit three miles down the road—finally. Traffic was flowing in that direction. He drove past Shelly's one last time and noticed something else. The power lines ran to a line of telephone poles that disappeared into the woods behind the parking lot. Those cables would deliver power, phone, and cable services to Gabe's establishment.

Just like that. Ray had gone from having time to kill to being on a tight schedule. Because now there were several stops he had to make.

CHAPTER 63

Computers and More was a secondhand electronics outlet on the north side of Raleigh. That section of Capital Boulevard was one mile of strip centers and convenience stores. The shop was supposed to open at nine, but the guy running the place showed up fifteen minutes late.

Ray thought about robbing him but instead walked inside and took a look around. It was exactly what he'd hoped it would be when he browsed the Yellow Pages. New equipment—that might or might not have fallen off the back of a delivery truck—lumped together with estate sale and flea market kind of shit. As such, you didn't walk into a showroom filled with shiny merchandise.

The store had a beat-up counter facing the front window. All of their inventory was in a large back room where you could walk in and look around. The storekeeper, a tall dude in his twenties with thinning hair, said nothing when Ray followed him inside. He just plopped himself on a stool behind the counter and started tinkering with a circuit board.

Ray checked out the back room. There were long work-benches cantilevered from each wall and a couple of office chairs on rollers. The center of the room was an island of long tables. Every shelf and tabletop was covered with radios, computers, typewriters, monitors, old TVs, you name it. Some of the stuff was worth a few bucks, like an IBM PC with the classic gunboat gray cover, which was hot shit during this era. But a lot of it was just sitting there in pieces, literally taken apart and never put back together.

"What do you have for radios and transmitters?" he asked the storekeeper.

"You need to be more specific," the storekeeper said. "What are you looking for?"

No, he wouldn't rob the asshole. He'd just gotten himself a new identity. He didn't need Felton Renfro getting jammed up with the law. But he was tempted.

"First off, a police scanner," Ray said. "Second, a receiver. Not a C.B. A Ham unit will work. But it has to have some range, and I need to pick up all frequencies."

The storekeeper let out a heavy sigh that meant he'd dismissed his potential customer as an ignoramus. "You've gotta have a license for that," he said.

"Not to listen," Ray said. "I'm also looking for a cheap computer to hook into it. Terminal programming, you know. Do you have anything FCC certified?"

The storekeeper responded with a blank stare. "If it interferes with your TV, we'll give you your money back," he said.

"How much for all of it?" Ray asked.

"Well, that depends. We can get brand new, and we have used stuff right here."

It would be so much easier to just knock the guy out and grab what he needed, but he had to play the game. "Walk back and browse with me," Ray said. "If you don't mind."

Fifteen minutes later, he came away with a police scanner still in shrink wrap and a Ham radio with some serious range. He trusted the scanner to work. But he made the guy plug in the

Ham unit for a quick smoke test. That probably convinced the storekeeper that he was a nut, but Ray really did have something in mind for them.

"What about car mounts?" Ray asked.

The storekeeper got somewhat helpful at that point. In seconds, he rifled through piles of shit in the back room and returned with metal brackets for both units. "I can't help you with installing it in your ride," he said.

"I'll handle that," Ray said. "I've got a nephew who's good with that kind of thing."

Then he bartered. Fifty dollars or five thousand didn't matter to Ray. His time was short. He wasn't on any kind of budget or savings plan. But he chiseled the price down to three hundred for all of it.

"You're buying this as is," the storekeeper said. "You've got two weeks to bring it back if it doesn't work. Then it's a twenty percent restocking fee."

Headshaking! Ray thought. *Crazy! Was he actually trying to talk himself out of a sale?*

He made a show of hesitating before saying, "Oh ... okay. Can I get a receipt?"

CHAPTER 64

By 10:30, Ray had worked up a sweat. He'd been scrunched down under the El Camino's console installing his new purchases. Every few minutes, he got out of the car to stand up and stretch his back. The storekeeper was still behind the counter hunched over something, not even glancing his way. His lie about the nephew helping him didn't matter at all.

Ray had both doors open with tools lying in the parking lot. That helped with airflow, but the truck's interior was in need of a good vacuuming. The smell hadn't been bad, or even noticeable, when he was driving. But hunkering down in the floorboard was a different story. It wasn't a bad stench, just a musty odor that wrapped around him like an old blanket, making him feel like part of the dirt and grime.

Normally, a car radio had to be professionally installed. But Ray Caldwell understood electrical systems. He mounted the scanner under the dashboard and secured the ham radio to the floor, drilling right through the rubber padding. But there was only one wired hookup available.

He solved the problem by ripping out the FM radio and

plugging the Ham unit into that power source. He didn't need to jam out to tunes. Even though some of the decade's hard rock would have been fitting on a day like today. (Actually, the Ham radio would pick up FM channels, but he wasn't going to be monitoring those.)

CHAPTER 65

LIBRARIES HAD ALWAYS REMINDED Ray of mausoleums. He doubted this body he occupied had ever been inside one. The moment the heavy glass door swung shut, he found himself missing the outside noises that normally went unnoticed. No traffic. No birds. No rustling of branches from squirrels or wind. This public library on Six Forks Road was quiet to the point of distraction.

The outside was brighter than yesterday. Warmer too. He'd needed his sunglasses for the drive over here. Fall was still fall, but mid-sixties in this region felt a bit above ideal. In that regard, he welcomed the cool of the air conditioner. He noticed, with satisfaction, that several people in this place were wearing coats. Perfect. He could wear the Duke hoodie and not roast. Better still, nobody would know he was weaponed up.

He made his way to the front desk and decided that libraries were undisturbed spaces where nothing actually happened. They housed books filled with facts and ideas. Through countless novels, they allowed their patrons to taste life without actually having to experience it. Everything happening out there amid the sun and the rain and the dark of night wound up here, recorded for posterity. A cause that Ray found both noble and pathetic.

The stereotypical librarian at the front desk was, herself, an undisturbed space. She served as an organic link, connecting records and catalog numbers to people wanting to find something out. Ray inquired about newspapers and periodicals on microfilm.

Fifteen minutes later, he had himself a temporary library card based on information from Felton Renfro's driver's license. That satisfied the requirement for microfilm viewing. Then the drudgery began.

His eyes were quick, and Ray Caldwell really did have awesome vision. So a mere glance at a page of newsprint was all he needed. Still, sifting through old newspaper records for information on a specific person was no exact science.

He caught his first break just before noon when he discovered that Shelly's opened its doors three years earlier. The article stated that the owner of this controversial new establishment, one Bill Quigley, could not be reached for comment. So Gabe wasn't listed as the owner—not that that meant a hell of a lot.

He narrowed his search down to a three-year span: 1982 to 1985. *News and Observer*. *New York Times*. What followed was another two hours of trial and error with a lot of close but no cigar moments. After a while, titles and dates started blending together. Then the words on the screen dissolved into a hazy blur of alphabet soup. Hunger pangs gnawed at Ray's stomach, giving him a headache that filled his ball cap to the point of bursting.

There was no food or drink allowed in the microfilm room, so Ray pushed onward, blocking out his own discomfort. A mental game that had nothing to do with sucking it up under extreme conditions. He convinced himself that his pain wasn't real, that it had never existed in the first place.

Then he spotted an article in the *Times* about Gabe Marshall being brought in for questioning in regard to a rent control scam in Manhattan. Ray didn't give a shit about that. But the black and white photograph allowed him to put a face to the name. The photo was a grainy head shot of a man in his forties with a mustache and thinning hair. Ray noted his fat jowls and broad nose. Given the deepness of his voice on the phone, Ray guessed him to be about six feet tall and two hundred and fifty pounds.

Gabe also had the jaw of a pitbull. He was probably slow and overweight, a stroke waiting to happen. But definitely not soft.

The article consisted of a small block of print in the bottom corner of page two. It mentioned him residing in Raleigh with his wife and family for several years. It also included a quote from Gabe himself: how could he know anything that happened five hundred miles north of him?

Ray couldn't have cared less about that either. But ...

Browsing the Raleigh news during the early 1980s rooted out Gabe's family. They'd definitely put down roots here in the capital city. His wife, June, not bad looking for a middle-aged mom, was involved in a garden club and Junior League. A son, Peter, was on the football team for a private school.

Gabe's daughter, Elizabeth, was a recent high school graduate who would be attending N.C. State University in the fall of 1983. Her yearbook photo was displayed in a full-page gallery along with her six hundred other senior classmates.

That caught Ray's interest.

She had her mother's dark hair and high cheek bones with a hint of her father's broad nose. Assuming she hadn't quit or flunked out, Elizabeth would now be in the fall semester of her junior year of college. Upperclassmen usually lived in apartments instead of dorm rooms. Usually.

Ray printed out the articles and photos. Now he had something to work with. He had Gabe's daughter's name and would probably recognize her if he saw her. And he knew where she attended school.

Folding up the printed pages and stuffing them into his back pocket, Ray left the library. He had to strike today. No way around it.

Thing is, hurting Elizabeth Marshall would only make things worse for Jill. Abducting her wouldn't work either. Finding her, learning her routine, setting up a place to keep her ... too much time and planning involved for all of that. Unlike Gabe, he didn't have cars with radios to dispatch to a known starting point.

So Ray decided on something else.

CHAPTER 66

FIRST PRIORITY WAS to eat and rehydrate. Get his strength back. Time was short, and Ray had a lot of shit to accomplish. That took about an hour at a Chinese restaurant where he scarfed down an order of pepper steak with an extra side of white rice. All washed down with several glasses of unsweetened iced tea.

When he was leaving, he noticed a TV turned on behind the counter and asked the cashier if there was anything interesting on the news. "No. Same old, same old. Going to be warm today."

He left the restaurant satisfied, but not sluggish, and used a payphone to call directory assistance. Two minutes later, he had an address and phone number for Elizabeth Marshall. Gabe's daughter. She lived in an apartment community ten minutes from campus. *Surprise, motherfucker!*

He wondered if he should return to the library and continue his hunt through the periodicals. That might turn up an address for Gabe himself.

No. He was going with his gut on this one. And Ray's instincts told him that Gabe wasn't one to mix the shiny and shady parts of his life. He wouldn't bring a hostage to his fancy house, wherever that happened to be. Like as not, Jill was locked up in a back room at Shelly's. Or in some other sleazy location.

That was the smart assumption. So why was he questioning? His weakness was why! He'd never second-guessed anything till this misshapen mission. Now he was struggling to trust his own judgment. That's what happened when you had something at stake. Something to lose.

Once again, he tried reminding himself that nobody in 1980s Raleigh meant anything to him. And that forming personal attachments to anybody was bullshit. Furthermore, regardless of how things played out, his time here was limited; his life would end the moment they invoked the reverse transfer. So what the hell was he so worried about? Why did he care what happened to people in a time and place that wasn't his?

He slapped the side of his head, disgusted with himself. His mission was on hold for now—who was he kidding? It was aborted. His new objective was to save Jill, somebody that mattered to him.

CHAPTER 67

THE SUN HUNG high in the early afternoon, and the light breeze barely moved the air. Ray was sweating in his Duke hoodie. He made the decision to dress cooler. He kept the 38 in the ankle holster and the sheathed knife against his hip, hiding under a gray tee shirt.

He drove back to the grocery store that was one exit past Shelly's. There were about thirty cars in the parking lot. Enough for his truck to blend in and not attract attention.

All day, he'd been keeping his eyes peeled, but he hadn't spotted anybody tailing him. Gabe would have sent more people there; that was for sure. But would they know whether Felton Renfro arrived in his own vehicle? Doubtful. The computer in the bonus room stored still photos on demand, not hours of continuous video feed.

He took a quick drive past Shelly's and saw a black BMW and a pair of motorcycles in the parking lot. Somebody home. His pulse quickened. He parked at the grocery store and turned on the Ham radio.

The lower channels, the legal ones for Ham operators with valid call numbers, were awash with amiable small talk. Ray worked his way upward, keeping a close eye on signal strength. Whatever unit Gabe had hooked to that antenna would be putting out some serious amps. Or maybe they weren't on the air at all right now; maybe this was all a waste of time.

Ray cracked one of the beers and a bag of chips. Nothing to do but watch and wait for a while. Small adjustments, circling back. Patience and persistence.

But Ray felt something he'd never experienced before. Instead of his usual battle cool, he was ready to jump out of his skin. It was an antsy, nervous feeling of frustration, illogically wanting something to happen faster than it should. In fact, weak willed and stupid was a better description of his current condition.

Out of sheer nervousness, he placed the Beretta on the passenger seat beside him and unzipped the leather gym bag in the floorboard. He wouldn't need firepower here in this parking lot. It was just one more thing for some passer-by to notice. And he certainly wouldn't be using any of the weaponry in the gym bag. But a gnawing apprehension, an irrational sense of danger —that damn weakness—still had its claws dug into him.

He worked his way up the higher frequencies. Way less activity in that stratosphere. This was reserved territory, off-limits to hobbyists. Again, a gnawing apprehension made a mouthful of chips taste like sandpaper. He took another swig of beer and made another gentle adjustment to the radio dial. *Stay the course*, he scolded himself. *Stick with the game plan, dammit.*

By now, Gabe would know that the location Ray gave him for his stolen merchandise (whatever it happened to be) was bull-shit. More than likely, he'd have people on call waiting to move when he told them. They'd at least have to check in at regular intervals.

The needle on the radio kicked. Someone said, "Status quo." Then silence. For a full minute, Ray listened to dead silence. Then he inched upward to the next frequency, then the next.

The needle kicked again. "Nothing new." It was a different voice. Then someone else said, "Same here. Out."

Using the increment between those two signals, Ray adjusted his radio and waited. More voices. Same cryptic comments. They were in a zone that spanned ten thousand frequency units. They were keeping their comments short and cryptic and switching frequencies after each transmission. When they reached the ceiling, they'd drop to the bottom of the ladder and start over.

Now that he was tuned in to their pattern, Ray only had to start at the bottom and start jumping till he found them. This was big. Huge, in fact. Being able to monitor their broadcasts without them knowing gave him a massive advantage.

But something still bothered him. He didn't know what. Just a bad feeling that he couldn't explain.

The needle kicked again. "Guess whose truck I just spotted right here in the Winn Dixie parking lot." Nothing cryptic about that transmission. Winn Dixie was the name of the grocery store where he was parked.

"You sure about that?" Gabe's voice.

"Hell yeah, I'm sure. I'd know that truck anywhere."

"Okay. Sit tight and keep watching." Then the channel went dead.

Ray took a look around him. Shoppers were coming and going, some pushing full grocery carts to their cars. Most of the vehicles were empty, except for a mom and kids in a station wagon. Without turning, he checked his rearview mirror and spotted a brown sedan with two guys.

They were definitely looking in his direction.

CHAPTER 68

STARTING HIS ENGINE, Ray glanced at the men in the sedan one more time and confirmed they were staying put. It was a warm afternoon and their windows were up. That meant they had their car running with the air conditioning on.

He switched to the next channel and heard "On our way." And "No change here." *No change here* meant Ray hadn't moved and they were watching him.

The anxiety had quit gnawing at him; those claws of trepidation had released their grip. A steady burn of anticipation melted away his apprehension and dread. The difference between waiting and action. Perhaps his new weakness was of some use after all, as an early warning signal if nothing else.

As with most grocery store parking lots, the parking spaces were parallel to the storefront. The sedan was parked behind Ray to his left. Both his vehicle and the sedan were backed into their respective spots so they could drive straight out without ever backing up. If those goons in the sedan didn't know he'd spotted them, and they were sitting tight and waiting for help (always a bad move), Ray could probably gun it out of there and lose them. *Probably.*

A family of four with an infant and a toddler got out of their car and crossed Ray's path. Two girls pushed a shopping cart in front of the sedan. It wasn't that Ray gave half a shit about collateral injuries. At least that's what he told himself. He needed a high percentage play, and *probably* wasn't going to cut it.

Gabe's voice came back on the radio. "Sit tight," he said. "They're almost there."

Grabbing one of the tear gas grenades from the gym bag, Ray got out of the truck and walked straight over to the sedan. He could see two faces behind the windshield going through momentary confusion, not sure whether to hop out and grab him or sit tight like the big man said.

Ray marched right up to the driver's side window. He could see the passenger reach for his door handle and reconsider. Amazing how people froze up when something unexpected contradicted specific instructions.

The driver rolled down his window. He had a pockmarked face and a thick black rug of fake hair that looked like something he'd knitted himself. For a moment, Ray thought he might tell him to leave them alone and go wait in his truck.

"Get in the back seat," he said. He cocked his head at his passenger. "Joe here's going to be right there with you."

Ray unclipped the tear gas grenade and tossed it in the dude's lap. Then he got out of there quick and headed back to his truck. Fumes poured from the driver's open window. The inside of the sedan was a nasty gray fog, so thick that the driver and passenger were barely visible.

As Ray pulled out of his parking space, he saw the driver literally fall out of his door onto the pavement, flailing at his face and eyes. The passenger was still struggling to get his door open. Ray considered driving out of the parking lot. But their backup was due to arrive at any second, and that would mean another high-speed chase. He needed time and space to operate without interruption if he was going to rescue Jill.

He drove around to the back of the grocery store and hoped no deliveries were being made right then. The loading dock entrance was closed. He was alone back here. No other vehicles or people. And there was a large brown dumpster, longer than his truck and at least ten feet tall. He parked alongside the dumpster and grabbed the Beretta. Then he walked back to the front of the store.

Dropping to his knees, he poked his head around the bottom corner of the building and surveyed the parking lot. Two motorcycles were parked near the sedan. And two big men in tee shirts and leather vests were walking the parking lot, apparently looking for Felton Renfro's El Camino. Ray had to admire that. No wasting time rescuing those other guys and helping them wash their eyes out. Instead, they were determined to find Ray Caldwell if he was still around.

One of them said something and the other one shook his head. After conferring for another few seconds, they sauntered over to the sedan. One of them pulled open the passenger side door and moved away. The other one was standing at his bike talking into something that was probably a radio mouthpiece.

A crowd had started to gather. Curious shoppers were standing at their cars, too busy gawking to get the groceries out of their carts. Two drivers almost hit each other from not paying attention to the simple act of leaving a parking lot. A middle-aged woman in a green smock came out of the store to see what the hell was going on.

Ray hurried back to his truck and tuned the radio. He might be able to drive around the perimeter of the parking lot unnoticed by anybody.

In the meantime, the radio was kicking up a fuss. "You're sure he's gone?" Gabe's voice.

"Yeah," a gruff response. "In the wind. For now."

"Damage?"

"Both dudes inhaled tear gas. But they'll live."

"Talk later," Gabe said.

Ray switched to the next frequency interval and stayed with them.

"What now?"

"Get out of there," Gabe said. "I'm coming up there to smooth things over and keep the law out of this."

"Got it," the gruff voice said.

"And keep looking," Gabe said. "That little shit couldn't have gone far."

"There's a highway right here."

"I know there's a fucking highway!" Gabe shouted. "You think I'm stupid?"

"Right, Gabe. We're on it."

The radio went silent. But Ray had what he needed. He switched to the police scanner. There was the usual radio chatter, but nothing about an incident at a Winn Dixie. So far.

He drove around the side of the building and stopped short of the parking lot. Then he got out of the truck for another look. The bikes were gone. A store employee and a woman in a pink hospital shirt were bent over the sedan guys. Another guy came running out of the grocery store with a white towel, probably wet.

Ray drove out of the parking lot, taking his time, leaving by the furthest exit from the highway because Gabe would be barreling through the nearest one any time now. Right on cue, a transmission came across the police scanner about the incident he'd just caused here. Police would be arriving in the next ten to fifteen minutes and Gabe would have to deal with them.

All of that presented Ray with an unexpected window of opportunity.

CHAPTER 69

BACK DOWN THE ramp and around to Shelly's again. It was beginning to feel like a never-ending merry-go-round of lap after lap, each one the same as the one before it. Only this time, he was getting off.

Pulling into the parking lot, he drove around to the back of the building. It only took a moment to secure the Beretta in the shoulder holster and clip the can of mace to his belt. Then he got out of the truck and grabbed the chainsaw and flashlight.

A cluster of thick black wires ran from a tall wooden power pole to the roof. The pole itself was wood, about ten inches in diameter. Ray cranked up the chainsaw. Attacking the pole at a downward angle, he sawed into it like a logger taking down a tree.

In a roar of smoke and splinters, the chainsaw ate its way through the wood in short order. The pole started to list and vibrate, leaning away from the building. Then, amid a loud cracking of wood, the power pole fell.

Ray got the desired result. When the power pole crashed down on the asphalt, the wires connecting it to the roof were ripped away. A cluster of black cables lay strewn around the toppled pole, hissing and spitting sparks.

He'd just cut the electricity and phone, which meant any alarm system was good as dead in this decade. Now he had to get inside. Which posed a problem. The building was solid cinderblock. He wouldn't have time to chisel through it or even blow it up. Both the front and back doors were solid steel, as were their frames. And he didn't have lock picking tools. He did, however, have a hammer and a crowbar.

Then the back door opened. Ray dropped the chainsaw and moved to one side, drawing the Beretta. A woman looked out. An unarmed, drop-dead gorgeous girl in her late twenties wearing a clingy blue dress with long sleeves and a short hemline. Chlorine blue with a glittery sheen. Ray had been so wired for a shoot-out that he barely stopped himself from pulling the trigger and blowing her head off.

Holstering his gun, he grabbed the chainsaw (that was still running) and approached quickly. He ran his eyes all over her, mainly checking for a weapon. Mainly. She was willowy with long brown hair and a face and body guaranteed to stop traffic. His eyes couldn't help but gravitate to her long legs.

She was a shade taller than Ray. Her perfect lips formed a surprised "O" of recognition. "Ray? Oh my God! What are you doing here?"

He shoved past her, and his nostrils caught fire. She was wearing some nasty perfume. Too much of it. *Did she use the whole bottle?* he wondered. Then he recognized it: that same cheap perfume that had saturated Ray Caldwell's trailer right after the transfer into this puny brain and tight skull.

It was dark inside. That was because the place had no windows and he'd knocked out the power. He turned on the flashlight and scanned his surroundings. It was like standing in a cavern with plenty of shit to trip over.

Right across from him was a bar, the mirror behind it

reflecting Ray's flashlight beam at weird angles. All of the tables had chairs turned upside down on top of them. And an elevated stage, a circular platform with two evenly spaced poles.

As his eyes adjusted to the darkness, Ray realized it wasn't pitch black in here. A little bit of sunlight managed to squeeze its way through a set of vents beneath the roof.

He could smell the girl's awful perfume as she followed him inside; she was keeping herself glued to him. Her voice was breathy; he could barely hear her over the idling chainsaw motor. "You've got to get out of here," she said. "They'll kill you."

"Anybody here now?" Ray asked.

"No. But you have to leave."

There was a glittery curtain around the back half of the stage and plenty of dark space behind that.

"What's back there?" Ray didn't wait for an answer. He headed back there to see for himself.

The girl grabbed his left arm with both hands. "No! You can't."

Ray shook her off and proceeded. She let out a startled squeak but came along with him. He shined the light on a closed door. "What's there?"

"Dressing rooms. You know that."

Ray figured she probably wasn't bullshitting him, so he kept going. All the way to what had to be a corner office in the back of the building. This door was solid oak mounted in a metal frame. A white placard with red letters said, PRIVATE.

"Gabe never leaves it unlocked," the girl said. "Now get out of here. I won't tell them I saw you here. Swear to God."

She got his heart pounding when she said that. Jill might be —hell, she could definitely be!—behind that locked door. He could try pounding on the door and calling to her. But a direct approach seemed preferable.

Laying the chainsaw on the floor, Ray grabbed the girl's

dainty wrist and shoved the flashlight into her hand. He ushered her to one side. "Keep that light on the door," he said.

Then he picked up the chainsaw.

CHAPTER 70

RAY STARTED at the top and made one long cut right down the middle of the door, splitting the I and the V in PRIVATE. The door remained upright, the hardware on either side holding both halves in place. Barely. One kick from Ray's boot launched the non-hinged side into Gabe's office.

The girl followed him in and handed him the flashlight. She'd stopped talking. Instead, she stood too close for his liking, given her perfume. "You're not Ray," she said.

No shit, he thought. Why did it take everyone so long to figure that out?

Unfortunately, Jill wasn't here. A wasted effort. Perhaps.

It occurred to Ray that he could have just asked this girl if Jill was here and saved himself some time. She would have told him the room was empty. On the other hand, he wouldn't have believed her.

Gabe's office was zero frills. The outer walls were unpainted cinderblock. No pictures or personal effects. Even with the lights on, this room would look, feel, and smell purely utilitarian. Ray turned off the chainsaw and scanned the place with his flashlight. There was a free-standing walk-in closet with two suits of clothes on hangers and an extra pair of shoes. Also a refrigerator and mini bar.

Against the back wall was a desk with a swivel chair behind it and a TV screen on the opposite wall that would have displayed outdoor camera footage if there'd been electricity. The desk had a rotary phone on it. No answering machine. Ray also spotted Gabe's radio on a rack behind the desk. Like the camera and TV, it would still work fine with electricity.

The desk drawer was unlocked, so there was probably nothing valuable in there. Ray rifled through it anyhow, slinging the contents all over the floor. Then he noticed a slight unevenness under his feet. A plastic mat—opaque gray—underneath the wheels of the office chair. Presumably to allow it to roll more smoothly without scratching the floor. Except ... the floor was a concrete slab. No rolling resistance, nothing to worry about scratching up.

Shoving the chair out of the way, Ray pulled up the mat and found the door to a floor safe staring back at him. The girl's breath caught in her throat. She'd been hovering over his shoulder the whole time. "You wouldn't happen to know the combination?" Ray asked.

"God, no. I never even knew this was here."

Ray thought quickly. Because an unexpected opportunity had presented itself, he'd come here hoping this was where they'd stashed Jill. That hadn't panned out. And now, in addition to everything else, he had to deal with Felton Renfro's El Camino being recognized by these assholes. Given time, he could probably crack this 1980s safe, no problem at all. The key word being *time*.

"I'm going to try to open it," Ray said. *Why am I telling her?* he wondered.

"You can't open that," she said. "Oh ..." She remembered he wasn't Ray.

"If the combination's three numbers or less, we have time," Ray said. "Otherwise, screw it." *Again, why did she need to know?*

Then he stopped and listened. The roar of high-powered engines filtered through the building's thick walls. It seemed that those motorcycle dudes had arrived.

———

No need to kill the lights. There was no power, no phone, no nothing in this place.

The roar of the engines ceased. Ray pictured the bikers dismounting. They were parked in front of the club. That meant they hadn't seen the El Camino they'd been looking for parked around back. If Gabe trusted them with a key to this place, they'd enter through the front door.

Ray wrapped his fingers around the girl's bicep, digging in just enough to let her know he wasn't shitting her. "Nothing personal," he said. "But one peep out of you when they come inside ..."

He let go of her arm. She wasn't going to call out or make any noise. He sat her down on the floor, back against the wall. Told her to stay there till he got back. Then he eased his way through the office door and into the corridor behind the stage, questioning his sanity (for just assuming she wouldn't screw him) every step of the way.

The front door opened, and a raging voice called out: "What the fuck?"

"The lights are out," said the other one. His voice was more along the lines of crazy mellow.

"No shit."

So there were two of them. Confirmation that they were probably the same two from the Winn Dixie parking lot.

Ray killed the flashlight and didn't move. No point in a firefight if that didn't get him any closer to his objective.

"Prop the door open," the raging voice said. "Can't see shit in here."

"Power must be out," Crazy Mellow observed.

"Fuck it. Let's get Heat and get the hell out of here. Hey Heat! You here?"

Ray heard the footsteps in the bar. Then a curse, followed by the clatter of wood on concrete. One of them had run into a table and knocked down a chair.

The question was: would they actually say, "fuck it," and leave? More specifically, would they leave without Heat, who Ray now knew to be the hot girl sitting on the floor in Gabe's office? Or they could decide to check things out. They'd need flashlights for that.

"Phone's dead," Crazy Mellow's voice said.

Too bad, too sad. They wouldn't be calling anybody.

"Heat! Just yell if you can hear me. We'll come get you."

Ray's skin prickled. He could smell his own sweat through the lingering stench of Heat's overdone perfume. If she called out ... he'd have to kill them all.

"She ain't here," Crazy Mellow's voice said. "Probably left."

"In what? She didn't have a car."

"Who knows? Who cares? That bitch is crazy."

"We've gotta bring Gabe up to speed."

A couple of minutes passed. Ray could hear glass clinking in the barroom, probably one of them raiding the booze. Presumably, the other one was outside talking to Gabe on the radio. So Ray's detour to this dive might still pay dividends. If the man himself decided to make an appearance, Ray would take out the bikers and then dig Jill's location out of Gabe. Literally.

Then the owner of the raging voice kicked his volume up a decibel. "Lock up and leave. We're looking for Heat now."

"Fuck, man. Seriously?"

"What do you think? That means going by her place and

reaching out to anybody she might be with. Same drill as always. Gabe's too stressed out about that other shit to worry about her."

The front door slammed shut. Then the engines roared to life and faded into the distance.

Ray made his way back to Gabe's office and shined the light on the girl. She was still sitting against the wall, knees drawn up to her chest. A picture of sensuality.

"Heat ..." he said. "Is that your real name?"

The girl nodded. "Short for Heather," she said.

"Okay, Heather," Ray said. "Let's open this safe and get the hell out of here."

CHAPTER 71

ALL COMBINATION SAFES worked on the same principle. A set of wheels on a spindle, each one representing a number. Get the notches on all of the wheels to line up, and paydirt! The problem was figuring out what those numbers were and selecting them in the right order.

While Heather held the light, Ray put his ear to the safe and turned the dial clockwise, listening and feeling for that definitive click. One unique click per number. The first one was 10.

Ray turned the dial counterclockwise. He'd already decided on a three number limit. If the spindle clicked on a fourth number, meaning a probable six-number combination, they'd cease and desist. The next number was 28. Then after a clockwise rinse and repeat, 34. Another clockwise turn yielded 10 again.

So three numbers. Six possible combinations. The safe opened on the third try. Took fifteen minutes.

"Holy shit," Heather said. "You're really not Ray."

"Nothing gets by you, does it?"

She leaned in close enough to brush against him. There was a longing in her voice. "Where were you last week?" she said.

Right in the middle of mission prep, Ray thought.

He shifted away from her. "What are you doing? Flashlight beam inside the safe, please."

"Anything you want," Heather said. Then she gasped.

The safe was a two-foot square eighteen inches deep. One side was filled with stacks of banded bills, lots of hundreds and nothing smaller than twenties. The other side was documentation for two identities that weren't Gabe. Passports, birth certificates, social security cards. Everything you'd need to become someone else. There was also a fat envelope from a lawyer's office. Plus some formal-looking letters.

They wrapped the bills in one of Gabe's shirts from the closet and the business documents in another. Ray tied the knots himself, making sure nothing was going to fall out. He'd dig through the printed matter later. Then he closed the safe, locked it, and placed the mat back over it, then rolled the chair on the mat.

Time to go. They were hitting on the thirty-minute mark.

Ray carried the chainsaw (couldn't leave that behind) and tied the bundle with the documentation to his belt. He let Heather carry the bundle with the cash. If she dropped it on the way out or pilfered any, he really didn't care.

She'd left her purse behind the bar and insisted that he shine the flashlight back there so she could get it. It had been darkness and a stroke of luck that neither biker had noticed it back there. Ray let her delay him for another minute because keeping her compliant would make things a hell of a lot smoother down the road.

The sunlight outside was blinding after being in the dark for so long. Ray loaded the chainsaw in the back of the truck but put the bundle he was carrying under his seat. Heather got in the passenger seat and fastened her seatbelt. *Just invite yourself, why don't you?* Ray thought.

Saying nothing, he started the truck and hit the highway. It was approaching mid-afternoon now. And the timetable had shrunk. He had to make some immediate moves fast. Like another car. He looked at Heather with the slim black purse in her lap and the bundle of cash under her feet. Her eyes, a soft shade of brown that actually matched her hair, were filled with ... trust?

Why in the hell should she trust him? Especially with what he planned to do next.

CHAPTER 72

RAY STAYED ON THE HIGHWAY, figuring miles of open road would make it harder to spot the El Camino. He asked Heather if she knew of any car rental places nearby. She did not.

He turned onto an exit that touted food, gas, and lodging like thousands of its kind, then pulled into the first parking lot he could find.

Reaching into the gym bag and grabbing the map and phone book, he found a rental car place fifteen minutes away on South Saunders Street. Otherwise, that location sucked. There wasn't much nearby commerce. And Ray had this truck he was driving and Heather to contend with.

He remembered seeing a place called Budget Car Rentals on Capital Boulevard. Right across from a shopping center with several businesses and a full parking lot. Nearly a thirty-minute drive from where they were now. It would have to do.

"Why are we renting a car?" Heather asked.

"We aren't," Ray said. "I am."

"What's wrong with what you're driving now?" Heather said.

So Gabe hadn't told her anything. She had no clue about Felton Renfro's El Camino being on his radar.

"What does Gabe have on you?" Ray said.

"Nothing." Heather started straight ahead. Her lower lip was trembling.

"You're hooked, aren't you!" Ray jerked up her left sleeve and turned her arm over for inspection. Healthy skin. No track marks. That made her more reliable but less controllable.

She was crying now. "You asshole! I'm not a stripper and I don't do drugs."

"And yet, you just happened to be at Shelly's."

"That doesn't mean anything."

"And wound up in Ray Caldwell's trailer."

"You know what—just let me out here. I'll get a cab home."

She reached for her door handle. But Ray drove out of the parking lot and didn't slow down. "You don't have to go back to him, you know."

"I said I don't want to talk about it," Heather said.

"No, you didn't. You said you weren't a junkie or a stripper. And that Gabe has nothing on you. That means—"

"Are you an idiot? He'll kill me if I try to walk out on him!"

"You keep forgetting I'm not Ray."

CHAPTER 73

Budget Car Rentals took almost an hour. It was now four o'clock in the afternoon. The sun still hung high in the sky, but you'd definitely need sunglasses if you were facing west.

Ray rented a burgundy Honda Accord and paid in cash. It was a middle-class businessman's type of vehicle. One you wouldn't look for Ray Caldwell to be driving.

So the logistics of two vehicles and a hot babe he didn't trust ...

First, he dropped Heather off at the car rental place. Then he parked the El Camino across the street in a shopping center on the other side of the road and walked over. By the time he got there, those guys at the car place were too busy fawning all over Heather to ask any questions.

The downside was they'd remember them. For sure. He was also signing Felton Renfro's name to the rental agreement. It would have to do.

Ray put on his cap and sunglasses and drove the Honda across the road to where the El Camino was parked. This parking lot was perfect for his needs. It was busy, most of the parking spaces already filled and lots of traffic going in and out.

There was a payphone outside of a large variety store. Even better, it was situated in a shallow basin below the main road. You had to drive downhill on a short service road to get here. Come nightfall, he could park behind the small thrift shop next door and have a bird's-eye view of this lot.

He had Heather wait for him in the Honda with the air conditioning on and hoped she wouldn't decide to drive off. Then he removed the radios in the El Camino, leaving their racks bolted in place. No time for removal and reinstallation. He put the Ham radio in the back seat of the Honda and the police scanner in the trunk. Electrical hookups would also have to wait.

Then he transferred the rest of his stuff over to his replacement car. Lastly, he wrote down the number of the payphone.

Heather came at him the moment he got behind the wheel. "Let's get out of here," she said. "Just leave together."

"You don't mind lowering your standards," Ray said.

She twisted around, positioning herself between him and the steering wheel. Heather was tall and slinky, but she was also heavy in the chest and had tight hips with just the right curvature. Even through his tee shirt, her body sliding against his chest made the blood rush to his head.

"C'mon, man." She brushed her lips across his, her tongue giving his mouth a quick taste of heaven. She pressed in tighter. "Like you said ... you're not Ray."

That almost did it. A pulsating surge started in his groin and gave him a head-to-toe body rush. Ray Caldwell definitely had a cannon between his legs. And Heather was reaching for it, not having to hunt around either.

That did it. Screw Gabe (well, actually Heather). No more rescuing Jill. Justin could fend for himself. Game, set, match. Turn out the lights. Drop the curtain. Thanks for playing. Type "The End" and move on to another story because this one was over.

Except ...

Her damn perfume made him want to gag.

Still ...

He was balanced on a seesaw that could tip either way.

"Please ... I'll make you feel like a king."

Ray shoved her off of him. "Is that what you tell Gabe?" he said.

"Ray! No. It's not like that."

"Just shut up. Okay?" He started the car and drove out of the parking lot.

But it wasn't that simple. With his heart pounding, his body still tingling all over, he was teetering on the edge of changing his mind and shacking up somewhere private with this babe till the reverse transfer took him out. No doubt about it: he wanted to take Heather up on her proposition over and over again.

But that perfume! She'd be better off bathing in piss.

CHAPTER 74

RAY ROLLED his window to let in some fresh air. The Honda smelled like pine-scented air freshener that was half a step up from Heather's perfume. Maybe.

To get untangled from Heather, he'd had to yank her out of the car and shove her into the back seat. Anybody who saw him driving might think he was her chauffeur. He drove further down Capital Boulevard just to put a little distance between himself and the El Camino in the parking lot.

He glanced at Heather in the rearview mirror. "Smoke if you want to," he said.

She responded with a cold glare.

"Do you know where Gabe lives?" he asked.

She slid over to the passenger side and stared sullenly out the window. This was a girl who'd never been rejected in her life, at least not for a hookup.

Ray decided to give her a few minutes and was immediately disgusted with himself. Why not just grovel and beg like a mangy dog while he was at it?

A few miles later, he stopped at a steak house to fuel himself up with protein and calories. He was going to need his strength for what lay ahead. Heather waited till he'd parked the car and turned the engine off to speak to him. "I don't eat meat," she said.

And yet, you see fit to climb all over Ray Caldwell, he thought. But he said out loud: "I'm sure they've got salads here."

"Forget it, Ray. I don't eat crap."

What a spoiled, selfish brat! "Well, I'm not leaving you in the car, so you can watch me eat," Ray said.

"I'm not going in."

"Restaurant booth or the trunk. Your choice." Then he watched her pretty face—a face that ought to be on a billboard somewhere—melt from petulance to despair.

"Heather, please. We're in this together. You don't want me now any more than that night in that trailer park. Thing is, you don't want what you've got. You need for your life to be different, but you've got no way out."

"Thanks a lot," she said. "Now I feel awful!" She stretched out sideways across the seat and covered her face.

"You can be free," Ray said. "You never have to go back to Gabe again."

"No. He'll find me."

"I'll handle Gabe, but you've gotta help me out. Okay? Will you do that?"

Heather sat up and wiped her eyes. "Okay," she said.

"But let's eat something. I'm about to cave in."

CHAPTER 75

EATING DIDN'T TAKE LONG. Still too early for the dinner crowd.

Ray decided to go back to the same library he'd visited that morning. Why not? It was open till eight. Nobody in Gabe's outfit would think of looking for them there. And he needed a quiet place to look over the documents he'd taken from Gabe's safe.

Or ...

Maybe he could wrap things up right here and now. He stopped at a convenience store and used a payphone to call the number he had for Gabe. The response was a recorded message, where a nasally female voice informed him that the number he was trying to reach had been disconnected or was temporarily out of service.

Disconnected meant disabled in this case. It was a safe bet that Ray had just dialed the number to Gabe's back office at Shelly's. There'd be no calling there for a while after what he'd done to their power pole.

It also told him that Jill had been there soon after they'd grabbed her. When Gabe put her on the phone and let Ray talk to her, the call had been on that number. So they'd moved her at some point.

No. There hadn't been time to transport her all the way over to Shelly's while he was still in that big house in the nice safe neighborhood. Yet, he *had* talked to her. At *that* number.

It didn't make sense.

He got back in the car. "How do you contact Gabe?" he asked.

"I don't," Heather said. "He calls me. Or sends somebody to get me. I'm not allowed to call him. Ever."

"So this guy doesn't want his wife or anybody in his other life finding out about you."

"Thanks, Ray."

"Actually," Ray said, "this is good. We can use that. So onward. To the library."

"The library?"

"Sure," Ray said. "You like books, don't you?"

CHAPTER 76

RAY COULDN'T HELP but smile when Heather flinched at the sudden silence. The moment you walked into the library, all of those sounds you took for granted—traffic noise, voices, even wind—were just gone. It was also fun to watch all of the heads swivel as she walked past.

The weather outside was cooler now, but the air conditioner was still cranked up in here. Ray concealed his weapons underneath his Duke hoodie. He let Heather borrow a long-sleeved shirt so she wouldn't freeze. Wearing it over her shimmery blue dress should have looked silly, but everything she did worked. Some girls were like that.

They sat at a corner table behind a full shelf of books. This was as private as they were going to get. Ray laid out the documents and went through them one at a time.

The passports didn't really matter. Gabe had a checkbook for a bank account in Lima, Peru. That was interesting as a source of possible leverage. The money wouldn't do Ray any good. Not with his mayfly existence in this time and place. There was also a bill of sale from South Africa for a large quantity of uncut

diamonds, straight out of the mines by the looks of the paper-
work. Also nothing of immediate help.

Then he found a document from a law office in New Jersey. It
was a signed contract where the law offices of Saul Williamson et
al. agreed to represent Gabe for a fifty-thousand-dollar retainer.
The heading at the top of the first page was all Ray needed. A
street address for Gabriel Marshall in ritzy Middlebury Heights.
Paydirt! This was where Gabe bedded down with his family. Ray
glanced at Heather and figured Gabe usually had better options.

Useful intel. But Gabe's wife was there. And his teenage son.
It was a near-sure thing that he'd stashed Jill someplace else.

Next move?

He knew where Gabe lived. He knew his daughter's name and
where she lived. But he really didn't give a shit about any of that at
the moment. Ray's prime objective—his new mission—was to get
Jill back. Because somewhere along the way, he'd stopped thinking
about her as only Justin's mama. Somehow, someway, he'd formed
an attachment to her. An unprecedented mental deficiency that
would have to be addressed before his next assignment.

What made things harder was this: the best way to get Jill
back was to trade Heather for her. And he hated doing that—
absolutely no clue why. Still, looking at it logically, he cared for
Heather less than Jill. So that was the tiebreaker. Emotional
attachment was a ponderous burden. How people carried it
throughout their lives was nothing short of mind-boggling. At
least in his case, that reverse transfer was going to come along
and bring him sweet relief at some point.

So he'd made his decision. A trade. Heather for Jill. The next
question was how to contact Gabe since he'd taken out the
phone line with the number he knew. He could hook up the
Ham radio and dial into the right frequency. That would do it.
But he'd also lose an eavesdropping advantage in the process.

The day was sliding by in a hurry. It was already half past

six. He could call this Saul Williamson at his law firm using the phone number on the contract's cover sheet. Assuming he was still there at this hour. And also assuming that if he did take Ray seriously, he'd actually be able to get ahold of Gabe.

Then he remembered Jill's pager. It was worth a try.

CHAPTER 77

DAYLIGHT HADN'T GONE AWAY. But the sun hung low on the horizon—as always, an intensified glow of bold orange and bright yellow, as if fighting for its very existence. Ray's favorite time of day in any era.

When they returned to the car, Heather was mollified enough to sit in the front seat. Ray grabbed the Ham radio off the floorboard and set it in her lap.

"What's that?" she demanded.

"We had to change cars. So you're my radio rack now."

"Really?"

"Trust me," Ray said. "You'll like this."

He snaked his hand under the console, hoping he wouldn't have to remove the FM radio to get behind it. That would take time. "Hang on a second." Thirty seconds later, he pulled down a single braid of red and black wire with a connector at the end of it. He plugged in the radio and started the car.

"Check this out," he said.

Feeling the heat from Heather's lap, he tuned the Ham radio to the beginning frequency in Gabe's transmission pattern and worked his way upward. Nothing for ten minutes. Heather started to fidget. Patience was not one of her assets.

Then a hit. Two voices, neither of them Gabe's.

"Nothing yet."

"Keep looking."

Then dead static. Ray switched to the next frequency in the chain. Next transmission, he'd be ready.

"Is that from Gabe's radio?" Heather said. "The one in his office at the club?"

"Nobody's broadcasting from there," Ray said. "But they just told me they haven't found the truck I left in that parking lot." He started the car and merged into traffic.

"Oh my God!" Heather said. "That is so cool. Where are we going now?"

"Nearest payphone," Ray said. "I'm going to try to get in touch with the man himself."

CHAPTER 78

LEAVE it to a convenience store to be inconvenient. The lone payphone out front was taken. And the guy using it wasn't in any hurry.

Ray sat in the car and tamped down his frustration. Nothing to do for now but wait.

Heather came out of the store with a package of oatmeal cookies. "I thought you didn't have Gabe's number," she said.

"I don't. I'm going to call Jill's pager and leave a message."

"What callback number would you leave? Oh ... this payphone."

Ray responded with a blank stare. Then his brain shifted to figuring out his next move. He could wait this guy out. Or try to get him to end his call without assaulting him. Maybe Heather could walk up real nice and distract him.

"What are you going to do if they don't call back right away?" Heather asked. "You'd have to keep everybody else off this phone. You should have brought an Out of Order sign to put on it."

He ignored her and tuned the Ham radio to the next channel. Still nothing. He'd give the guy five more minutes, then head someplace else. Maybe he'd have to break radio silence after all. It was getting late, and this thing had already gone way too far.

"Bad idea," Heather said. "*Really bad.*"

"You gonna eat those cookies?"

Heather shook her head and put them in the glovebox. "Don't know why I bought them," she said. "I don't eat crap."

"Everybody buys shit they don't need," Ray said.

Right then, the guy on the phone hung up. But he didn't leave. No. He started fishing around in his pocket for more change.

Getting out! Ray opened his car door. He'd been steadily losing patience, and Heather had gotten his blood simmering just now. This was going to be one epic beatdown if that asshole didn't clear the hell out of there.

"Ray, stop!" Heather had both hands on his right forearm.

"I'm only going to say this once," he said. "I like you. But stay out of my lane."

"Idiot!"

Ignoring her, Ray got out of the car. The guy was dialing another number but was about to experience a true disconnect.

Heather yelled after him. "If you're going to risk cops and jail, at least go for an indoor phone!"

The asshole was leaning back against the wall with the receiver to his ear. He glared in Ray's direction, as if daring him to come over. He was three inches taller than Ray and looked to be in his mid-thirties. He'd already way underestimated the situation.

Ray gave him a casual wave and got back in the car.

CHAPTER 79

RADIO SHACK at North Hills Mall was still open. Ray paid way too much for a plain white phone with push-button numbers. Whatever. One stop shopping. And they sold phone cable there. He needed at least thirty feet of it. He also bought a phone jack.

Now he was driving back to the thrift store that overlooked the parking lot where he'd left the El Camino. Ray took off his sunglasses. There was barely enough remaining sunlight to call this part of the day dusk instead of nightfall. The perfect time for what he had in mind.

At this hour, the shop would be closed. Probably. If not, he'd have to go inside and persuade whoever was in there to help him out. As Heather had said: *take risks that pay off.* Well, she didn't exactly say that, but her comment about the convenience store payphone still rang true.

Neither of them spoke during the drive over. Ray tuned the Ham radio to a new frequency every couple of minutes and picked up a few snatches of info that he already assumed to be the case. They were still looking for Felton Renfro's truck to no avail. Not surprising. Raleigh was a big city with cars every-where. Ray studied the inflections in their voices and guessed that they'd all but given up for the day, that they were just keeping up the chatter to make Gabe think they were looking a hell of a lot harder than they really were.

Heather broke the silence. "What are you going to do?"

"If I tell you, it'll spoil the surprise."

"You're going to try and make that phone work, aren't you?"

"I think it already works fine," Ray said. "Or I need to get my money back."

She shifted in her seat. Getting antsy. It was scary as hell to break free from a bad thing. But it was worse afterwards. That's when all the uncertainty and second-guessing cranked up. Heather had no clue what the future had in store for her. Ray didn't have that problem; he knew he wasn't long for this world. Period. That simplified things.

"Look," he said. "When we get things hooked up, I'm gonna tell Gabe some things that you're not going to like hearing. All bullshit. So ignore it. Can you do that?"

"I feel like I've been ignoring bullshit forever," Heather said.

When they reached their destination, dusk had given way to nightfall. The shop was about forty feet from the road. As Ray predicted, there was a closed sign in the window. A couple of lights mounted on the building illuminated the storefront and half of the parking lot in front of it. Headlights from passing cars lit up the other half.

A strip of pavement ran around the left side of the building, wide enough to accommodate a trash truck. That's because there was a dumpster on that side set just far enough back to not be a major eyesore. That also meant you couldn't park there without having half of your car in plain view. A chain-link fence stood at the edge of the pavement, separating this lot from the property next door.

On the right side of the building, nothing. A steep hill over-grown with weeds and brush dropped straight down to the shopping center where Felton Renfro's truck was parked.

This whole thing might have been easier if the place was still open. But they were here. And Ray was going for broke.

He killed the headlights and backed the car up to the dumpster, letting the front half stick out. Then his first roll of the dice. Drawing the 38 from his ankle holster, he took aim at the nearest outdoor light. He took a deep breath before squeezing the trigger. The 38 wouldn't be as loud as the Beretta, but it wouldn't be silent either. There might be a master switch on an outside electrical box that would enable him to simply kill the power. But this entire property going black would be more likely to catch the eye of a passing patrol car. A partially lit building, on the other hand ...

Ray shot out the nearest light with better results than he'd hoped for. The pop of the gun and the tinkle of breaking glass didn't rise above traffic noise on the busy road. About one-third of the storefront went dim, but not completely dark. Close enough to pass for a store that was closed for the night. And unless you drove in and looked, his car was hidden now.

He retrieved his Radio Shack purchases and also the flashlight, pliers, and wire cutters. At his behest, Heather stood by with the black jacket in hand. "There's something in your coat," she said. "Feels like a hunk of metal in the lining."

Ray thought about the bladed brass knuckles and almost smiled. "An insurance policy," he said.

Luck was with them. The power meter and phone lines on the side of the building were behind the dumpster. Ray handed Heather the flashlight and showed her where to hold it. Then he cut the phone line and went to work. Tiny wires from the two pieces of line had to be matched with their colored counterparts on the phone jack.

Fifteen minutes later, he had himself an outdoor wall jack on the outside of the building. Ray plugged in the phone and held his breath. If this didn't work ...

Dial tone!

Ray punched in Jill's pager number. Knowing full well he might be wasting his time, he started talking.

"Guess what, Gabe? I've got Heat." He gave the address of the shopping center below and the location of the payphone. "I don't talk to Jill on that phone in one hour, Heat's not gonna look so hot anymore. And you'll never get your stuff back. I'm calling that payphone. One hour. Be there."

Ray hung up.

"What now?" Heather asked.

"We get set up around back and wait."

CHAPTER 80

THE JACKET WAS black as ink, darker than the night around them. Ray held it in front of him, waist-high like a matador's cape, to hide the flashlight beam. He focused the light on the ground and walked around the back of the store without revealing any sign of himself.

There was no cover back here, only a ten-foot stretch of dirt and gravel between the rear of the building and the drop-off. He'd have binoculars at the ready when the time came, but he could see the shopping center and the payphone without them.

He stretched the phone cable around the building and plugged it into his makeshift wall jack. Now, from the top of the hill, he could call the payphone and also watch it.

Forty minutes to go. Ray and Heather got back in the car to wait. If nobody showed up, if they didn't pick up any radio transmissions, Ray was going with Plan B. That meant breaking radio silence and talking to those assholes directly. He didn't want to give up his eavesdropping advantage, but sacrifices had to be made sometimes.

After a painstaking ten minutes crawled by, the radio came to life. Gabe's voice no less. A simple question. "What's the word?"

And the response. "Almost there."

Ray switched to the next frequency. "It worked," he said. "They're on their way."

"But Jill won't be with them," Heather said.

"She'd better be or it'll suck to be them."

"What about me? You gonna mess up my face to spite Gabe?"

"Don't be stupid," Ray said. But that option wasn't off the table if Jill wasn't okay. He was a man capable of anything. Normally. The corpses at that fancy house were proof of that. But it also wouldn't surprise him if this strange weakness inside of him extended to Heather. It was a cancer of sorts, attaching itself to every fiber of his being.

The radio crackled. "Turning in now. Don't see anybody yet."

That was Ray's cue to get in place. Armed with the Beretta and binoculars, he made his way around back, again using the jacket to conceal his flashlight beam. There were still plenty of vehicles in the parking lot below, but it was only about half-full at this hour. The El Camino sat alone about twenty yards from the payphone. The nearest car was parked two spaces away.

Ray checked the time. Still ten minutes till the hour deadline he'd given them. He decided to call the payphone at the one-hour mark—and not one second before.

He watched the shopping center entrance through the binoculars and spotted the two bikers. They split up and went to opposite ends of the parking lot. A black BMW started at the far end and weaved its way through the rows of parked vehicles, coming to a stop next to the El Camino. It was them.

The BMW's windows were tinted too dark for Ray's binoculars to see inside. Maybe Jill was with them. Probably not, according to Heather.

Two men got out of the car. One of them sauntered over to the payphone. The other was checking out the El Camino. Ray wished for the radio; there'd be communication with Gabe happening for sure. But this setup had inherent limitations. Heather was in the car with the Ham radio beside her, but they were switching frequencies with every transmission (smart), and she wouldn't be able to keep up with that.

Nothing happened for the next seven minutes. Then Ray called the payphone.

CHAPTER 81

FROM TWENTY FEET above and about a hundred yards away, Ray focused his binoculars on the payphone. He couldn't hear it ring. But he watched the man standing next to it reach for the receiver. This guy was cleaner cut than the others they'd sent after him. Smooth shaven with short dark hair and looked to be wearing a suit without the jacket and tie.

"Hello. Ray?" He sounded like a white-collar guy answering the phone in his office.

"You're not Jill," Ray said.

"C'mon, Ray. Let's talk—"

"My instructions were pretty fucking clear!" Ray said. "I talk to Jill. Not you, Jill! On that payphone you're on right now."

He hung up and watched. Business Guy stepped away from the phone and said something to the guy at the truck. Ray called the payphone again and hung up right before Business Guy could answer it. If they had Jill with them and he could make them get her out of their vehicle, or if they didn't have Jill and he could make them bring her here, those evening shoppers would have a story to tell their grandchildren.

Business Guy went over and spoke with whoever was inside

the BMW. Then he walked back to the phone with a black object in his hand. So there were at least three of them. One at the truck, another at the phone, and at least one other in the car. Plus the two bikers.

Ray's pulse had amped up. His heart rate remained slow and steady as ever. But the pulsation of blood flowing through his body had intensified; each beat of his heart caused a throbbing in his head. He could feel an army of insects racing up and down his spine till he wanted to jump out of his skin. It happened sometimes ... ready to fight but forced to wait. The thirst for battle threatened to overwhelm any vestige of judgment and patience.

He called again and almost forgot that Gabe's people had no clue that he was watching them. For all they knew, he was miles away in a hotel room or some phone booth.

Business Guy answered on the second ring. "Jill's right here," he said. "Hang on a second while I put her on." Then he held the black object to the receiver.

"Ray?"

Jill's voice! She was slightly muffled by static on the line that wasn't there before.

"Are you alright?" Ray heard himself say.

"I'm fine. They haven't hurt me. Yet." It was Jill talking. She'd answered a question, so that thing in Business Guy's hand wasn't a tape player. Her voice was tight. She was being coached on what to say.

"One more time," Ray said. "You're really alright?"

"They're treating me like family," Jill said. "But they need their stuff back."

The whole time, Ray kept the binoculars focused on the object in Business Guy's hand. Depending on who was talking, he was moving it between the receiver's earpiece to mouthpiece. And whenever Jill talked, there was a burst of static ...

Now Ray got it. That thing in Business Guy's hand was a

portable radio. Which explained the static. Jill could be anywhere. That's also how they'd contrived putting her on the phone during Ray's conversation with Gabe.

"Where are you now?" Ray asked.

Business Guy spoke into the phone. "She's right here with us, Ray. Just what you asked for."

Bullshit, Ray thought. Jill wasn't anywhere nearby. But at least she seemed okay. That was the good news. The bad news for Ray was having to forego a bloodletting with this vermin.

"Look," Business Guy said. "We all went too far. But let's iron things out. Why don't you come here and bring Heat with you? Even trade. No hard feelings. Then we can talk about that other thing. What do you say?"

"I want Jill out in the open where I can see her," Ray said.

"Absolutely," Business Guy said. "We'll both be right here at that phone you're calling me on."

Meanwhile, Business Guy's partner was in the process of jimmying the driver's side door of Felton Renfro's El Camino.

"Twenty minutes," Ray said.

"Twenty minutes, Ray? Really? I can see your truck from where I'm standing. Why don't you come on out?"

"Best I can do," Ray said. "By the way, I hope none of you messed with the truck. There's a bomb in there on a delayed timer. Opening the driver's side door cuts a piece of transparent filament, and then it's a five-minute countdown to glory."

Ray hung up. It was a pointless bluff. There was no tactical advantage to be gained from it. Just the satisfaction of making those assholes change their underwear.

CHAPTER 82

ONE THING WAS CLEAR: there'd be no rendezvous in the parking lot below. No swap. No bloody battle. No nothing. Jill wasn't there. They'd never intended to bring her. If he'd called from someplace else—the convenience store phone, for instance—where he couldn't see the parking lot, he never would have guessed their radio-talking-into-the-phone scheme. He would have battled it out with those dudes for nothing.

Ray made his way back to the car, careful to hide his flashlight beam. When he opened the car door, the passenger seat was empty. Heather was gone.

What did she take? That was his first thought. Probably cash. But that didn't matter to him. The radio was still there. Well, no shit. What would she do with that? And he had most of his weapons on him. He'd have to park somewhere and do a quick inventory once he got clear of this area.

And getting clear could be a problem in itself. What if she was headed down there, ready to inform Business Guy and his pals that Ray was perched right above them? Hell, she even knew what kind of car he was driving.

That left two options: circle back behind the store for one last look. Or just get the hell out of here. Ray chose option two.

Keeping his headlights turned off till he pulled out of the parking lot, Ray merged into what was now a light flow of traffic. At least he was planning to put his remaining life (short as it was) to good use. He hoped Heather was going to do the same. Usually, adult humans, members of the rank-and-file public, didn't get a chance for a do-over. If Heather blew her opportunity by running back to Gabe ... it would really suck if she did that.

Why do I care? Ray thought. But he knew the answer already. Weakness. Weakness. And more weakness. Anyway, it didn't matter now.

Then he saw her. She was way on the other side of the four-lane road with a median between them. She'd taken the Duke hoodie. It was baggy on her, and she had the hood up, concealing her head and face. Forget that Ray Caldwell had awesome vision. Even at night, that body was impossible to miss.

Driving on was a given. Yet another scenario where the right move required no assessment whatsoever. Ray made the wrong move without hesitation. Making a hard U-turn, he bounced his car over the median and pulled onto the shoulder in front of her.

Heather stepped out of her heels and tried to run. Ray caught up with her in a couple of steps. "Get in," he said. "They'll scoop you up if you stay out here."

"Get away from me!" She swiped at him like a feral cat; one of her long nails dug into the side of Ray's neck. Hitting her, grabbing her, forcing her in the car was not an option. He had to stop. Any second, people would be slowing down to gawk.

Ray turned and walked away, trying to fight off a strange feeling that he'd never experienced before. It was a longing for things to be different and extreme disappointment that they were not. In plain English, that translated to sadness and regret.

And there was no reason for it. Jill was the priority if he couldn't save both of them. It really was that simple. And yet, the empty feeling in the pit of his stomach said otherwise.

He got in the car, and the passenger door flew open. Heather got in with him. Her hood was still up, and she was staring at her feet.

Ray backed the car up a few feet. Then he got out and retrieved her shoes.

CHAPTER 83

THE BUS STATION was drab and gray with the carbon smell of exhaust in the air. This was a stopping off place for people on their way somewhere. You could feel it the moment you drove up to it. Ray already knew what the inside would be. A concrete floor and rows of plastic chairs with coin-operated televisions. Anybody voluntarily loitering here must be half dead, he decided.

They sat in the car, neither of them saying a word. Finally, Heather pulled down her hood and looked at Ray.

"I don't feel right leaving you," she said.

"You said it yourself. You need to catch a bus out of town."

She nodded and shifted in her seat. "You should come too. Or at least drive away from here and never look back."

Ray didn't know what to say. He'd never had a conversation like this one. His had always been results-oriented action. Never had it occurred to him to ponder the best outcome for any person. But in Heather's case ... "You're getting out at the right time," he said. "Things are about to get real. You don't need to be part of that."

"What are you going to do?"

"Take things to another level."

Heather gave him a long stare. "I guess you need your hoodie back," she said.

"Keep it."

"Ray. I stole from you." Heather reached into the hoodie's front pouch and pulled out a stack of hundreds.

"Half of it's yours," Ray said. "We both stole it." Retrieving the bundle of cash from the back seat, he got out four more stacks.

Then he unclipped the can of mace from his belt. "You know how to use this?"

She nodded.

"Put it in your purse. Just in case."

Heather slid the canister into her purse and folded the cash into a grocery bag that she stuffed in the hoodie's pouch. Then she sat stiff as a statue, like she was posing for a sculptor or painter.

"Thanks for not handing me over to those goons back there," she said.

"No big deal," Ray said.

"Something I've gotta tell you ..."

Here we go, Ray thought. He hated shit like that. She was searching for the right words to express whatever she was trying to express. And he was way more clueless than she was in the realm of personal connections. He knew what to say, but anything he said would be bullshit. All part of his training. To instill fear. Inspire loyalty. Or give a false sense of security. All for the sake of manipulation.

Finally, Heather got it out. "Nobody's ever really helped me out before. Not like you. Oh, guys fall all over themselves to buy me shit, but when it comes to really doing something ..."

"Quit stalling and go," Ray said.

Heather got out of the car.

"Hey Heather," Ray said. "Take care of yourself."

Fighting back tears, she blew him a kiss and walked away.

Maybe it wasn't bullshit after all.

CHAPTER 84

As it turned out, Ray and Heather's destinations were in close proximity to one another. She needed to catch a bus out of town, and Ray was going to pay Gabe's daughter a visit. Her apartment was a fifteen-minute drive from the bus station.

The place wasn't hard to find. Much like the apartment community where he'd taken refuge with Justin, it was comprised of rectangular buildings—living spaces with dwellings stacked next to each other like shoeboxes. Except these buildings were faded brick instead of wood and only two stories tall. Most of the residents here would be college students.

Ray drove through the development, reading numbers off the buildings. Each building had its own number and was divided into four apartments with letters A through D. Elizabeth Marshall's apartment number was 390D on the top floor.

He drove two buildings over and backed into a parking space near the exit. A straight shot from there to the road. Then he listened in on the Ham radio and picked up a conversation between Gabe and a voice that matched Business Guy from the shopping center.

"You spooked him," Gabe said. "All you had to do was lure him in and you tipped him off."

"C'mon. This guy's smart. He knew all along."

"Smart! He's a fucking moron." Gabe was ranting now. "We're doing it my way from here on in. Next time he hears his girlfriend's voice, she'll be screaming."

"And then we'll never get our stuff back," Business Guy said.

They switched channels, and Ray followed their pattern.

"He's got one of yours, remember?" Business Guy trying to reason with a jackass.

"Think I give a shit about Heat? After what she let him do to the club?"

They'd been smart about not using names or giving anything away. But Gabe was starting to slip up. Getting Heather out of town might be the only time he could ever say he'd taken a bad situation and made it better. And now he was going for a repeat. One long day.

Gabe ranted while the saner, smarter dude tried to chill him out. Keep looking. No panic. Stay the course. But Gabe was losing his shit. That made things dangerous for Jill. If he got more restless and scared, he'd take it out on her.

Ray had heard enough. As he suspected, the shit was amping up to a new level, and Ray was going to have to amp up with it.

He loaded up the gym bag with the hammer, crowbar, cordless drill and bits, and two of the three remaining tear gas grenades. He changed into the red corduroy shirt and put on the shiny black jacket and cowboy hat. With the boots, his ensemble reminded him of ancient times when warriors never bothered with camo or subterfuge. When they donned helmets with bright plumes and carried shields with bold emblems. No stealth. No misdirection. Just direct confrontation.

Well, maybe a little misdirection. He added the Ham radio and AC adapter to the gym bag.

Before getting out of the car, he checked the Beretta to ensure there was a round in the chamber and slid the 38 into its ankle holster. The jacket concealed the hunting knife strapped to his side with a six-inch blade sharp enough to slice paper or flesh. Ray Caldwell was ready.

CHAPTER 85

HIS DIGITAL WATCH told him it was 10:13 PM on a Friday night. Over eighty hours elapsed since the transfer into Ray Caldwell's body. There was no set time for giving up on a mission and invoking a reverse transfer. But this one had already lasted longer than most.

Dusk had given way to nightfall. The parking areas were lit up. As were the sidewalks and entryways to the buildings. Nobody outside. Half of the parking spaces occupied. Apparently, many of the student occupants were out for the evening.

As Ray approached building 390, he heard loud music coming from the unit below Elizabeth Marshall's apartment. He walked up the stairs to 390D and knocked on the door. Paused a moment to listen. Knocked again. There was a flaw in his plan, a chance that Elizabeth could be at her parent's house. Home for a visit. He'd find out soon enough; no plan was perfect.

The door was locked. After checking under the doormat for a key and finding none, he used Felton Renfro's plastic bank card to spring the lock on the doorknob. But the deadbolt had been thrown. Removing the outer plate and drilling out the screws would hide outward signs of forced entry. But that would be loud and time consuming. Instead, he opted for the crowbar. Ray leaned into it, and the door swung open. Part of the frame had torn away, littering the threshold with splintered wood.

Ray swept the splinters under the mat with his boot and went inside. The door didn't fully catch anymore, so it was basically hanging open. *Screw it.*

Inside was a living space with a kitchen, dining area, and den. The scent of hairspray and perfume was noticeable but not unpleasant. (Heather could have used some tips from these girls.) He could feel the thump of music from the apartment below. Good. That would provide extra cover.

He didn't know what a typical college girl's apartment looked like, but this one had some nice furniture. A plush gold couch and two matching chairs arranged around a glass coffee table with several empty beer cans and a half-consumed wine bottle. A varnished oak cabinet housed an entertainment system. And the dining room table, littered with textbooks and papers, screamed expense. As did the paisley curtains across the back window. There were several pairs of shoes on the floor in random spots, and a pink skirt was draped over the back of the sofa.

Ray glanced in both bedrooms to confirm that the place was empty. Then he checked the most logical places for phone numbers. There was a phone hooked to an answering machine on an end table next to one of the gold chairs. Nothing there. There were photos of family and friends at parties and gatherings secured to the refrigerator by pink magnets shaped like bows.

Then he found what he was looking for without having to start tearing the place apart. Taped to the wall next to a phone in the kitchen was a list of emergency contact numbers. Two numbers for Elizabeth's family: one for Dad, another for Mom. Two separate phone lines at the same house, Ray assumed.

He erased the greeting on the answering machine and

recorded a new message of his own. The first thing a frantic parent would do was call his kid's apartment. When they heard Ray's message, they'd know for sure he'd been here but wouldn't have a clue as to his (or Elizabeth's) current whereabouts.

Which parent to call? June, the mom, would more likely panic and call the police. He called Gabe. Dad would want to handle things himself.

"Hello?"

It was a man's voice that Ray didn't recognize. Chances were that Gabe had some flunky on an outside line acting as an answering service for him. That would help insulate him from wire taps. So nobody could call him directly, not even his daughter. Or the number on that emergency contact list might well be for Elizabeth's roommate to use if necessary. Either way, Ray could make this work.

"Ray Caldwell here."

Silence on the other end.

"I can hear you breathing," Ray said. "Tell Gabe I've got Elizabeth. Apartment 390. 'D' as in dumbass."

He ended the call and set up shop at the dining table, attaching the AC adapter and plugging the Ham radio into the wall. In a few seconds, he was tuned in. No chatter yet. He'd wait five minutes and then call Mom's number.

Then the phone rang. After four rings, the machine picked up and played Ray's message. *Too late, asshole! Elizabeth and I are long gone. So listen carefully. You're going to release Jill to a place of my choosing. She walks there alone and unharmed. Or you'll find out how loud your daughter can scream. I'll call your home number with instructions.*

A couple of dead seconds followed by a beep. Then a total emotional core dump from Gabe. He'd come completely unglued. He was screaming threats and profanities at the top of his lungs. Ray worried for Jill. But instilling a sense of panic was all part of the process. He'd sure as hell succeeded in doing that. Gabe was still yelling when the machine hung up on him.

Nothing happened for eleven minutes. No phone calls. No radio chatter. Ray kept an eye on the door. If Elizabeth or her roommate came home, he'd have to deal with them. This was *not* a flawless plan by a long way ...

The phone rang again. Another risk. If this was a friend calling, if that caller heard Ray's message ... most people would dial the 911 crisis number. Not a bad idea for later, depending on how things played out.

Four rings, and the machine played Ray's message. The caller listened to the whole thing and waited several silent seconds after the beep to softly hang up. This had to be one of Gabe's people, somebody way more cool-headed than his boss at the moment, calling to hear exactly what Ray had said.

A couple of minutes later, the radio came to life. Business Guy trying to talk some sense into Gabe again.

"I know. Look, he's probably not there, but we'll send people."

"Everybody!" Gabe shouted. "Including me."

"You need to sit tight. The rest of your family's still gone?"

"You know they are. Touring colleges. Both of them."

Ray listened intently. Gabe's wife and son were gone, leaving Gabe with the house to himself. He had Jill at his house! Ray should've figured that out earlier, based on what Jill said on that fake phone call they'd staged: *They're treating me like family.* She'd left him a clue and he'd been too dense to pick up on it.

"How many with you?" Business Guy asked.

"Four. They'll stay. I'm going down there."

"I've got a better idea," Business Guy said. "Stay and send them. You can hold down the fort alone."

Gabe paused for a moment. "I want to cut his balls off!"

"Hey!"

"Alright. I'm sending them and everyone else. And you get down there too!"

"On my way."

The transmission ended. And that was all Ray needed to hear. He figured on about fifteen minutes before the calvary showed up. All of this shit he'd set in motion did create an awesome diversion.

He was packing up the radio when the door flew open. Damn. Fourteen minutes early.

"Don't fucking move!"

The boy was six feet tall and skinny with a mop of brown hair. He was pointing a hunting rifle.

CHAPTER 86

THE BOY'S fear oozed off him so thick that Ray could almost feel its touch against his skin. The wide eyes, the sweat on his forehead. This kid's heart had to be pounding out of his chest. What made things really bad was: he had his finger on the trigger and the safety catch was off. (Ray Caldwell had great eyesight.) One false move, anything to spook or startle this guy, and the gun would go off.

Ray put his hands up. "C'mon, please ... Don't shoot!"

The kid took a step forward. "I said don't move!" He sidled over to the phone, keeping the rifle on Ray. Obviously, he hadn't worked out what to do next. How do you dial a phone and keep a rifle trained on somebody a few feet away? You didn't.

"Can you please not point that thing?" Ray said.

"Shut up and don't move." Gaining some confidence now.

"Look," Ray said. "I'm—ssshh!" He made a show of trying to stand, then he gulped and grabbed at his chest and keeled over on the floor.

"Hey!" The kid stood over him, not knowing what to do. At least the gun wasn't pointed right at him anymore.

Ray thought about drawing the 38 from his ankle holster. An

easy shot. But too noisy. Instead, he somersaulted to his feet and buried the hunting knife in the kid's right hand just above the wrist. He snatched the rifle away before the boy could howl in pain. Textbook. No chance at all of the rifle getting dropped and maybe going off.

The kid's eyes were glazed over. He cradled his hand against his chest and backed away whimpering. A dark stain spread across the crotch of his jeans. And he was gushing blood all over his tan windbreaker.

Ray grabbed the pink skirt off the back of the sofa and made two long slits. A six-inch tourniquet. Going against all things even remotely intelligent, flying in the face of survival in its most basic form, he slung the boy onto the couch, jerked his hand away from his body, and wrapped it tight.

Then he set the phone down next to him. "You dial 911 when I leave," he said.

The kid nodded and thanked him. Un-freaking believable.

Ray checked the rifle. It was a 12-gauge shotgun with two shells loaded. Not enough for going after an intruder, at least in Ray's opinion. Grabbing his bag and the rifle, he headed out the door.

Standing in the breezeway were the two bikers. At least Ray assumed it was them; he'd never seen them up close in the light. They were big dudes, well over six feet tall and easily two hundred and fifty pounds. A human wall if they stood side by side. One of them was smoking a cigar.

The one who spoke was leaning against the wall with his arms crossed as if he were waiting on a bus. "Where the hell do you think you're going?" He was smiling. Not intimidated at all. Why should he be? Either one of them was nearly twice the size of the runt they'd come to stop.

Ray didn't hesitate. He was standing ten feet above them at the top of the landing. The rifle in his hands had two shells in it. Overconfidence carried a high price tag.

Normally a shotgun blast would blow its target backwards. With these two, it was like hunting large game. They both fell. But took their time doing it. Two mountains of flesh slowly crumbling under their own weight.

The door to the loud apartment flew open, and a two college students, a boy and a girl, stepped outside to investigate. While they were gaping at the two bodies on the sidewalk, Ray came down and pointed the rifle at them. "Back inside," he said.

They didn't waste any time arguing with him. As their door was closing, Ray tossed one of the gas grenades in after them. He was taking no chances on alcohol convincing anybody in there to be a hero.

CHAPTER 87

RAY DROPPED the rifle (no more ammo) and made for the rear of the building. Then he started running. A half-moon hung high in the clear night air. He avoided walkways, kept to the shadows. Blended with his surroundings like a hint of cloud in a dark sky.

In the car, he hooked up the radio and pulled out of the parking lot slowly and smoothly. As he turned onto the drive leading to the road, he had to swerve to avoid an oncoming car that was pulling in way too fast. One of Gabe's people or some drunk coming home early? No way to know, and no reason to care.

One thing he did need to worry and care about was the timing of it all. They'd gotten people over here faster than he'd anticipated. How long before they figured out this was all an elaborate bluff, that he didn't have Elizabeth? Probably a while. In this era, if you wanted to talk to somebody on the phone, that person had to be home when you called. She was not. And all Gabe's people would find at the scene were bodies and chaos. Not to mention police and paramedics in the next few minutes. Nobody was going to contact Gabe and tell him everything was peachy keen.

And if they did ...

Ray tuned the radio to the next frequency and heard plenty. More people on their way to the apartment complex. Gabe frantic for info on Elizabeth. *Not much fun, is it, asshole?* Ray wanted to grab the mike and say it over the air. But he kept the thought in his head.

It was all falling in place. He was headed for the posh Middlebury Heights neighborhood to pay a visit to the man himself. Allowing for traffic, it would take about twenty-five minutes to get there if he pushed it. That meant it would take them nearly half an hour to come to Gabe's aid. Plenty of time. Well, not really. But he'd make it work. Because Ray Caldwell didn't give a shit about odds. He knew where to go and what he had to do when he got there. That was all that mattered.

As for a specific plan, he'd figure that out when he saw the place.

PART SEVEN
A REALLY, REALLY LONG DAY

CHAPTER 88

BELLINGHAM LANE LED RIGHT UP to the gated entrance of Middlebury Heights. Driving up, Ray noted that the entire perimeter of the neighborhood was protected by a wrought-iron fence with spiked pickets at the top of it. It would be about a ten-foot climb. Then he'd have to find Gabe's house on foot. And he might trip an alarm in the process.

The gate at the entrance looked formidable on the surface, sure, an imposing grid of black metal protecting the road that led into the place. On the left side of the gate, a guy in a call box was looking at Ray as he drove up. The dude was wearing a gray uniform like a fucking doorman!

Weak link! The human element. Not like the robotic sentries where Ray came from: with them, you got one warning if you were lucky, regardless of the circumstances. Broken leg? Still two seconds to retreat or else. But humans placed excessive value on the lives and welfare of their peers.

Ray slowed to a stop about twenty feet from the entrance and hunched down beneath the dashboard. He grabbed the oatmeal cookies that Heather left in the glovebox and shoved three of them in his mouth. Then he cracked open a can of beer, the last one in the floorboard, and took a big hit off it. He didn't swallow. He chewed the nasty combination of beer and cookies down to mush. Then he put the car in gear and rolled forward.

The gatekeeper slid his window open as Ray approached. He wasn't much of a physical specimen. No taller than Ray without his boots and a soft roll around his belt line. But he had tiny round eyes with pupils like black marbles and the long jawline of a hunter. Not a predator that attacked and imposed his will. This dude was an opportunistic scavenger that picked up scraps.

"Hey. You can't go in there," he said.

Ray rolled down his window and gave him a blank stare.

"This is a private neighbor—"

Ray spewed the beer-infused cookie mush down the side of his car door. Then he opened the door and spilled out of the car. Crawling on his hands and knees, he ejected more fake puke onto the pavement.

All the while, he kept an eye on the seedy gatekeeper and watched him exit the call box and head his way. He stood over Ray, disdain etched across his ferret face.

"Hey? Loser! You hear me?"

Ray responded with a dry heave.

"You can't stay here. I've gotta call the police if you don't leave now."

Ray feigned an attempt to stand and slumped backward against the side of his car. "Can't make it any further," he said, gasping.

"I can help you," the gatekeeper said. "But I need your wallet and keys."

Nice guy. A real public servant. He was going to call the police to have Ray arrested. Then he'd park his car somewhere and help himself to his cash and anything else of value. If Ray had really been drunk, he might have come back to find his car gone.

Ray reached into his coat and hopped up. Just like that—the gatekeeper found himself pinned against the side of the Honda with a razor-sharp hunting knife against his throat.

CHAPTER 89

FIVE MINUTES LATER, Ray was on the other side of the gate, driving into the heart of posh Middlebury Heights. The traumatized gatekeeper cowered against the passenger side door and directed him to Gabe's house at 1 Lakeview Drive.

The fact that Ray was doing the driving and the gatekeeper was sitting next to him with his hands free wasn't a problem. All he'd had to do was draw a little blood when they were in the car to reinforce who was running this show. This clown had too many brains and not enough guts to try attacking him.

Ray had also looked through the gatekeeper's wallet and knew who he was and where he lived. Not that he would bother hunting Artie Stover down at his residence if he tried running. Instead, Ray would shoot him like the mangy cur that he was. They were clear on that point as well.

This was an all-brick neighborhood. The houses back here behind the gate were huge, with plenty of space between them and mature trees towering overhead. Everywhere you looked, streetlights illuminated the sidewalks. A safe haven where you could go for a leisurely stroll at three in the morning. A place inhabited by the likes of Gabe Marshall, a dirtbag who didn't mind using helpless people as pawns.

"Hey look," Artie said. "You're picking a dangerous man to mess around with."

"Why are you talking?" Ray said. He was hell-bent on this course of action. Not much time left before the reverse transfer. So it was now or never.

"Left up here where they're building a house," Artie said.

A construction site. With a house still in the idea stage. Building materials—bricks and long planks of wood—were stacked on pallets. But the actual building process had not been started. They'd left two big oaks standing near the road, but the rest of the lot had been cleared and flattened out. There was a bulldozer parked near the entrance and a dump truck filled with logs and brush that had been cleared. A sign with red letters warned against trespassing.

Ray killed the headlights and turned the corner. Lakeview Drive was a cul-de-sac with a single house situated at the very end—hence the number one as Gabe's house number. The road was like a gauntlet leading up to the front door. There might be an alarm system; there might not. A guy like Gabe wouldn't want police in his house. And contacting the police about a crime taking place in your home gave them all kinds of probable cause.

Still, even without an alarm, and with manpower diverted, coming in through a door or a window carried a ton of risk. Ray paused to think things over. He turned on the radio. Really didn't matter if Artie heard anything. Maybe even better if he did.

It was better than he could have hoped for. Gabe was frantic. There was a shitstorm in full swing at Elizabeth's apartment, compliments of Ray, and they still hadn't located her.

"Holy shit," Artie croaked. "Holy shit!"

Ray cracked him between the eyes with the back of his hand.

Nothing serious. Just hard enough to blind him for a couple of seconds. "No talking."

The radio chatter continued. From what Ray could gather, Gabe had a guy named Stu in the house with him. If Jill wasn't there, he'd have to hurt them very badly to find out her location and hope he didn't run out of time.

Ray killed the radio. Reaching into the back seat, he plucked a stack of hundreds out of the gym bag and shoved them into Artie's sweaty hand. "That's five grand," he said. "You get another five when this is over."

"Man, I'm not made for this shit."

"Shut up and listen. All you have to do is walk up to the front door and ring the bell till somebody answers."

"Jesus!"

"Tell them anything you want. Yell for help. Say I'm standing behind you with a gun. I don't give a shit. Just get them to answer the door."

Artie tried to look at Ray and couldn't. He stared straight ahead, his mouth sucking air like a fish out of water.

"Really no decision," Ray pointed out. "You do it or I'll kill you dead."

CHAPTER 90

ARTIE'S FACE looked pale as curdled milk. But he stuffed the cash down the front of his trousers and trudged the sixty feet of road towards Gabe's house.

"I'll be behind you," Ray said. "Maybe I'll hang back. Or I might be right on your ass. But don't even think about looking over your shoulder."

Ray followed close behind him for a few steps, then peeled off into the shadows. Wearing the black leather jacket and cowboy hat, he blended into his surroundings with the fluid movements of a trained warrior. The Beretta was fully loaded in his shoulder holster. The 38 in his ankle holster. The hunting knife sheathed at his hip. And inside the jacket: a nasty surprise in the form of brass knuckles with a pop-out blade.

Overkill really. The fight would never require all of that. But that was the way of it. Armed for a long campaign that would likely entail a thirty-second skirmish. He also carried the flashlight, pliers, wire cutters, a screwdriver, and the crowbar. He was also over-killing it on tools, but better to overdo things on that front as well.

Climbing onto the bulldozer, he unscrewed the plate housing

the control panel and found the necessary wires. Didn't need the crowbar to persuade it. He put it under the seat. Time was against him. Not just his remaining time here, but the next thirty seconds. Artie would be approaching the front door at any moment. Or he might decide to turn and run. None of that mattered. Ray was locked in, totally focused. That was the main thing. The *only* thing.

The bulldozer coughed a couple of times before the engine came to life. Ray knew the basics: start, move forward. He wouldn't be stopping. He'd figure out how to control that wide metal blade by the time he got there.

The dozer barreled across a shallow ditch at the edge of the construction site, nearly pitching Ray out of the driver's seat. Full speed ahead, he rolled into Gabe's side yard, raising the blade ten feet off the ground.

Artie was standing on the front porch under the house lights. He was waving his hands in gestures of innocence. Really all Ray needed from him. Not a *good* distraction. Just a distraction.

Eight ball in the side pocket. That's what Ray thought when he spotted his target—a huge bay window, at least twelve feet wide, on the side of the house. Swinging hard right, the dozer pitched forward and smashed through the window. All the way through.

The impact shook the house and cracked a second-floor window. Grabbing the crowbar, Ray scrambled across the dozer's hood and positioned himself behind the waist-high blade. He laid the crowbar next to him and drew the Beretta.

He'd crashed into a fancy dining room. Underneath him was a piece of wooden furniture, some sort of fancy table with a lace cloth and silver service on it. Dead center was a crystal chandelier above a long mahogany table on a longer oriental rug. Two entrances. One to his left behind the table. Another directly in front of him.

At the sound of approaching footsteps, he pointed his gun over the top of the metal blade and waited. A guy with broad shoulders and a combover burst into the room. Ray shot him twice. Then he used the crowbar to knock down the sharp fingers of glass reaching down into the entryway he'd just created. Even after widening his opening, getting inside was still not easy. Ray slid himself over the dozer's blade. Holding on to the top edge, he glanced down and realized he was far enough inside to avoid landing on furniture. And totally vulnerable if anybody walked in right now.

Ray let himself drop. His boots made a loud bang on the wood floor. Gabe knew where he was—no question. No point in sneaking around. Might as well make himself known and get down to it.

"Gabe!" he shouted. "Gabe Marshall!"

No sound. Ray listened for the creak of floorboards, the sound of footsteps. Nothing.

Ray kept yelling. "We're in your fancy dining room," he said. "I'm about to un-tape Elizabeth's mouth so you can hear her screaming. Bring Jill in here. You've got twenty seconds."

CHAPTER 91

HE COULD SEE his shadow stretched to twice his actual height across the lacquered floor. This whole thing was a huge bluff. But the die had been cast. He'd give Gabe fifteen seconds and then come after him. No bluff there. That was as real as it got.

Ray didn't need fourteen of those seconds. They entered through the door behind the dining table. Jill first, Gabe right behind her. He had his left arm around her neck. His right hand held a pistol near her head. Ray recognized his mustache and beefy face from the photo he'd found in the library. He was a big dude, alright, easily twice the size of Jill. He was wearing trousers with suspenders and a white dress shirt with the sleeves rolled up.

The man Ray had shot, presumably Stu, was splayed against the wall next to the nearest door. Gabe never noticed or cared. He didn't even gape at the front end of a bulldozer where his bay window should have been.

"Where's my daughter?" That's all he wanted to know.

Ray stepped forward, assessing the situation. Gabe's eyes were wide, his face flushed crimson. Even though he wasn't moving, he looked like someone in the middle of an intense exercise session. He shoved the barrel of his pistol against the side of Jill's head. "One more step and I'll kill her," he said.

"And you'll never see Elizabeth again," Ray said. That was true. If Gabe pulled the trigger, Ray would empty the Beretta into him as a final act of futility in a totally failed mission.

"You think you can threaten me? Cocksucker!" Gabe was coming unhinged. Always a dicey thing to deal with.

Then he regained a tiny bit of composure. "It's over, Ray," Gabe said. "Put down your gun. I might let Jill live if you play your cards right. She's a good girl. She doesn't deserve this."

The shithead managed to make himself sound halfway reasonable. He wouldn't, of course, spare Jill. But Ray had no cards to play anyhow. So he just stared at Gabe and said nothing.

"I mean it," Gabe said. "Drop the gun or I kill her."

Jill kicked and struggled. She tried to sink her teeth into his beefy forearm.

Gabe tightened his grip, choking her. He leaned down and snarled in her ear. "I swear to God, I'll break your neck," he said.

Really stupid, Ray thought. For a brief moment, his gun wasn't pointed at Jill's head. Ray put three bullets in his right eye. Blood spattered on an opulent oil painting on the wall behind him.

Jill rushed forward, barely getting out from under Gabe's bulk as he fell. She looked different than before. Same blue-green eyes and blonde hair. But she had a healthy glow that was missing before. Forced clean time would do that for a person.

"Ray!" She ran up and flung herself into a tight hug around his neck. "Oh, Ray! I thought you were dead."

Ray's heart leapt. She smelled fresh as rainwater, nothing like that nasty perfume of Heather's. Her skin was smooth, her hair soft. Ray had to draw himself up sharply to avoid kissing her, to force himself to push her away to arm's length.

"Listen to me, Jill. We've got to—"

Then he seized up. From the crown of his head right down to his toenails. It was happening. The reverse transfer.

"Got to ... get ..." he said.

Had to tell Jill ... get the ... Go! ... Leave him behind. He tried to open his mouth, but nothing doing. He was going away.

CHAPTER 92

RAY FELT himself hit the floor with a distant thud. Always in the past, when a reverse transfer kicked in, he'd just drift back to his own world without knowing or caring what became of the host body. Occasionally, he'd check into a hotel after a mission was completed and literally sleep through the process. He'd never tried to stay. That was the point: no host selected for a transfer had a life worth hanging on to.

Once again, he called out to Jill, but nothing came out. He couldn't see or hear her anymore. Couldn't move or even breathe. His entire being had completely stopped. No pulse, no breath, no movement or feeling. Not a damn thing.

Reclamation ...

A brief glimpse from above—his real self in the hexagonal transfer chamber. Nearly three hundred pounds of him. Lean muscle perfectly distributed on a towering frame. The eyes were closed as if in sleep. But this was no catnap. He was in a state of suspended animation, a nice way of saying clinically dead. His body was being sustained by life support, ready for the reverse transfer to infuse life back into him.

He looked down at himself, dreading reclamation. His

mission was a total failure. He'd never even started on it. Worse still, he'd affected untold timelines with his actions. It was going to be an ugly debriefing.

Worst of all, he'd never see Jill and Justin again, never know what had happened to them. And he wouldn't be Ray anymore. Instead, he'd be an overdeveloped asshole with the face of a wolf who made everyone around him cringe.

Something wasn't right. Normally, he'd catch a quick glimpse of the room and the chamber. Then everything would go blank as he settled into his rightful body.

He watched his real self in the transfer chamber go limp.

And then his head was too small. He was lying face up on a hard surface with somebody trying to drive his chest through the floor.

He was staring up at a chandelier. That wasn't right. It looked like the same chandelier in Gabe's dining room. Wait!

Jill leaned over him, her face a mask of concentration. With a determined effort, she pressed down hard on his breastbone with both hands. Hurt like hell. Before he could speak, she pressed her mouth over his and pinched his nostrils shut.

He pulled her fingers off his nose; her mouth could stay where it was for now.

She sat up and touched the side of his face. "You're back," she said. Tears flowed down her cheeks. "You died. You were gone for at least a minute."

Ray tried to sit up and felt dizzy. He put his head between his knees and tried to ignore the splitting headache in that tight skull he'd just reoccupied. His chest felt like an elephant had stepped on it.

"What the hell did you do to me?" he said.

"CPR. I'm a nurse. Remember?"

CPR. Cardiopulmonary resuscitation. Brings dead people back to life under the right conditions. That's what happened.

The reverse transfer hit him, he dropped like a rock, and Jill sprang into action and pulled him back.

Which meant ...

His real self was now his formal self. A transfer projected one person's consciousness into another. The sender had to be kept alive on sophisticated life support, but both beings could coexist simultaneously.

But in the case of a reverse transfer, somebody had to die. And it wasn't going to be Ray Caldwell. Somewhere in a future era, a wolf-faced asshole was dead in his transfer chamber.

So that was that. No more timeline. No reverse transfer pending. He no longer occupied this male human called Ray Caldwell; he *was* Ray—for the duration of his remaining lifespan.

It was going to be a really long day.

CHAPTER 93

Ray closed his eyes and focused on not puking. The headache was already subsiding. Probably because he'd never fully left Ray Caldwell's body.

Restarting a stopped heart in a discarded host's body during a reverse transfer ... that was a new one. The result was obvious. Those brainiacs who'd engineered the process probably hadn't thought of that. Or it had been raised as a potential issue and nobody cared.

He took a couple of deep breaths to gather himself. Jill was kneeling next to him, holding his hand. Her warm touch radiated all the way up his arm. She should've gotten the hell out of here and left him for dead. He'd been trying to tell her to do just that when his body locked up.

Getting to his feet, he staggered backwards a couple of steps and found himself leaning against the front end of a bulldozer. (Yeah, it had been a wild few hours.) A guy named Stu was splayed across the threshold of the nearest door. Gabe lay crumpled against the far wall.

He took a step forward, pausing to let his head clear. He was settling back into Ray's body—his now lifetime host—just fine.

But there was one small problem: Ray Caldwell had just been brought back from death via CPR. That took a lot out of a human.

"We've got to get out of here now," he said.

"Too late for that."

Ray recognized the voice. It was the self-assured voice of an executive in the corner office. Smooth shaven and not a hair out of place, Business Guy stood in the doorway next to Stu's body. A guy stood next to him pointing a gun. Another dude came in from the far door where Gabe had entered. And from behind and above: the telltale click of a bullet being chambered. One or more of them had climbed in over the bulldozer.

Nothing he couldn't handle, even in his current condition. Except ... the shoulder holster was empty. Of course it was. He spotted the Beretta ten feet away on the floor, where he'd obviously dropped it when the reverse transfer hit him. He wasn't wearing his jacket either, nor the cowboy hat. Jill must have pulled all that off of him as part of her life-saving efforts. So here he was ... a serpent without fangs.

He still had the hunting knife on his hip. One diving throw would take out the man next to Business Guy. Then a rolling grab for the Beretta with the 38 in the ankle holster for backup if that didn't work out.

All totally doable. He could feel his nerve endings coming to life; the brain of a killing machine from another era was firing high-voltage signals through his body. The stakes were higher now, of course. If he got himself killed, it was game over. No reverse transfer to yank him back to where he'd come from. That was fine by him. He wasn't going to live out his days in this era avoiding danger just to prolong his inevitable death. That was pure cowardice.

But Jill was here. She could get hit in the crossfire. And her life wouldn't be worth a nickel if he tried to fight his way out of this and things went wrong.

"Why don't you lie down on your face and spread-eagle?" Business Guy said. "Or I can have one of these fine gentlemen shoot you in the kneecap."

Ray did as he was told. Rough hands patted him down and found the 38 (that he'd never even fired) and the hunting knife (that he'd used plenty).

Business Guy let out a low whistle. "You're a walking arsenal," he said.

They cuffed his hands behind him tight enough for the metal to bite into his wrists.

"Here's how it's going to go, Ray. You're going to tell us where to find our merchandise or Jill's gonna start losing teeth."

He spoke to one of the guys with him. "Sit him up against the wall so he can watch."

"You know the police are coming," Ray said. "All that shooting in a gated neighborhood. The whole side of a house caved in. You've gotta get out of here."

"Way ahead of you, Ray. Artie's already contacted the police and told them everything's a-okay. He is the nighttime security guard, after all. I know, pathetic. But he can follow simple instructions. How about you, Ray? Can you follow instructions?"

Two dudes sat Jill up in one of the wooden chairs. Ray had made a bad move. Better to have taken the fight to them while he was armed. Yeah, Jill might have gotten clipped by a stray bullet. But look at her now.

That damn weakness was still alive and well. Only it didn't feel like such a weakness now. At any rate, thinking about it didn't bring on self-contempt anymore. It seemed right and natural to care what happened to someone close to him. Not a liability or a weakness.

Now that was weird!

But it sure didn't seem like an asset either. Not where he was sitting at the moment.

Business Guy turned out to be a cocky son-of-a-bitch. He couldn't help gloating.

"I've gotta tell you this, Ray ... I kept saying to myself: how is this slimeball always one step ahead of us? It's as if he was listening in on everything we say. Then it hit me. You had yourself a radio and somehow figured out our frequency pattern. Impressive."

He snapped his fingers. "Then I got an idea. You got everybody scurrying down to college land to rescue Gabe's poor kidnapped daughter. Nice ploy, by the way. So I played along on the radio for your benefit. And Gabe's. And we did send everybody down there. Except for a few of us stayed behind.

"So there you have it. You took care of Gabe for us. And now we'll return the favor and take care of you."

"What's your name?" Ray asked.

"Does it matter?"

"Yeah," Ray said. "It matters to me." *It'll make killing you a personal thing,* he thought.

"I'm Tony," Business Guy said. "Tony Spidero. And this big guy standing next to me is Andre. He's a dentist. Show him your special toothbrush, Andre."

Andre, a fireplug with a crewcut and snug red tee-shirt, reached into his back pocket and pulled out a pair of vice grip pliers.

"Okay," Tony said. "The patient's prepped and ready. Let's go to work."

Jill struggled and kicked. Andre walked over to her, actually looking bored, as if he had all the time in the world. Two guys were holding Jill to keep her from getting up. Andre grabbed her around the chin with sausage-like fingers and forced her mouth open.

Ray glared at Tony, imagining that smooth face busted open. He had to do something, couldn't let those assholes mess Jill up like that. If only he'd acclimated a little bit faster after getting slammed back into being Ray Caldwell for keeps.

Jill let out a scream as the vice grips went into her mouth. And then it hit him.

"Don't do it!" he yelled. "I know where your missing diamonds are."

CHAPTER 94

YEAH, diamonds.

Ray remembered now. He and Cory had stolen a satchel from Meathook. Cory had the idea and saw the opportunity but didn't have the balls to go for it. Old Ray, as Justin called him, had been crazy and stupid enough to actually do it.

Those future era eggheads would find it fascinating, right up there with the reverse transfer backfiring. An occupant never had access to a host's past memories. Nobody chosen as a host had anything in his past worth remembering anyhow. Ray Caldwell was the first, it seemed.

Apparently, under sufficient duress, those deep recesses of Ray Caldwell's unused mind had dredged the memory up. Maybe that bill of sale for uncut diamonds that he'd taken from Gabe's safe had jogged something loose. But Ray guessed it was his connection to Justin and Jill and imminent threat to them that did the trick.

At any rate, back to Meathook ...

Cory had guessed there was a fair amount of dope and cash for the taking. He was right about that, but only half right. He never expected diamonds. Big ones. Worth a fortune ... well, that was way too hot for dudes like them to handle. Really too rich for Meathook's blood as well.

Even Ray Caldwell had enough sense to figure that out. Which is why he'd stuffed all that glittery bling back in the leather pouch it came in and tried to flush the whole thing down the toilet. And then tried to unclog the toilet with a towel rod. (Having enough sense to figure out they were in deep shit didn't make him smart.) That's why the plumbing in Ray's trailer was backed up. Yeah, that bag of diamonds had some bulk to it.

Three full seconds of still silence had elapsed since Ray's shout-out about knowing where the diamonds were. Tony gave him the same appraising stare that a parent might give a difficult child. "Of course you know where they are," Tony said. "That's why Jill's going to be eating applesauce from now on. Get on with it, Andre."

The wide-bodied Andre positioned himself in front of Jill and reached for her mouth. She kicked him hard in the nuts.

Andre sank to one knee, then staggered back to his feet, drawing back to hit her. Ray slid his feet between his hands and got the cuffs in front of him. It was on. They had guns. He didn't care.

"You're going to have to kill me," he said. "Then you'll never get your ice back."

"You're not the moron everybody says you are," Tony said. "You're actually a pretty smart cookie. But we're holding all the cards."

"I'll keep coming," Ray said. "Either these assholes will stop me with bullets or I'll fuck you up. If I bleed out and die, there's no more game."

With that, Ray started walking towards Tony. Andre left Jill and moved between them. And Ray could sense (more than hear) one of Tony's goons coming up behind him. Instincts honed from countless hours of simulations and field experience.

Ray actually felt a slight change in temperature when his opponent got within reach.

Then Ray sidestepped and tripped him, sending him stumbling into Andre. And then he shoved both men to the floor. They landed in a pile, one on top of the other. The two guys holding Jill looked confused. They looked to Tony for guidance. *What should we do? Come over? Keep ahold of this girl?*

Tony had a gun out. He was pointing it at Ray from a safe distance. One of the guys holding Jill had a gun to her head. The other was aiming his piece at Ray. Andre tossed the dude on top of him aside and jumped up, snorting like an enraged bull.

"Alright, Ray," Tony said. "No reason to get excited. We're all friends here."

He was slinging shit with both hands. Even dimwitted Old Ray could have seen that. But there was a glint in Tony's eye, a tension in his face that he tried to hide. He'd just come up with a new plan.

"No more games," Ray said.

"Well put," Tony said. "No more games. No more interrogation sessions where we piss each other off. We want our diamonds back. You want to be left alone. So you're going to *show* us where they are."

CHAPTER 95

5:45 AM.

With most of the city still asleep, the first hint of sunrise dulled the blackness of the night. Two cars turned down the dirt road leading to Ray Caldwell's trailer. Their headlights pierced through a light mist of morning dew looking for a place to settle.

Ray was driving the Honda Accord that he'd rented under Felton Renfro's name. He was still wearing handcuffs, so both hands were positioned on top of the steering wheel. Tony was in the passenger seat with his gun pointed at him.

His black jacket was folded neatly on the back seat with his cowboy hat on top of it. They'd gone through the pockets but hadn't found the bladed brass knuckles hidden in the lining. That could be important at some point.

Andre followed in a black BMW. He had Jill with him. Tony had instructed his other goons to stay behind to clean up the mess at Gabe's (whatever that meant).

Ray had been told that it would go bad for Jill if he tried anything. But he knew it was going to go bad for both of them no matter what. They were loose ends. Once Tony had the diamonds, they would kill both of them and get rid of Ray's car in the process.

He couldn't help noticing that the smell of pine-scented freshener had finally dissipated. Remnants of Heather's perfume still lingered, though. Ray studied Tony's face and posture for clues, but Tony took no notice of the smell. That meant he'd probably never had anything going with Heather. Not that it mattered now.

Slowing down to a crawl, Ray broke a line of yellow crime scene tape stretched across the drive. Nobody allowed in or out of there. That meant there was nobody home in any of the three trailers here. His trailer and the one belonging to Jill and Cory were empty by default.

Whoever lived in the third trailer near the back of the lot had decided to get the hell out or been evacuated by the police. Ironic —if that trailer hadn't had its phone turned on when Ray had wasted Meathook, the police wouldn't have been contacted till much later. Like as not, he would have dropped Justin off some-where safe and proceeded with his mission. The reverse transfer would have yanked him back a couple of hours ago. None of this would be happening right now.

No regrets, though. This was how things were—the way they were supposed to be.

The Honda's wheels crunched on the graveled dirt as he shined the headlights at his old trailer. It was just like he left it. A rusted-out box with a deck that was about to fall off of it.

Tony was visibly annoyed. This was clearly *not* where he'd expected Ray to take him. "You're kidding, right?"

"Under my trailer," Ray said.

"Please," Tony said. "Our guys went over this dump from top to bottom after that bullshit story you told Gabe about the latrine at the bottom of the hill."

Ray saw no reason for secrecy at this point. "They're stuck in the plastic pipe that connects to the shitter," he said. Then when

Tony didn't respond right away, he added, "We're gonna need cutting tools. I've got some with me."

Headlights filled the rear windshield as Andre pulled in behind him. Ray got out and popped the trunk. Tony followed close by, keeping his gun on Ray. Thick, round-bodied Andre poured himself out of the BMW. Ray didn't see Jill.

"Where is she?" he demanded.

Andre opened the rear door in a grand sweeping gesture. Jill lay across the back seat with her hands tied behind her and her feet bound together. She looked up at Ray, her blue-green eyes grabbing his gaze like a tractor beam. An unspoken signal passed between them. *We're in this together. To the end. However long that happens to be.*

"I'm alright," she said. "Don't worry about me."

Do whatever you have to. That was her message to Ray.

"Should've stuffed her in the trunk," Andre said. His voice sounded too high and reedy for his massive chest.

"Up your ass," Ray said.

"Enough!" Tony said. "We just need our merchandise, Ray. Can you do that for me?"

"No problem," Ray said. "Just send Fatback there under the trailer to get it."

Tony laughed and shook his head. "Look at Andre; look at the space underneath your trailer."

"Looks like it's up to you," Ray said.

"That's not happening either," Tony said.

"I guess that leaves me," Ray said.

"I guess it does," Tony said. "Now step away from the car."

"We need the chainsaw out of there. I'm gonna have to cut through some pipe," Ray said.

Both Tony and Andre had their guns out. When they weren't waving them around, Tony carried his gun in a shoulder holster under his jacket. Andre tucked his pistol in his waistband. Probably a phallic thing for a big dude with no nuts. Ray committed those details to memory for future reference. *Near* future in this case.

Both guns were also equipped with silencers. Another detail Ray picked up on. He and Jill weren't getting out of this alive if these two got their way.

"I say we waste him now and send our guys in," Andre said.

"Shut up, Andre," Tony said.

Ray knew he couldn't risk it. If Tony killed him and this alleged location turned out to be another ruse, he'd be shit out of luck on retrieving those diamonds.

"The chainsaw would cut through plastic PVC, no problem," Ray said.

"Dream on, if you think we're putting a chainsaw in your hands," Tony said.

Tony took a look at Ray's inventory of tools. "Reach in there and get that hacksaw," he said. He and Andre stepped apart and away, angling their guns in Ray's direction.

"You know how long that'll take?" Ray said.

"Don't sweat it, Ray. You're not getting paid by the hour."

Andre laughed in appreciation of Tony's wit. His high-pitched giggle was the byproduct of nerves.

Doing as he was told, Ray retrieved the hacksaw. "I assume I have to keep the cuffs on," he said.

"We're in no hurry," Tony said. "You've got as long as it takes."

"Can I take my jacket with me?" Ray asked. "For something to lie on under there?"

Tony gestured with his head. "Get the man his coat," he said.

Andre tossed Ray's black jacket at him. Good deal. Now he was weaponized.

Then Tony reached into his pocket and pulled out the bladed brass knuckles. "Nice try," he said. "Those geniuses that checked your pockets didn't find this. Good thing I know to check behind them."

Okay. So now he *wasn't* weaponized. But he wasn't going to let a little thing like that stop him. Shrugging in feigned resignation, Ray headed to the trailer.

"And Ray," Tony called after him. "Don't even think about coming out of there empty-handed. We'll shoot you dead and then make Jill wish we'd shot her too."

CHAPTER 96

THE CRAWLSPACE under the trailer was about eighteen inches. Ray had to crawl on his elbows to reach his destination. Fortunately, the trailer was, at most, twenty feet wide. That meant traversing ten feet of wet mud to get underneath the toilet.

It was past 6:00 AM now. The sun had brightened, but it was still dark as hell under there. Ray probably would have wanted a flashlight for this job on a sunny afternoon. But he hadn't asked for one. Darkness and shadows meant Tony and Andre would have problems seeing him. Besides, Ray Caldwell had awesome vision.

He heard footsteps crunching in the gravel and saw two sets of shoes standing near the trailer. "I'm gonna sit," Tony said. "You keep an eye peeled."

From underneath the trailer, Ray couldn't see where Tony went, but the only place to sit would be the steps to the deck. He might get a butt-full of splinters out of the deal. Andre was still standing next to the trailer at the spot where Ray had crawled under. Not that there was anything for him to see.

Ray got on his back and flicked on the black Shelly's lighter for a moment. The white PVC pipe was within arm's reach.

Sawing out the clogged section with the diamonds in it was a simple matter that wasn't so simple. The inside of his nose had already begun to feel dank and musty. And the stench of rotted sewage made his stomach churn. He'd eaten stuff that would make a billy goat puke, and this smell of shit and stale water was as bad as it got.

Really, the right way to do this job would be to attack the problem from above. Pull up that loose bathroom floorboard that was rotting out and saw through the pipe from above. But being under here, out of sight for the moment, gave him an edge.

"How's it going under there?" Tony called out.

Ray started sawing. Not on the pipe, though. He wasn't inhaling any more of that stench than absolutely necessary. He'd found a nearby metal strut that would produce a good grating noise. "Thought you said I had as long as it takes," he said.

"Yeah, well, hurry the hell up."

Here's where he had to perform simultaneous, yet unrelated, actions with his hands and feet. While sawing away on the metal strut, changing location every half minute to never cut through completely, he tested the rotted piece of plywood on the bathroom floor with the heel of his boot. It was just as loose and precarious as when he'd almost stepped through it—seemingly ages ago at the start of this long day.

His plan was simple and stupid. At an opportune time, he'd break through the floor and come up into the trailer; from there, he'd have options. Maybe find a weapon. Take them by surprise through a door or a window when they were expecting him to be underneath the trailer. Unarmed. Wearing handcuffs. What could possibly go right?

So far, the best execution strategy he could think of was: retrieve the diamonds and feign being stuck or injured. Maybe toss the leather pouch halfway out. Make one of them have to come in after it. Anything to create a diversion. Even wearing cuffs, those brass knuckles would have come in handy, for the blade if nothing else.

Eventually, he was going to have to saw his way through that PVC pipe, which would be tough going with this hacksaw. It already stank down here. But releasing the trapped water from Ray Caldwell's toilet would make those tear gas grenades seem like air freshener. And it wouldn't be a fast process. That shit-infused sewage would drip down on him with every stroke of the saw.

That made his best weapon a contaminated hacksaw. Outstanding!

A medium-sized rock skittered across the ground. It bounced off the bottom of the trailer, missing Ray by about a yard. "Wake up under there!" Andre said.

"That's what your mom always tells me," Ray said.

Andre cursed and picked up another rock. But he didn't get low enough for a good angle and wound up throwing it into the dirt.

Then Ray noticed something. From his prone position, he could see the bottom half of the BMW—some fifteen yards away. The rear passenger door swung open. Something happening ... Jill fell out onto the ground. She was still tied up, but she'd somehow managed to get the car door open.

With total disregard for his knees and elbows, Ray gripped the hacksaw's rubber handle between his teeth and belly-crawled to the edge of the trailer where Andre was standing.

Andre raised his voice to a near shout. "Hey Tony, Gabe wouldn't let us touch her. But he's gone now. I say we do Ray's old lady right here and make him watch."

That was it. He was about to turn around and see Jill ...

Ray lunged with the hacksaw and scraped the blade against Andre's left shin. It didn't cause serious damage. Ray knew it wouldn't. But it damn sure ripped his pants leg and broke the skin.

Andre howled, mostly from rage. He dropped to his knees, going for the gun in his waistband. Tony jumped off the deck and grabbed his right forearm with both hands. "What the hell are you doing?"

Andre stood up and shook Tony off him. Tony slapped him hard across the face. "What's wrong with you? Leave him the hell alone."

"Know how I met his mom?" Ray said. "She was toting a mattress on her back."

"Gonna kill that little bastard!" Andre yelled.

"Get rid of your gun and I'll let you try," Ray said.

Before Tony could stop him, Andre yanked the gun from his waistband and tossed it on the ground. It landed about ten feet away from him. Ray noted that it had a silencer on the barrel. More confirmation of what he already knew: they'd brought them out here for disposal.

He also watched Jill roll under the car. She wasn't trying to escape. How could she? Instead she was hiding. Not a bad idea.

"Come on out!" Andre said. "I'll rip your goddamn head off."

"And you'll be the one crawling under there to fetch those diamonds," Tony said. He stood nose-to-nose with the big man. "C'mon. Smarten up. He's not worth it."

"Yeah. C'mon, Puss-gut," Ray said. "Let's bury the hatchet. After all, you're the fruit of my loins."

Andre roared and slammed into the side of the trailer like a linebacker making a tackle. The whole trailer shook from the impact.

Tony knelt down out of arm's reach and made eye contact with Ray. "Play time's over," he said. "Get my stuff. Now."

Ray deliberately avoided Tony's stare and looked past him. He had an opening. A decent opportunity. He had to take it.

But if it backfired ...

No choice. Nothing was ever going to be one hundred

percent safe. *Not* taking it would constitute weakness in this case.

"I'm done playing around," Tony said. "You've got fifteen minutes before I let Andre climb in the back seat with Jill. Hey! I'm talking to you."

Ray let his eyes widen and shifted his gaze. Barely enough to give Tony something to pick up on. Then he waited till that exact moment Tony was about to glance over his shoulder.

"Keep running, Jill!" he shouted at the top of his lungs. "Don't stop! Keep moving!"

CHAPTER 97

TONY SPUN AROUND. Saw the door to the BMW hanging open. Nobody in sight.

Ray thought about it. He could come out and jump Tony from behind. But Andre was right there. Instead, he stayed under the trailer and moved towards the spot where Andre had tossed his piece. His next move depended on Tony.

"Watch him," Tony said. "Don't let him out of your sight." Then he sprinted to the car and looked inside. Panic was setting in; Ray could see it in his body language, in the way he shuffled his feet this way and that, unable to make up his mind which way to go.

It was time.

Ray slid out from under the trailer and grabbed Andre's gun off the ground. The big man wasn't intimidated at all; he just seemed more pissed off than ever. The fact that he didn't even hesitate before charging caught Ray slightly off guard. Nothing he couldn't handle, though.

Calmly, deliberately, he leveled the gun and fired.

An empty click.

Not the satisfying recoil that Ray expected. No choice but to dive out of the way of the human locomotive coming at him full steam.

Ray landed on his back. With maybe eight inches of chain tethering his wrists together, unjamming a gun—while literally being under the gun—posed a challenge.

He rapped the butt of the pistol against his knee.

Very much *unlike* a runaway train, Andre had regrouped with surprising agility. He loomed over Ray the way a dinosaur might attack a rodent. "You're dead!"

Racking a fresh round into the chamber was hard. The cuffs bit into Ray's wrists as he willed himself to not drop the piece.

Andre reached down and snagged a handful of Ray's corduroy shirt.

Bang!

Well, not an actual bang with a silencer involved. But a definite recoil followed by the click of the next bullet chambering.

Ray jerked free of the big man and squeezed off two more rounds. A tight pattern focused on Andre's left eye. That was it for him.

But he didn't see Tony anywhere. The back door of the BMW was shut. Jill was probably still hiding underneath it. Where else would she go?

Tony emerged from the back of Jill and Cory's trailer, visibly angered. The sucker had engaged in a quick search for a runaway captive who hadn't gone anywhere.

The smart move would be to rush him. Run straight at him and start firing as soon as he got in range. A hardcore gunfight with zero formalities. Except—Tony had a rifle in his hands. Must have gotten it out of the BMW. He could plug Ray before he got anywhere near optimal range with the pistol he'd taken from Andre.

Obviously, Tony realized that too. He raised the rifle and fired a round into the dirt, right next to Ray's right foot. The loud crack of gunfire splintered the still morning. No silencer on that baby.

Ray never flinched. "You're going to wake up every cop in Raleigh," he said.

"What if I do? You're the wanted criminal. Me and my pal, Andre, tracked down the scum that busted into Gabe Marshall's home. You just killed him, by the way."

"There's an escaped witness that'll say different," Ray said.

"That bitch!" Tony said. "We'll scoop her up. No problem. And when we do ..."

"You should've taught your boys how to tie a knot," Ray said.

"Drop the gun," Tony said. He stood where he was, about ten yards behind the BMW, with the rifle aimed at Ray. So twenty-five yards apart.

You don't want cops, Ray thought. *And you don't want your crew involved either. You want those diamonds without anybody knowing you've got them.* No, Tony wouldn't enlist outside involvement unless absolutely necessary. Still, with that rifle pointed at him, Ray thought about saying that out loud as a reminder.

He dropped Andre's pistol.

"Now kick it away," Tony said.

Ray kicked the gun towards Tony. It slid about five feet across the dirt.

"Now get your ass back under that trailer and start sawing or I'll drop you right here. I'm gonna be right there with you, lying flat on my belly with my gun on you. Fifteen-minute time limit. Then I'm going to shoot your legs and work my way up."

Ray didn't move. He just stood there and looked at him. A blank stare.

"Do it, damn you!" Tony said.

Ray took his time turning around. Tony strode forward and fired a shot in the air. Ray stood still.

"Move, I said!"

By the time Ray took his first step towards the trailer, Tony was at the rear of the BMW. Adrenaline would do that to a pissed-off dude coming unglued.

The BMW was parked behind the rented Honda. And Ray was between the Honda and the trailer. That decreased the distance between them to ten yards and change. Acceptable range for a shootout if Ray had the gun in his hand. Having to snag it off the ground would not be good.

Ray took a couple of half-hearted steps and paused to look over his shoulder.

"Seriously, Ray, if you don't fucking move—"

Tony pitched forward. Face first. A swan dive into the gravel.

Ray sprinted. Not straight at Tony, but to the opposite side of the Honda where Tony would have to stand up to have a clear shot at him. That meant not going for the pistol.

As Tony was getting to his feet, Ray leaped onto the hood of the Honda and launched himself. The rifle came around. But not in time.

Ray's angle was a little off. Instead of hitting Tony head-on, he'd targeted the space behind him. Reaching and twisting, he managed to snare Tony's forehead—but not his neck—between his forearms. They both went down in a tangle of arms and legs.

The handcuffs were up around Tony's eyebrows. And he did the wrong thing. He tried to angle the rifle to get a shot at Ray from behind. That wasn't going to work. There was a reason why a person committing suicide with a rifle usually pulled the trigger with his toe.

Ray dropped the cuffs down across Tony's windpipe and put his knees in his back for leverage. Tony fired a useless shot in the air. Then he let go of the rifle and struggled to free himself. The metal bit into Ray's wrists. Blood streamed down his forearms. He held on. For ten seconds. Twenty. A full minute, just to be sure, even after Tony became dead weight on top of him.

The chain between the handcuffs had dug so deep into

Tony's throat, Ray had trouble ripping free. Most of the blood on his arms and the front of his shirt was Tony's. But some of it was from the divots in his wrists.

Jill! Where was she?

Then he saw her legs sticking out from under the BMW and realized ...

With Tony's focus on Ray, she'd managed to trip him as he walked past her. Beat the hell out of his plan with the rotted floorboard.

"Damn, girl," Ray said. "You're something else."

At 7:30 AM, Ray and Jill had already done more than most people would do all day.

PART EIGHT
JUST CALL ME RAY

CHAPTER 98

FIVE MONTHS HAD PASSED since that fall morning in Raleigh.

The news stations reported that a bulldozer plowed into a house in the posh Middlebury Heights neighborhood, causing a fire that destroyed the home. Police said that the bulldozer had been parked at a nearby construction site. Gabe Marshall, who had been home alone that night, perished in the fire. The incident was still under investigation. The most likely culprit: teen vandalism.

There was nothing reported through any news outlet about the literal pile of dead bodies at the house on the hill on Boxelder Road. Not a thing. All concerned parties had cleaned things up on their own.

For Ray Caldwell, February was a new year in a new city. Nobody who'd known him would recognize him anymore. His beard had filled in black as coal. The mullet was gone. He'd let the hair grow out on the sides and chopped it shorter in the back. Jill dyed it to match his beard. His body had filled out too. He'd never be the monster he'd been in a future time and space, but insert his mind into anybody, add some serious conditioning to the mix, and stud-li-ness was a given.

On a Saturday afternoon in Alpharetta, Georgia, Ray was with his family at Chuck E. Cheese. It was loud, with kids coming at you from all directions. And, of course, there was the six-foot mouse.

Justin was running around having a blast, too keyed up to eat anything. They'd probably have to wait till they got him home to feed him a proper dinner.

Jill wasn't drinking; she'd been clean and sober for almost five months and had her nursing license back. Ray wasn't drinking either; it wasn't worth it for him. Why not just order a coke? It had caffeine, woke you up, and blunted the greasy burn of the lukewarm pepperoni pizza they'd been eating.

They were sitting in a booth across from two other nurses from the medical center where Jill worked. Preston was a big guy with a soft body and a softer heart. Carla was married with a daughter about Justin's age. Her husband, Mark, was trying to keep an eye on the kids while nursing his first beer of the two-drink limit here.

Everybody here knew Ray as Daniel, compliments of the new identity he'd set up for himself. Daniel Eugene Raeford. He'd picked that name because of Justin. No matter how much they tried to coach him, the boy couldn't break the habit of calling him Ray. This way, Ray could just be short for Raeford. Besides, the boy was right. He really *was* Ray.

Jill leaned into him, her body always a degree or two warmer than his own. Since going back to nursing, she always managed to smell both clean and alluring. She put her lips against his ear. "You're a good man, Ray."

He heard that. Amid the screaming kids and the bells and whistles from the arcade, and with the animatronic band cranking up yet again, he heard that clear as day.

They could relax and enjoy each other now. In large part because Ray had tied off one final loose end on that fateful morning in the trailer park ...

To Jill's consternation, instead of getting the hell out of there, Ray grabbed the chainsaw and gas mask and got those diamonds out of the pipe beneath the clogged toilet. A nasty job. But he had to do it.

He didn't know much about the people he'd been battling and avoiding, but he was sure they were hooked into an organization with some serious resources. He, and especially Justin and Jill, didn't need people like that hunting for them.

So Ray wasn't going to give them a reason. He packaged up the stolen diamonds and mailed them to the law offices of Saul Williamson in New Jersey along with the bill of sale from South Africa. Williamson was a high-profile attorney who represented the interests of some bad people. He wouldn't have the balls to screw them over.

Gabe's checkbook to the offshore accounts, on the other hand, was fair game. And Ray managed to divert a tidy sum into an account of his own. Eventually, he'd have to go out and find ways to replenish their funds in this strange society where he'd landed. But they were good for now. They lived in a nice house. Safe neighborhood. Justin was in a good school. It wouldn't last forever, but nothing did.

In the meantime, Ray had his mission to attend to. He glanced at his watch. Details to come in the next five minutes by his estimation.

On cue, Justin came charging up to the booth and grabbed his arm. Ray knew the drill. The boy had posted a top score on Defender, and it was up to Ray to beat him if he could. His mission: come as close as possible to Justin's score, but still fall short.

He was up to the task.

ACKNOWLEDGMENTS

First, thank you for reading my book! If you are on this page, you probably read it all the way to the end. That means a lot to me as a writer.

Also a big thanks to my family, who encouraged me to write since childhood.

Finally, a huge shout-out to Emily Nemchick for her awesome editing job. She finds everything!

Sign up below for information about my upcoming projects and free offerings.

https://bonnerlitchfield.com/mailinglist.html

ABOUT THE AUTHOR

Bonner Litchfield lives with his wife and dog in North Carolina. Some of his hobbies and interests include CrossFit (painful at times), hanging out with friends and family, reading, traveling, and cheesy TV shows.

Visit him at <u>bonnerlitchfield.com</u>

Milton Keynes UK
Ingram Content Group UK Ltd.
UKHW030154051224
452010UK00010B/458

9 781965 975008